THE RETURN OF THE PLAYER

ALSO BY MICHAEL TOLKIN

The Player
Among the Dead
Under Radar
Three Screenplays: The Player,
The Rapture, The New Age

THE RETURN OF THE PLAYER

Michael Tolkin

Grove Press
New York

Selection from pages 374–377 of *Commentary on the Torah* by Elliott Friedman
copyright © 2000 by Richard Elliott Friedman,
reprinted with permission of HarperCollins Publishers.

Published simultaneously in Canada
Printed in the United States of America

FIRST EDITION

Library of Congress Cataloging-in-Publication Data
Tolkin, Michael.
The return of the player/Michael Tolkin.
p. cm.
Sequel to: The player.
ISBN-10: 0-8021-1801-1
ISBN-13: 978-0-8021-1801-1
I. Motion picture industry—Fiction.   2. Hollywood (Los Angeles,
Calif.)—Fiction.   3. Satire.   I. Title.
PS3570.O4278R47 2006
813',54—dc22   2006041171

Grove Press
an imprint of Grove/Atlantic, Inc.
841 Broadway
New York, NY 10003

Distributed by Publishers Group West

www.groveatlantic.com

06 07 08 09 10   10 9 8 7 6 5 4 3 2 1

For Stephen, Garen, Teddy, and Leo

Some of this book was written at Yaddo.
I am grateful for the privilege.

I invited W. D. Howells to come with us to the first night of Clyde Fitch's dramatization of *The House of Mirth*. The play had already been tried out on the road, and in spite of Fay Davis's exquisite representation of Lily Bart I knew that (owing to my refusal to let the heroine survive) it was foredoomed to failure. Howells doubtless knew it also, and not improbably accepted my invitation for that very reason; a fact worth recording as an instance of his friendliness to young authors, and also on account of the lapidary phrase in which, as we left the theater, he summed up the reason for the play's failure.

"Yes—what the American public always wants is a tragedy with a happy ending."

—Edith Wharton, *A Backward Glance*

One

G riffin Mill was broke, he was down to his last six million dollars. No one knew he was ruined—not Lisa, his wife; not June, his first wife; not even his lawyer—but the $3 million in investments that he made in the late 1990s (on the advice of his business manager, convinced of a permanent new economy charged by an expansion of wealth made possible by technology), having reached $22 million in February of 2001, were now barely doubled; and what might have been $25 million—if the Studio's stock had once again reached $80, and he could have exercised his option for a half-million shares at $30—was now gone forever, because the parent company had made a stupid merger, box office was down, it would never return, and the stock hadn't seen better than $17 in five years. He owed June and their two children, Ethan and Jessa, $300,000 a year out of his salary of $1.5 million before taxes, but since his income after taxes was barely $750,000 a year, that left him only $450,000 to spend after the alimony. He paid two mortgages. If he sold his house with Lisa he might clear a million, but where would they go? The distress of his situation made him impotent, and he was allergic to Viagra.

It was Griffin's impotence and depression that had sent Lisa to a divorce lawyer, who asked her to secretly make copies of Griffin's financial statements. Griffin, who loved his second wife and believed in the strength of their marriage much as he once believed in the value of Global Crossing (high of $61, low of zero), had never established a way of hiding his assets, and his prenuptial agreement with Lisa was generous, so it was a shock to her when the lawyer wrote some numbers on a paper and showed her how she could not afford a divorce, since her share of the stock would be less than $5 million, which, invested at what the lawyer suggested should be a conservative 3 percent, would generate about $150,000 a year. She might win more stock after a lawsuit, but even with $300,000 before taxes, she would bump around in coach, collect her own bags, and never again enjoy Christmas in Maui in a suite that cost $1,000 a day. The lawyer advised her to stay with Griffin until he beat her.

"Do you think he will?" she asked.

"Shit happens," said the lawyer, an expression of resignation so infinitely repulsive to Lisa that in the rebound from the meeting she located some pity for her husband, who in secret carried his financial ruin at the cost of his cock.

The lawyer's suggestion that she return to work was ridiculous. She had been a bad actress, her talent limited by her reflective intelligence and by a murmur, just next to her conscience, of her mother's last words, before she had died of lymphoma five years ago, written in her impersonally elegant cursive on hospital stationery, expressing dismay that her bright and gracious daughter *would follow a path so pebbled with crushed vanity.* Lisa was thirty-seven; she was old. Griffin was fifty-two; he was old.

After the meeting Lisa went to pick up her daughter, Willa, from Children's Lincoln, the school founded in 1940 by Hollywood Communists sympathetic to the Lincoln Brigade, who set their mission statement on a bronze plaque at the entrance.

DURING THE SPANISH CIVIL WAR, 1936–1939, TWO
THOUSAND EIGHT HUNDRED AMERICAN VOLUNTEERS
TOOK UP ARMS TO DEFEND THE SPANISH REPUBLIC
AGAINST THE FASCISTS AND JOINED THE ABRAHAM LIN-
COLN BRIGADE. THE "LINCOLNS" CAME FROM ALL WALKS
OF LIFE AND INCLUDED STUDENTS, SEAMEN, LUMBER-
JACKS, AND TEACHERS. THEY ESTABLISHED THE FIRST
RACIALLY INTEGRATED MILITARY UNIT IN UNITED STATES
HISTORY.

CHILDREN'S LINCOLN IS DEDICATED TO HONORING
THEIR SELFLESS EXAMPLE. IT IS THE SCHOOL'S MAN-
DATE TO RAISE UP CHILDREN FROM ALL BACKGROUNDS
WHO WILL, WITH DIGNITY AND RESPECT, SUCCEED
WHERE THE LINCOLN BRIGADE FAILED, FOR LACK OF
COMRADES, AND FIGHT BRAVELY IN THE ADVANCING
LONG STRUGGLE AGAINST NAZISM AND FASCISM.

Well, things change and in 1992, without ceremony, the
plaque showed up on the wall behind the manual skills shelf of the
library, and though everyone in town now referred to the school as
Children's *Mercedes*, almost everyone wanted in. The Children's Lincoln original motto, **CHILDREN OF THE WORLD, UNITE!**
became **WHERE ROOTS TAKE WINGS**, as common among
West Side private elementary schools as **SHE GOT THE HOUSE**
in a yacht basin. Tuition at Children's Lincoln cost $19,000 a year.
None of the school's fathers were lumberjacks, although a few
dressed the part.

Lisa usually sent the housekeeper to pick up Willa, because
Griffin's two children with June Mercator were also, as friends of
the school say, *in the Lincoln Community*, but instead of graduating

directly to middle and then upper school at Coldwater Academy, Griffin's first choice for him, Ethan was now in the eighth grade of a public school program for something called gifted children at the Walter Reed Middle School in Studio City, along with the children of gardeners, auto-body repairmen, public defenders, and the children of the people the public defenders defended. Jessa, though, was still in Children's Lincoln, a year behind Willa, and June almost always met her at school, and Lisa didn't like being in the line of cars with her, and there she was, two cars ahead. She saw June look at her in the rearview mirror, and nodded.

Willa, from his second marriage, was twelve years old, seven months older than Jessa, the second child of his first marriage.

Though he still lived with June the year of Willa's birth, the marriage had already decayed, and it was felt by everybody in town that it was June who betrayed Griffin by getting pregnant when she knew his affair with Lisa was serious. He was still married to June when he bought a house three blocks away and moved in with Lisa.

And their daughter, Jessa, was still in Children's Lincoln. He had made no promises to June that Jessa would also go to public school. Griffin surprised June by not calling his lawyer to threaten institutionalization for her if she persisted in trying to send Ethan to public school. She expected from Griffin the legal version of a pig screaming to death, but impersonating guilt, he respected her social agony and knew or guessed that she felt naked and covered in bed sores in any room with the wives she held as friends in the years of her marriage, because they had all known the truth about his affair and kept it from her.

Forced by custom to carry the burden of decorum, submitting to the rules, June saw her life twisted by inexplicable geometries while she saw Lisa, at worst, circle Griffin's needs whorishly as he moved forward in the world. Other than the second wife's required public demonstration of restrained benevolence and good manners (Sherman, this time sparing Atlanta), whenever the two women faced each other—say, Griffin and Lisa dropping Jessa and Ethan at June's after a custody weekend, and Lisa is in the car with Griffin and June comes out to the street because she has to remind Griffin of some mundane obligation to the kids, and she's wearing Griffin's old sweatpants and Lisa is dressed for something that looks like fun with other adults—June might have burned with the question, What cost does Lisa pay? if she didn't have the one grand consoling ugly answer: Her rival's only child was a little bit stupid. No fear that the spawn of Lisa's sin would humiliate Ethan and Jessa by taking not only their father but also an Ivy League degree and a smooth ride for the duration. Children's Lincoln would never have accepted such a dull girl without the pull of connection, because Willa was darling but slow and—well, actually, not so darling. Annoying. Willa annoyed the world. Slow shifting eyes and a crinkle of disgust around her perfect little nose made folks happy to hate her. Other kids avoided her, and without the Children's Lincoln's rule that every child in the class must invite every other child in the class to every birthday party, none of them would have given her three seconds out of school. Behind her face, the only part of her body or spirit remotely enviable about her, Willa's tongue knocked against her palate, and when she spoke quickly, in one of her frequent rages, the words died in her mouth like a gasping fish slapping the wet floor of a canoe.

June knew that Lisa did not love her own daughter, and worse—or better—June knew that Lisa preferred Jessa, in part because a cruel God had impressed Jessa's face with his opinion of the father and his crimes, dredging from Griffin's genetic history the loutish mug of a drunk peasant in the corner of a Brueghel, eyes forced nickel-thin by freckled porky cheeks. What an awful deity, to give the stupid one the look of intelligence, and the brilliant one the look of low brainpower, capable of nothing more than dung-hill feral greed. In the mirror, each saw the face the other deserved.

Jessa Mill was a strange child. With a fraudulent amiability, she accepted Lisa's fussy affections, because if she rejected Lisa her father would blame June. Her favorite phrase in the universe was "Instant Messenger." She wanted to start a band called The Instant Messengers of Death. From the murderous current of the age, she attracted drifting thoughts of assassination.

June did not know this about her, but neither did Lisa. No one knew much about her.

About Ethan, June knew that Ethan hated Lisa only from loyalty to his own mother, and she told him not to say how much he hated the weekends when he left his mother alone while he and Jessa stayed at their father's hated house.

And Griffin, always difficult to read, probably knew all of this better than she did and had traded Ethan for Jessa, since he needed at least one child in the school to use as a tool for his ambitions in Hollywood. Griffin was on the board of Children's Lincoln, where an active role in the parent community served as another front in the battle to stay alive in Hollywood. As chairman of the school's annual fund-raising dinner, he had license to call every parent in the school and ask for donations to the two auctions, silent and public. They answered his call with scripts signed by the full casts of a dozen television shows, bottles of important wine, weekends at a spa in Ojai, all-access passes to concerts, the free use of a private jet anywhere in the country, baskets of chocolates, toys, clothes, musical instruments, records, and a catered dinner cooked by three private chefs. He even told June that he took this active role in his elementary school's fund-raising to put his children at the top of Coldwater's acceptance list and also to add a social pretext for work. When the acceptance letter from Coldwater arrived, a thick packet of medical forms and appeals for donations, Griffin told her it felt like a film inhaling a hundred million dollars on the first weekend of release, and then said, "Look, this helps with the other stuff too," meaning it was imposing and sexy and helped purge the scandal that was now as old as his two daughters.

It shocked June that everyone accepted every new social arrangement so long as two of the three adults in any rearrangement consented and one of them was powerful or rich, but she tried hard not to let rage become indignation. There wouldn't be those biblical admonitions to defend the widow and the orphan if God hadn't seen the need.

The bell rings in the alley, and the children are called outside.

June wants to resist Griffin's gloomy expectations of a collapsed world, but the parents she knows are worn out from the burden of children, and she believes that the death of purpose, the death of the family as a unit of physical survival in a nature that yields food only by the work of a group, is the omen of global death, because the parents feel the uselessness of their efforts. No matter how much they tried, the children were awful, even the sweetest. They graduated from high school with the strength of a potato chip, fried and fragile. The narrow desperate ambition for their children to get into Brown and Stanford was proof to June that Griffin was right: The panic about the saving power of a degree from the Ivy League was the canary in the mine shaft, the best evidence of the human species' deep sensitivity to impending extinction. The parents in other countries who raise their children for suicide martyrdom express the same alert recognition. Better for a child to die immediately in the name of a cause than waste away slowly in a world without safe water. Blowing yourself up on a bus on Ben Yehuda Street is an early acceptance to Princeton.

. . .

What the divorce lawyer told Lisa made her want to throw up, not so much because of her husband's financial statements as for the waste of those years in her life when she might have done something smarter than act, when she might have become a healer like her friend Elixa, or a lawyer or a reporter or a social worker or an astronaut or a civil engineer or anything but a bad actress. She wasn't stupid, as her mother's ghost reminded her too often, and she might yet give her life a meaning she could look back on with satisfaction when she was old, but . . . but. But what? She thought, I have failed my husband. He left his wife for me, he sacrificed two children for me, he suffers for his new family, and in what way have I given him the consideration a man deserves? In what way have I given up something of myself to him, given the father of my child, whatever my bad thoughts about her, a gift of the pain of my own sacrifice, even the sacrifice of my pride, burnt on the altar of conceit, my disdain for the Hollywood that rejected me, the Hollywood that was personal when it said *It's not personal*—in what way can I help bring his focus back to his difficult work, give the man the pleasure he needs? What does he need, another woman or, finally, my ass?

And here comes Willa.

"Hello Wills, get in. Tell me about your day."

Willa opened the back door, and by the sullen refusal to talk and the disgusted vehemence with which she threw her heavy backpack to the seat Lisa saw the coming tantrum like a squall line beyond the reef.

"Do you want to talk about it?"

Willa buckled herself in and said, "They hay me."

"They *hate* you," said Lisa, with emphasis on the *t*, stupidly trying to correct and, instead, affirming.

"Maaaaaameeee. I cahn helh myseff. Thass why they hay me. Thass why they may funna me."

No, Lisa wanted to say, they don't may funna ooh, they just don't like you, and it has nothing to do with the way you talk because you only flub your words when you don't get your own way. Speech therapy didn't help because Willa liked her power; there's one of her in every class, the spoiled bilingual brat, her two languages English and Baby. In time she might drop the pre-K act to protect her marginal place in the group, but the inner baby of this type never really grows up. Lisa worried for her daughter's future, especially without a father rich enough to save her from starvation in the world, because she was of that tribe in Hollywood who either rise to the top, with their tantrums excused for their genius, or last about five years before everyone gets sick of them and they're fired and disappear. Lisa worried that her daughter was nothing more than a pigeon. You never see old pigeons.

She watched Jessa Mill get into June's car. She wished she knew more about June.

. . .

She doesn't know that June goes to Goth clubs, sometimes alone, sometimes with her hairdresser, and doesn't tell anyone from real life. She's forty-two and not so old for the clubs, but the wives of Windsor Square were never Goth, even when they were young, and she keeps her industrial music collection a secret from them. It's too complicated, she tells herself, to let them see this part of her. She likes the feeling of being a superhero, playing the role of June Mercator Mill as her alter ego. That's how she feels about her trips to Goth clubs a few nights a month. Her Goth self is wrapped up in a weird blend with Mormonism too, from a forty-five-minute tour of Mormon

Square in Salt Lake City, and whatever Judaism she inhales from the Jews around her. She's not the oldest woman in the club, and the lights are low, and she wears spectral makeup, darker than Siouxsie Sioux, covering the lines around her eyes with delicate gore, so that she looks like the Mistress of the House of Usher after a raven croaking "Nevermore" has blinded her, artfully.

She doesn't fuck anyone, doesn't talk to anyone, she just floats until she lands near the DJ's booth. DJs have a look, a glance that's ironic, courageous, deliberate, hilarious, and profound, and she likes to humble herself in the aura of what she believes is the DJ's superior knowledge of life.

She wastes time and makes herself miserable chasing men who are chronosocio appropriate. The men who are the right age for her are mostly creeps. All men without women are creeps, she believes, until they have a woman. They may turn out to be jerks, but that's a different burden and part of the deal.

And then there was the Mormon afternoon that started when she answered this ad on Match.Com.

VERITASEXY: 45. Attractive humanoid (I'm told) professional, intelligent, clean (body, not necessarily mind), non-player (looking for "the" relationship), witty/sarcastic sense of humor. I like a wide variety of things, and I am very open-minded (I'll try anything at least once, and if I like it—I'll try again!). Will eat just about anything, but preferences are BBQ/Grilling, Mexican, Indian (eastern), Asian and sushi. I like most music (no rap or hip-hop, though). I love to ski. I love to play tennis. I like Maui. I like Milan. I like camping via tent, travel trailer, or Four Seasons hotel. Romantic, cuddler, generous. I'm looking for . . . you.

She fell for Veritasexy because he was a Harvard guy and she really wanted someone smart, and she liked the combination of Ivy League and BBQ, sarcasm and generosity; especially that. Her profile at that time had been:

JUNEBUG4PLAY: 42. I know better than to look here, or really anywhere for that matter, for love. Instead I look for just really good companionship. Love follows or it doesn't. And sometimes we don't want love, we just want release. Like sometimes I just want the release of a good run down a slope in Deer Valley (love the snow there, love the service, hate the prices), sometimes I just need to jog an extra mile in the morning, sometimes I just need good cause to scream and hope the neighbors don't mind. And sometimes I don't care what the neighbors think. But I am a single mom, so I have to say that, but I'm also free most weekends, so I have to say that too. If you're a man with a sexy phone voice, a man who understands what's going on in the world and can tell me about it, a man who can make me laugh, and a man who lives not too far from where I live (Los Angeles), let's talk. Let's even . . . chat?

Everyone would know what she meant by *chat*. She needed fucking, she wanted holding and cuddling, but she also needed to come, and she didn't want to jack herself off watching thirty-second porn clips; when she wanted connection with someone, she'd join a chat line on the phone, or pick a guy from Craigslist who lived anywhere in the country, it didn't matter, trade a few e-mails, then give him a cell-phone number she kept just for e-dates, and if he liked to talk hot, she'd lie in bed with a vibrator in hand and talk about sex. June liked hearing a man come; she liked to hear the way a man, while he's talking about all the ways he's going to fuck a woman hard, loses his theatrical aggression as he gratefully accepts the woman's breath to penetrate his hand, his coming softening his voice. She liked to hear him lose contact with her for the few seconds that he came, didn't hate him for the depletion of his interest in her, and didn't mind that she usually couldn't come until after they finished talking, when she could edit the fantasy she shared with him, make it exactly what she wanted but always keeping the image of a man, somewhere in the United States, maybe a hotel room, maybe alone in his apartment, maybe in his office, working late, holding his cock for her, staining his underwear for her, *because* of her. She supposed some women beat themselves up about this kind of thing, inscribing their names on the walls and floors of an infinite memorial to the death of spirit by confusion, but the Goth part of her spirit let her off the hook; it was all more of the horror of the world and not so dreadful to feel guilty about, or else, even if she felt suicidal after hanging up the phone, it was just part of the joke.

After a late-afternoon coffee with Veritasexy, then dinner at a barbecue place in the Valley, they talked on the phone about fucking and he invited her to ski in Park City two weekends later. They flew to Utah on a Friday morning after she sent the kids to school. He took a suite for them at the Deer Valley Inn. She skied better than he did, which turned him on, he said, and they smooched on the chair lift. She didn't like him, but she couldn't have said why until they were sitting in the hot tub, after skiing but before dinner, and they talked about how hungry they were and he said he was looking forward to a "premium-brand margarita." A voice in her head, not her mother's voice but its understudy, said, "You cannot fuck a man who talks about premium-brand margaritas, no matter where he went to school; trust me on this." But after two margaritas, both premium-label, she fucked him. All the time he was pumping her, forcing himself to fuck harder because the head of his dick was premium-numb, double numb through the condom, she heard herself trying to tell Griffin about this, about what she missed about him, his fucking when he was strong, before Ethan was born, and to her own dismay, for her body's betrayal of her self-respect, she even came, thinking about Griffin.

In the morning she packed and left Veritasexy, who said, agreeably, "I think you have some issues about intimacy, but if you ever want to see me again I'm there for you." The earliest flight she could take was at 2 P.M., and with four hours of nothing to do she went to Temple Square, to see the Mormon Temple, which she couldn't get into because you have to be a Mormon in good standing with the Church. In the plaza before the granite temple, about a dozen girls in long dresses, with name tags on their breasts, stood like a flower shop's unsold lilies in the last half hour of Good Friday.

A cold wind blew from the Wasatch Mountains, and the girls wore insufficient cardigans. Some of the girls were talking to visitors, some walked backward while they towed the faithful and the curious on a guided tour, and to collect her for the next group, two of them approached June. They were Shifra, from New Zealand, with a high wide forehead and at her hairline a few sad little pimples that acne creams can't touch, and Puah, from Idaho, a virgin in every way, June was sure of this, and June wanted for herself that quiet faith in chastity and fidelity. This little girl didn't talk dirty at midnight to men whose faces she would only ever know from their digital profiles.

June followed them, her intellectual curiosity knocked aside by the determination of faith awakened. Jesus resurrected came to America and preached to the lost tribes of Israel. When the Mormon faithful die, each becomes a god of his own world, like the God of this world, this worst of all worlds. And the generosity of our God, who not only gave his only son that we should live but allows us a baptism even when we have died. "If you're interested," said Shifra, "you can visit the Mormon genealogy center across the street from Temple Square, where we compile the names of the dead and baptize their souls for eternity."

Eternity!

June became a secret Mormon, without an official conversion and without study, but the eternity of the soul had never made such sense before, since only the eternity of the soul explains the recurrence of agony. Her soul and not her ego cried out for what Griffin had torn away from her, not physical company but his own soul. If she felt pain, then so must he, because if she was torn, then Griffin was also shredded where their souls once were knit. Hating Griffin, then, was hating part of herself, although she knew how thin was her knowledge of the Mormon God, the Angel Moroni, the gilt figure on top of the Mormon Temple in Los Angeles, pointed toward the building in Salt Lake where she saw the truth revealed.

Her husband's second marriage confused her, not because he fell in love with someone else but because she now knew that her soul was still married to Griffin, no matter what papers they had signed, no matter what the judge agreed to. She could not marry anyone else because Griffin was her husband. But he was also married to Lisa, and she supposed that Lisa's soul was also bound to Griffin's for eternity. They would have plenty of time to talk about this when all three of them were dead.

Two

I f he converted his job into sound, Griffin heard nothing but a drone, an almost white noise, and against one's expectation that such a terrible buzz would leave him drained of the creative intelligence necessary for deciding which films to make, the almost white noise sustained a fantasy of the muffled engines and rush of air outside a company jet, and within the jet, Griffin could live forever, immune to bad luck. Having worked for twenty-five years at this game—for a while even running his own small film company, until the backers decided that municipal bonds would make them more money—his was the business of relationships, and he supervised—no, he supported—the harder work of six producers who worked exclusively with the Studio. The producers, given millions by the Studio, bought books and paid for scripts and then tried to develop them into movies. Griffin read the scripts himself, but assistants with degrees from the best universities in America also read the scripts and compiled the notes. No one could call him lazy, he did read the scripts and he did have his suggestions, but every change he advised came from the inner voice that first spoke to him about six months into his service, when he understood how to anticipate the notes from Stella Baal, President of Production, who did have the power to say, "Yes, we will spend a hundred million dollars on this picture. Congratulations." Stella was five years younger than

Griffin but she understood two things better than he did: the movie business and the taste of the audience. Lisa, trying to make Griffin feel good about his role as a messenger, told him that he was a midwife. He saw himself as the eunuch referee at an orgy.

Griffin rotated a special vocabulary through his notes—a practice that began in fear, when he started at the company and wanted to make certain that he sounded like a man with a vision—and over the years the producers, who at first mocked Griffin's jargon, soon respected what he said and, in advance of Griffin's notes, would guide the writers toward the goal of meeting them. A memo from Griffin always included, depending on his mood, such words or phrases as *objectives, decisions, code of behavior, abstract objects, sub-goals, jeopardy, call to the quest, first confrontation with the mentor, resurrection, the return,* and *the second return.*

Not that his notes really mattered to the producers Griffin sent them to, since his six producers also had staffs of genius readers, and then the directors and stars whom those producers hired or wanted to hire paid their own sacerdotal councils to prepare their own notes. None of this should imply that Griffin slid through the day—no, his movies made money, so he was doing what he was hired for—but he had learned from Stella to give up his own taste and keep before him the memory of every test screening and the subsequent grosses of every film he'd seen and to surrender to the audience, admit that the audience knew what it wanted, and his hard job was to help put old wine in a new bottle. He consoled himself with the example of Eric Clapton, a brilliant musician who might have been as difficult for the masses as Bob Dylan, or Hendrix if he had lived, but Clapton pursued the middle way. Let someone else take a film to Sundance; if the director was good, Griffin would offer her a commercial script (no loose ends, no irony, clean justice for all) and teach her the secret of how to keep working until the choice to leave is yours.

Over the years with Stella, Griffin understood that Stella's prime objective was to keep her amazing job and that her *milk bath of purification*, her *substitute imperative*, her *third and successful attempt at killing the monster*, and finally, *Personal Will: the most important weapon in a Hero's arsenal*—all the stages and character attributes to bring forward the victory Griffin wrote about in his notes—were true and enduring in his boss's life. What was theory to Griffin was religion to Stella Baal.

But Stella would not keep her job forever, because *That's the way the cookie crumbles*, and Griffin wanted it; more than that, he wanted the crown privilege of the job, a seat on the board of the parent company with a view of all its divisions and, with that view, serious money, for Griffin wasn't afraid that the world was coming to an end; no, he was in a panic because he knew the world was already ten years dead and the future was just necrosis. All around him Griffin saw the blood pooling as it settled after the heart had stopped, and he wanted his own private island, and no metaphor of an island: he wanted an atoll in the Pacific, in Tonga or Fiji, forty acres with good soil; and to have that private island he needed to be very very rich. Before the crash he had most of the money he needed, but the lying shithead Stanford brainiacs in Silicon Valley, and the lying shyster Texas Republican goyim shitheads of Enron and their lying shyster Jew allies, and the lying shithead rabbis of the Houston Holocaust Museum who let the Enron shitheads goy and Jew together put their staining names on the museum's dedication wall to wash their names, and the not lying but still fucking culpable fucking gullible shithead who told him not to sell Lucent and Global Crossing because "Warren Buffett never sells" but skipped the lecture about how Warren Buffett never buys overpriced shit on the recommendation of carnival shills, had left him with only enough cash—forget his possibly worthless stock options which he was reluctant to exercise and sell because he'd have to file with the SEC and then everyone

in town would enthusiastically guess the reason—to charter a heli-
copter out of the city when the starving hordes turned Los Angeles
into a lifeboat eleven days at sea minus food or fresh water—and to
what armed skinhead haven in the Sierra foothills could that heli-
copter lift him without an invitation?

Everyone wanted a seat on that board, and all the boards like it,
because the only club better is the Senate. You had to deliver, but
even if you didn't, the whole point of being at the table in the CEO
cabal was power and action and helping each other make a lot of
money, fighting to get rid of the people who wanted your seat at the
table or whose strategies could bring attention to the scam and hurt
the stock, and then backing up your allies if the law or the share-
holders questioned the methods and executive pay. Even if he lasted
another three or four years, the buyout on his contract wouldn't be
enough for Griffin's purpose, not for an island, not even a farm with
deep good wells and solar power in New Zealand, with a bunker for
two thousand pounds of food.

Griffin lacked a *mentor figure, a shape-shifter,* and *two comic spirit
guides,* but with a *strong through-line for his super objective,* he believed that
the weapons he needed would come to hand when he least expected
them, so long as he had *faith,* which he might lose at the end of the
second act but which, by the *third-act bump,* would return. And there,
he knew, was the problem, because he had gained his piece of the
world at the cost of faith, in himself more than God or the future;
he had lost this faith too early in the story, at the end of the first
act; and at fifty he had passed the age at which most of the members of the club, men of faith in themselves more than in God or
the future, had already been recognized, tapped, initiated, and
branded. Finally, his premature loss of faith caught up with him,
because it always does. He knew from having outlined so many plots

that a lead character who starts the second act without faith is not the hero but the adversary, and *the adversary is always defeated by his own mistake.*

Taking an inventory, making a list of what his own bad faith had cost him, he surrendered his hatred of the shitheads, except for the senior managers who dumped their stock when they read the auditor's secret reports. He would not achieve the serenity of wealth until he accepted responsibility for the sin of losing his money, because he had felt the market's weakness but for dim, greedy, or stupid reasons allowed his business manager to have the final word when, three months before the collapse, as his secretary touted Nortel, Griffin felt the tremors of a crash inside the shelter made from all his pretty stock certificates, and watched it fall, and stood there.

And there were things he'd done he didn't want to think about, because he saw no way to ever make amends, since confession would be his ruin, even the end of his life, and how then could he help his children? Can the hero have a secret? Achilles had his heel. *A vulnerable hero* is a sympathetic hero, so when he *battles the adversary,* he is weak and the contest is *in ritual doubt.* Griffin knew his wound didn't qualify, because it came not from battle but self-infliction.

And was it really a wound or just a secret? There's always that thing, the dragon in my rearview mirror.

I'm not a Jew but I need a rabbi, thought Griffin. Everyone here is a Jew, and look at them. They know something that I don't: how to live with guilt. And they talk to God. I need to talk to God. No, God knows already. God knows the truth. Why take up God's time with what God already knows?

So, setting aside the horror of his moral inventory, and rejecting the pornographic luxury of his dread about the future, Griffin told his secretary, her nest egg emptied by Nortel, to hold all calls. There are men and women at the highest level of the parent company, above the motion picture division, who would love me if they knew me, but they see me, however well paid, as Stella's nicely groomed left hand, with no one on her right. Stella knows enough to keep me away from that table, because she knows I would make a good impression on the people she reports to and that, delicately and discreetly, a few careful weeks later, someone from that table would call me at home one night and ask me for my honest opinion of Stella, not for what I said, but how I said what I didn't say. And I would reply, "I can't tell you how much I've learned from her. What's smart about her, and I think what makes her so valuable to the company, is that she's not trying to hit a home run all the time; she gets up to bat and knocks out singles and doubles, almost every time. I'd say she knows how to consistently hit doubles better than anyone else in the game. She has fewer strikeouts than anyone else in the business. If you don't strike out, you score. She's incredible."

But the parent company doesn't want doubles, it wants big burly bases-loaded triples and homers, it wants triumph more than measured success, because this is fucking show business, and the company wants the show. And this is what scared Griffin about such a call, because Stella was younger than he was and good at an impossibly hard job and everyone in town still made fun of her, maybe because she was a woman though mostly because she was a pathological liar, but setting that one aside—on the shelf where he dropped his fearless moral inventory—since at least half the people judging her were demonic sociopaths themselves, aides to Beelzebub and lying when they called her a liar, Griffin worried that, if given the chance to make the big decisions, he would strike out.

So, having no faith but knowing enough that to pray without

belief in an answer marks the first step toward redemption, Griffin prayed.

Dear God I don't know what I'm doing here with my elbows on my knees and my face in my hands, staring at the carpet; and I know I'm pretending that I don't believe you're there so you'll be fooled into thinking that my effort to talk to you when I think you're just a fairy tale should be rewarded ahead of the prayers of the holy saints who feed the poor and fight for the widows and orphans; and I know you probably can't be fooled, which means I'm wasting your time, but since you, God, are infinite what's a few minutes here? I am confused and I ask only for clarity. I am agitated and I ask only for distance from that agitation, since I can't expect to be free of it. You know the wrongs I have done and, considering my sins, what you've given me is so amazing that this gift should be listed in the register of miracles. In spite of my sins you have rewarded me with three beautiful children and the ability to support my beautiful first wife, June, who doesn't yet have a career or a second husband but of course if she remarries I'll still pay child support for my son, Ethan, and my daughter Jessa; and also you have given me the ability to support my beautiful second wife, Lisa, and our beautiful Willa, but Dear God I have a terrible feeling based on recent evidence that maybe you've started my punishment, so hear me, O Lord: If your judgment against me has begun, why do you have to punish my wives and children for my sins? Because if I fall they will fall too. Can the merits of my grandparents and great-grandparents, who so far as I know were honest people, wash away some of the blood on my hands so it doesn't mess up my wives and children? Please, God, this has become a real prayer and I ask you God to give me another chance; I ask you God to give me some strength when I meet scary people; I ask you, God, to give me clarity so that when an opportunity for something real in this town shows up, I can recognize that opportunity and grab that chance, God, grab that chance and make it mine, and God I promise that I will make great charity and be worthy in every way I can and do good, as I understand it.

What is done is done. I will be judged in the balance. I have not done my best.

. . .

In the stuttering slow drive home, the traffic sluggish as though weighed down by a million guilty secrets, Griffin's secretary put through a call from the head of a network, a Children's Lincoln dad.

Griffin told him that he needed swag for the silent auction.

"Like signed scripts?"

"Like DVD packages of all your TV shows."

"It's yours."

Never ask a big man for a small favor; that's the rule, but in this case the small favor to help the kids gave the rich donors a fuzzy little glow of self-appreciation for not having shredded all their connections to simple gestures.

At home in time for dinner, he asked Willa about her day, then couldn't tune his attention to the sound of her voice. Willa could have used her suspicion of his disinterest as the reason for clotted speech, but she usually spoke clearly around Griffin because he gave her what she wanted.

A kiss good night, damp lips on his cheek, lights out, door open just this much and leave the hall light on, and back to the master bedroom, lock the door, to find Lisa on the floor, naked, sitting cross-legged before a scented candle in a votive glass. She had never done this before, and he didn't know what resolve had brought her to the inspiration for this ritual.

"What's this for?" He didn't want this to be about sex, but there she was naked, her body open to him. He was sorry about the way Viagra gave him a migraine headache and added a blue filter to his vision, but he consoled himself with the thought that he wasn't alone with a limp prick, that Viagra was the answer science gave to society when society asked, Where did the erection go? At first he blamed his problems on the usual utilitarian quality of his pillow talk and that, to be fair to the rest of the day, his entire conversation with Lisa consisted of mutual temperature taking, assessment of the children's needs, and his obligation to schedule the sacrifice of a few hours of work every other week to see his two other children in school or pick them up in the afternoon. This surrender to the concession of humanity which few other executives bothered with did not give Griffin much satisfaction, because, while he enjoyed his children's company—in measured amounts that were always exceeded—after more than a few hours with them he felt like a fish given too much food. He assumed that every man he knew, or almost every man, had a few of those hard-on pills in his house all the time. Now he felt awful for his wife, who stared into the small flame without looking up at him.

Lisa said, "We need to talk. I like candles, the shadows move, you know? Shadows, moving. Stare at the flame, see the past, see the future. That's what we have to do. Sit down."

"Should I take off my clothes?"

"You don't have to."

He grunted as he lowered himself, knees hurting, but respected Lisa's concentration and withheld the complaint about his old body.

"I went to see a lawyer about getting a divorce."

Griffin had not expected this, had not thought it possible, and in one of those eternal instants in which revelation charges the mind with the knowledge that comes with rings of implications expanding on a few original causes, he understood without having to ask why: work and dick.

"Who did you call?"

"That's the wrong question, Griffin. Not who, why?"

"I know why."

"Tell me what you know."

"I'm unhappy at work and my penis is soft."

"It's more than that. Those are the symptoms. And I told the lawyer, and he said we couldn't afford a divorce."

"So you'll separate?"

She passed her hand over the flame before she answered him.

"I look in the flame and I see that you've been keeping your troubles to yourself, because you want to protect me from being worried about you, but I'm already worried about you. I see that you've forgotten your bad reasons for doing things, and all you remember is your good reasons. Take care of the family. Help the Studio. Be a good father. Be a loving husband. Make this marriage work. You forgot your bad reasons. You forgot about sex. You forgot about money. You forgot about competition. Or you're afraid you're too old for sex and money and competition. You have friends with their own jets, men who started out with you. You have a good life but you're six months from being broke. You're not saving any money, because you can't. You think you're too old to have your own Gulfstream, even a share in one. I see it's this kind of negative attitude that's the reason you've been held back. And I haven't helped you."

"You've been fine. Don't beat yourself up."

"I'm not. I'm looking hard, and I see some things about myself that I don't like. That I thought the deal was, Marry this guy who's an inch from the top, and in five years you'll have a house on the Vineyard and a condo in Aspen. Well, it didn't work out that way. Now what? What's my piece in this? What I didn't understand was that for me to get out of you what I married you for, you had to get out of me what you married *me* for—except you don't know what you married me for, and I don't either. It was something to do with June, but it's more than that. I don't know. The more the time passes, the less I understand why you left June . . .

Because her house was haunted by the ghost of David Kahane.

. . . but it doesn't matter that you may have had a bad reason to marry me, or no reason. What matters is that I be a good wife and create a reason. And I did not create a reason for you to have married me. I actually allowed myself to be a trophy wife, which I'm embarrassed to admit. So that's my piece. I let you hang yourself. I watched you tie the rope around your neck for my own entertainment. That's pretty stupid, because I didn't see that if you die I die with you. I don't know if you have enough juice left to actually help rescue yourself, but you won't get that juice if I don't help you. What the candle shows me is that you can't be strong without my help. So I can't watch you anymore, I have to be on your side of the camera. Okay. From now on, the deal is, If you do everything you can to make this thing work, I will do everything I can to help you."

"If you really help me, nothing can stop us."

"Hold my hand."

She held their hands over the thin column of heat rising from the flame.

"That hurts," said Griffin.

"Griffin, tell me why you're unhappy."

"Well, I guess in story terms, I'm still overcome with grief for my wound."

"Listen to yourself. You have a working vocabulary of about eight hundred words. That's all you need in this town, but I know you used to have more. When I met you there were more. And I had more. My vocabulary is just as thin as yours. So we'll start with simple language. What, Griffin Mill, do you want most?"

"I want to change jobs."

"What kind of job do you want?"

"A job with access to wealth."

"Good. Change jobs, take a risk. Don't be scared."

"You mean that."

"You took a risk when you told me you loved me. You left a wife who loved you. I'm not afraid to say that. I know you can leave me the way you left her, the way you left June."

"I wouldn't."

"You don't know that."

"Maybe that's my problem: that I won't leave you. Maybe leaving you would be proof of what you say I need, ambition. Maybe I'm too decent. I'm stuck. That's my wound."

"Now you're getting close. That's right. You're stuck inside yourself. What's keeping you there? Griffin, what secrets are left between us?"

"I haven't slept with anyone else."

"I know that. But what does that prove? You treat your fidelity like an endurance test. You're a white-knuckle monogamist; the airplane of your marriage is either going through heavy turbulence or it's crashing and you're grabbing the armrests, squeezing them until your knuckles are white, and there's a parachute but you're afraid to take the leap. Do you think that makes me happy? You should have slept with another woman. Maybe you'd be happier if you had a mistress."

"You wouldn't be happy."

"I can handle myself. I'm talking about you. I want to help you. Do you want my help?"

"Of course I do."

"Really? Because if I'm going to help you, I have to be rough on you. If you want to have wealth when you're sixty-five, it's time to quit the production side of Hollywood."

"That's what I've been thinking. How did you know that?"

"Because there's nothing else for you to do. If I had someplace else to go, I'd leave you, and when I realized there was nowhere to go, I figured out why. And then I figured out the one basic question to ask you. Who do you want to work with? If you could work with anyone in town, doing anything, who would it be?"

Griffin couldn't answer. He stared at the flame. The question humiliated him. He should have thought of this a long time ago. Lisa hummed the theme from *Jeopardy!* and Griffin smiled.

"Time's up," she said. "Just name someone, anyone. Now."

"The only person in town who has the power to take me all the way up, and who could use me, is Phillip Ginsberg," said Griffin. "He's the third- or fourth-smartest guy in town. I'm convinced of it."

"Call him."

"I can't approach him for a job directly because I'm too low on the totem pole."

"What about Ricky Mellen, could he call? Isn't that what lawyers are for?"

"I don't think it would make a difference."

"We can have a party and invite him."

"No. He would never come, and the inappropriate chumminess of the invitation could ruin me. The only place we intersect is Coldwater. He grew up in town, his father was an ophthalmologist, he graduated from Coldwater, and his son is in the eighth grade there. He's the president of the board of trustees, for the reason I help out at Children's Lincoln, not because he's devoted to the place but because if he needs something from someone who wants to get his kid into the school, he can get the kid in if the kid isn't brain-dead or autistic. I could get to Ginsberg through the school, but probably not until Ethan starts there."

"So you do that, and then what?"

"I don't know."

"I'm going to tell you something I really shouldn't talk about, but this is an emergency. It's life or death for us. Okay. His wife wrote a book."

"He's divorced. He's gay. Don't you know that?"

"That's what I'm talking about. Candace Ginsberg wrote a book after they split up. She typed it and made a copy, and the copy was copied. And circulated. It wasn't published and men aren't allowed to read it. I probably shouldn't let you read it, but this is for my family."

"You have this here?"

"In my closet, second drawer from the bottom, all the way back. Turn off the light and take it downstairs. I want to go to sleep."

"Why is it such a secret?"

"Second drawer from the bottom, all the way back. Read it downstairs."

. . .

Phil Ginsberg started in Hollywood as an agent, married Candace Netter, the daughter of the president of the agency, gave him his first grandson, and stayed with his wife until the boy, Squire, was three. Ginsberg was the most purely frightening person Griffin knew in Hollywood, more than any movie stars throwing tantrums over the size of their trailers; or directors refusing to shoot new happy endings to films, or even Stella Baal when she blamed Griffin for a failure, especially when the failure really was his fault and then his job was threatened, though her anger passed, because she believed in the team and he was on it.

No, Griffin trembled at the idea of Ginsberg because the man was everywhere and nowhere, now owning the music division of that company, which he sells and then buys an Internet store that he convinces the investment bankers will make a zillion dollars, and he sells the stock at its highest, six months before bankruptcy; having learned the Internet business he buys a cable system in New Mexico and returns to Hollywood and starts a cable channel dedicated to soccer, with English and Spanish commentary. He had also managed to slip between a few best-selling novels and the films made from them. He had started with a little more than nothing and was now worth $750 million but, lacking his first billion, suffered a manic insecurity ensorcelled with his manic confidence, a chemical bond for brutality. He was mean and worked alone like a troll beneath a bridge, demanding a tax of everyone who passed: money, gold, cattle, a first-born child. In the universe of billionaires, $750 million was play money, and Griffin knew there was still space in Ginsberg's world for someone to help him make the leap to really savage wealth, incomprehensible wealth: castles in Spain, a vineyard in Tuscany, a fleet of jets, counsel to presidents, and two Rembrandts if he wanted. But the great boom was over. People had to work for a living. Ginsberg surely lacked a few ideas, and Griffin wanted to help him find them.

The book was typed because Candace couldn't work a computer and then spiral-bound at Kinko's because, fearing Ginsberg, no publisher would take the book on. Candace gave it to her friends, who kept the book a secret from men, to preserve for themselves the wisdom of its loony truth. She called it *Sharing His Closet, a Memoir by Candace Netter.*

As I said, Phil was a brilliant confersationalist, and there was no one more sought after for the best tables in the best houses in Hollywood, which as I said earlier, is not just a geograpical area, but truly a state of mind spread across many zip codes and three area codes, and for that matter, even includes some of the most beautiful apartments and finest restaurants in New York City. I had grown up in the world of Hollywood, and raised in Beverly Hills, on North Roxbury Drive, just down the street from the home of Ira Gerswhin, the brother of the great

George Gershiwn, composer of many great songs, of which Ira wrote the words. Lucille Ball was also a neighbor, as was the incomparable Jimmy Stewart, who bought the house next to his just to tear it down and plant a garden! Everyone loved to trick or treat on Roxbury Drive.

But for all that I had become familiar with the homes of truly important people, it was not until my marriage that I was a guest as an adult. What I did not understand was that I was Phil's ticket (which by the way I almost used as the title for this book). Phil needed a woman on his arm because he was not ready to bring another man and going alone would present an awkward seating arrangement. He didn't have enough money or power in those early days of our marriage to make up for the difficult social problems presented by gay men, and in those days, at the height of the tragic AIDS epidemic, there was a stigma about gay men alone in straight company. Phil needed a child, our darling son Squire, to complete the picture. When Phil traveled to New York or London, where he often did business, he could go stag because he was a visitor. And of course it was in those cities where he wasn't known that he explored that side of his sexuality that he kept from me.

It may surprise the reader to learn from me that Phil was actually a very tender lover, and I had no lack of exciting orgasms, at least from his hands. The problem was that he could not re-

ceive pleasure from me. And over time, this became my wound, a term I borrow from the Journey
of a Hero, and I came to doubt myself awfully, I
asked my girlfriends what they did to give their
men pleasure, but it was not until I went into
therapy to find out what I was doing wrong that
my therapist had the insight to ask me more
questons about my husband than about me. My therapist, the practically psychic Dr. Teri Barr, saw
a picture emerging of a man who was holding something back. But by that time I had become a night-
mare version of the person I had been on the day
we stood beneath the white canopy and we said our
vows and Phil smashed the glass under his foot
and we were married. I had grown fat. To keep my
pain and confusion in a cage where it couldn't
take over my life I talked too much and for too
long. I became a cariacture of myself, a carica-
ture of a woman, I had become a kind of awful
shrew, so that when Phil left me I knew why people
in town wore saying to each other, "Married to
her, I'd be a fag too." And everyone felt sorry
for our son.

When Phil established himself at a high
level, and people needed him more than he needed
them, he dumped me. One kind friend said to me,
"Phil isn't a real homosexual, he's just homo-
expedient. It serves him to travel light, and
the baggage of heterosexuality, the need to share
attention with someone doemestic instead of
keeping the spotlight on himself, all of the

negotiation among couples at a table to include
everyone and the topics that matter to them, talk
about business, of course, but also talk about
soccer games and homework, the substance of a
normal or if that word offends you then typical
heterosexual family life, took away from Phil
the quality that he most needed in the world,
which was the appearance of invincibility and
self-sufficiency. He needs to be gay to be off
limits. He can't be a bachelor because then his
hosts will bring attractive single women to the
table, and he'll have to focus on them, or be
thought rude, and all of that will just get in
his way. As he is, he can come late and leave
early. This gives him power.

A better plan than sabotaging the unsinkable Stella Baal had
opened up to Griffin. Let her keep the job. I know how to approach
Phil Ginsberg, because now I understand him. Ginsberg uses father-
hood as another weapon in his campaign for wealth. Rumors of a sor-
did private life could hurt him with the investors he needs. The evidence
of his son and his dedication to the leading school for the children of
the town's most powerful parents, along with the usual run of fash-
ionable charities, raise the balance of his public account so high that
no one sees him in the shadows on the other side. He works alone
because he doesn't want anyone getting so close he'd be vulnerable to
blackmail. He needs a straight partner, me, so he doesn't have to work
so hard to look normal, which will free him to pursue the billions he
needs to justify his time on earth. He's stuck at $750 million for the
same reason that I'm stuck at work, because when you raise money for
a school it doesn't do enough for you in the world. You only impress

the other parents at the school, and then their gratitude is a little condescending, and when you give too much it's obvious what marker you're going to call in. The guy who gives a ton of money to a hospital is looking for political power, wants a moral laundry for his dirty money, or has a sentimental need to prove something to the memory of his annoying mother. Really big donations to the private high schools are remembered when the donor's son or daughter is competing for admission to the Ivy League or Stanford and the high school has the power to pick which kids get the nod. So the kind of man who puts his energy into fund-raising for a high school wants to lube the gears of college admission. It's still just for family. For all of Ginsberg's success, some part of his attention is not well focused on work. He needs me. Ethan's acceptance at Coldwater is the opportunity I prayed for, and it was already in my hands.

Griffin would answer the fund-raising letter that Ginsberg had included in the acceptance packet sent out to the "Coldwater Community" by making a serious donation. Calling producers to auction off their box seats to Laker games meant nothing to Ginsberg; worse, he'd look like a wife. In his letter to the school's parents, Ginsberg said the children of the community deserved a new media center. "If our children follow us into this crazy marvelous important world of ours, they need the future now." A direct appeal to nepotism; that was brilliant. That was acting like a Republican!

Griffin knew that, to shake the tree hard enough for Ginsberg to care about him, he had to pay for the media center, all of it, by himself. This was worth selling his stock. This was an investment in putting himself in front of Ginsberg. This said, I'm here, I'm wealthy, I don't need you, I believe in the school because I do not apologize for giving the children of privilege the tools that will help them maintain that privilege. And that's why I'm giving the school seven hundred and fifty thousand dollars. I believe in . . . us.

Three

T he next day, Ethan called Griffin at work and announced that he was not going to Coldwater. "Eli's father can't afford the tuition, so he's going to North Hollywood High. I don't want to go without him, and North Hollywood is a really good school."

Ethan's best friend was Eli Swaine. Until last year, Eli's father, Gregory Peck Swaine, had badly managed the division of the Studio created for buying and making low-budget films, reporting to Griffin. Greg complained that the studio never committed enough money for prints and advertising, which was true, because distribution didn't expect Greg's films to do well and only sustained the division so that the annual report could include pictures of the executives at the Sundance Film Festival as a validation of their devotion to film as art. When Greg released four of what he called art films one year, each set in the American heartland with roughly the same scenes of the local coffee shop, impotent highway patrolmen, intellectual commercial fishermen, and slutty but honorable waitresses, Stella Baal shut the classics division down finally and reluctantly and tossed Greg a generous settlement in veneration of his last name. Greg's father, Warren Swaine, had produced sixty-two movies and still, at age eighty-five, made a movie every few years. Greg and his father were not close. Now Greg was stupidly trying to raise money to run the same kind of company without a studio's support. He was the dullest of Hollywood types, a Nicholas Ray intellectual who knew the jargon of French film theory, a neutered film buff who whined about the bean counters and believed Hollywood had once been better. But Hollywood has always been the same.

Greg Swaine had five children, and while he was Hollywood royalty, his own achievements failed to open the doors at the elite elementary schools, and even if they had, he couldn't have afforded the cost, about $23,000 a year for the high school. Warren Swaine, indeterminantly wealthy in the style of his generation's barons, did not support Greg or the grandchildren. The son of Warren's short second marriage to a Sabena air hostess, Greg was three at the time of the divorce. Though Warren paid child support, father and son never knew each other well. Greg's mother never married again and smoked herself to death. Greg wanted to be a producer so he could prove himself to his father, a stupid reason by itself but even worse because that's what he told everyone.

The settlement for his job was just enough to support an office and secretary, which he needed, because if he worked out of his house, when prospective investors returned his calls there was the chance they'd hear a vacuum cleaner in the background. Elixa, Greg's wife, told Lisa, who told Griffin, that when Greg returned calls he sometimes ran the hair dryer near the phone and said he was on a private jet. Griffin kept this to himself because some people are so creepy that even to know this about them is a sign of dangerous proximity to contamination.

Eli and Ethan went to Walter Reed together. Ethan was there by his mother's moral and social choice, a patriotic decision that her son should know something about the class differences in the city and the nation, even from the protection of a privileged unit, and Eli was there because it was free.

That Greg's father would not pay the tuition for his grand-children's education was a secret that all of his friends knew, because Elixa told them. Greg was spending money, not making money, and it was Elixa, a chiropractor with a business she kept modest to give herself enough time with her brood, who paid the household bills. In the small community of Hancock Park, connections among parents crossed from work to nursery. Eli and Ethan had been friends since their mothers met in a class for the parents of infants, run by a Hungarian refugee whose cardinal rule from which all others depended was simple: no pacifiers for babies; leave them be and let them cry themselves to sleep. After three or four nights they would go down without a struggle. This was nothing to make fun of, for the graduates of her system had an emotional stability that was freakish in the zone between Beverly Hills and Malibu; they all said *please* and they all said *thank you.* The Hungarian rented a yoga studio for her classes, and the parents sat against one wall while their children, some still crawling, played by themselves or with each other. When two children claimed the same object, the Hungarian would say, "Ethan wants the truck and Eli wants the truck." With this, one of the boys would relent, calmly. None of the parents could follow this practice in their own lives. June and the others were there because in therapy they had each discovered the absolute failure of their own parents—even their parents' generation, the greatest generation ever to raise a generation of drug addicts and compulsive shoppers—to pass along to them any practical wisdom for raising independent and self-reliant children. Something in the water of the depression or the war years, at least through the release of *Rubber Soul,* maybe the fluoride, had turned all their parents into liars who promoted the same diabolical mendacity; that they enjoyed parenthood, saw a meaning in family, and worried when their children struggled or failed, not for the sake of the children's happiness or the security of their future but to save themselves from shame. It was always about them, *their* wound.

The parents in the yoga studio admitted to themselves that the urge to have children had the same force as the urge to buy something expensive, that their children were mostly awful because they came from parents who could not distinguish between narcissism and the force of life that demanded reproduction. What an ugly word: *reproduction.* Produce me again. Me. Again. Not: *Try another way out of the maze, combine these two different sorts of genes.* What impelled life originally to hide the codes of life in flesh, and then divide that flesh into men and women, and then call them together for sex, and then drown them in car pools?

Of course, June triumphantly supported her son. "I think this is a very brave and moral decision," she said to Griffin. "This is why I was so happy that he went from Children's Lincoln to a public middle school, where he learned that there's a real world outside the walls of the castle. And since that castle is going to fall sooner than later, I want our son to know how to live in the real world."

"Perhaps you're right," said Griffin, something so unexpected to June that she asked him to say this again, fearing that he'd said, "You're starting a fight." And when he told her that so long as these two best friends were together, he would be happy with North Hollywood High, which after all had an excellent program for gifted children; what difference did it make? But he emphasized *as long as the boys are together,* because he knew he would immediately call Greg Swaine and find out what was really going on.

. . .

He called Greg and asked him, "What is going on? Coldwater is the best private school in the country, probably. You know that, don't you?"

37

"And I can't afford it," said Greg. "I can't afford the school. You know I'm not making money, and the wife, to use that phrase, isn't making enough to keep the house running and cover a twenty-three-thousand-dollar-a-year tuition, especially since my four younger kids will want to know why their big brother goes to private school and they don't."

"Have you asked your father?"

"Yes. He said no. I barely know him. It was like going to an uncle by marriage. I've never felt so marginalized."

Griffin couldn't contain himself. "Marginalized? You know what that sounds like, Greg? *Marginalized* is what a college professor with an Italian last name says he feels when he's denied tenure by women and uses the language of gender and race identity instead of getting angry and going all Dago on them. Does he know how many children Coldwater sends to the Ivy League and Stanford every year? It's incredible. You've seen the facilities, you've seen the labs and the gyms and the library. The place is set up better than some colleges."

"He doesn't care. He won't pay. I can't afford it, so that's, you know, all she wrote. The fat lady has sung. All my life I tried to be Richard Widmark, and I end up whining like Dan Duryea. You know what I mean."

"No. Who is Dan Duryea?"

"Google him. Images."

"I don't want to Google him."

"He was an actor, a great character actor. I'm too caught up in my own life as a character actor. Maybe I'm not even Dan Duryea. Maybe I was wrong to aim for Widmark, maybe I should have set myself up as Glenn Ford, he's more of a family man than Widmark. I wasted years on my Belmondo phase, and maybe that's the problem too, instead of Delon. Alain Delon and Glenn Ford. You know what I mean about Glenn Ford?"

"No. I can't name a single Glenn Ford movie and I'd rather be listening to Glen Campbell while drinking Glenfiddich. I want to know one thing. Would you send Eli to Coldwater if you could?"

"*3:10 to Yuma;* and of course I'd send him there. I'm not doing this out of pride. *The Courtship of Eddie's Father.* I don't have contempt for the school just because I can't afford it. I've worked on myself. I'm more developed as a human being than that. *The Big Heat.* Fritz Lang directed it. Try finding that one at Blockbuster. And if they had it, they'd probably put it in the foreign film section. Jerks."

Griffin thought, If you were really developed, you schmuck, you'd have made money with the classics division. You'd have made films with sex and blood instead of coffee shops. You'd have taken what you love about film noir and bought up some Korean cop movies. Or you would have made big brilliant comedies about stupidity and vanity and the way love can't blossom until everyone, the hero especially, knows the truth about themselves.

Griffin asked his secretary to get Warren Swaine's phone number but to let him make the call himself. Griffin gave his name to the assistant—a man with a soothing voice that to Griffin sounded like he was one of those genetically modified casually handsome beauties of the concierge class—and asked for Mr. Swaine on a personal matter. Everyone knew Griffin's name, and Swaine was on the line quickly.

"Young Mr. Mill himself, Warren Swaine here. I'm sorry we've never had the pleasure."

"At least we have that pleasure now, sir."

"And what is this personal thing you want to talk about? You have a movie?"

"No, sir."

"You don't want my car, do you?"

"Sir?"

"*Sunset Boulevard.* DeMille is calling Gloria Swanson for her old car. I have a Bentley, six months new, so it's not for that."

"Could I come and see you about this?"

"Why the mystery?"

"It's a personal request, and I think we need to be in the same room."

"One condition. After a pitch like this, I'm too old to wait while you fit me into your schedule. So either you're here in an hour or whatever you want from me . . . you can't have."

. . .

Swaine lived at the top of a street Griffin had never been to, high in Kenter Canyon, in Brentwood. The house was a broad hacienda, filling a promontory with a view of the city, wealth turning the air into a magnifying glass that also filtered out the brown stain of pollution. Looking toward the ocean over the ridges and arroyos of the Santa Monica Mountains, one could believe that everything was right with the world.

Swaine answered the doorbell himself, though the butler was in the background, handsome as Griffin expected from his voice, groomed like a marine with a trust fund, but out of uniform, just a guy who was there for the pure pleasure of service.

"Thank you for seeing me, Mr. Swaine," said Griffin. The only other people to whom he spoke so respectfully were his children's teachers, but with them the custom of such honor was a condescension in exchange for their low pay.

Swaine took him around the pool to his office, in a small house surrounded by roses. Beyond the pool, Griffin didn't recognize the canyon to the west, which he hadn't seen when he was at the front door of the house. This should have been Mandeville Canyon, but he saw from here that Mandeville was actually two canyons over, and the unmapped canyon he was looking at had three riding rings and a broad polo field, something too large for Griffin to have missed after so many years in California. The large houses along the canyon were evenly obscured by their gardens, which ended in a neat line against the border of a few dozen long rows of grapes on the vine, a vineyard, which surrounded the deep green polo fields and riding rings. Griffin counted five small children on Shetland ponies, who were learning to jump in one of the rings, supervised by a couple of lanky women in riding clothes.

"That's a pretty sight," said Griffin. "But what canyon is that? It should be Mandeville, right? But it isn't."

"Why are you here?" said Swaine, and Griffin didn't want to divert the conversation into his own confusion about geography.

Swaine took the big seat behind his desk, instead of taking an armchair in the sitting area of the room, so Griffin had to face him across a skyline of awards. Swaine wasted no time. "What do you need from me?"

"This is very awkward," said Griffin. "This is not about movie business."

"If it were, you'd have told me what you wanted on the phone."

"It's about your grandson."

"From which one of my children?"

"Greg."

The producer's face was so obviously set not to tell his true feelings about his son that he might as well have held up a sign that read READY TO KILL THE FUCKER.

"It's about Eli. I know him pretty well because he's my son's best friend. They go to Walter Reed together."

"Well, it's a surprise that you send your own kid to a public school, and I have to say I already like you for that."

"Why is that a surprise?"

"Because you're one of them. I hate to say it, but you know what I mean. I learned too late about the problem of private education, and the one who paid the price for that is Greg. But you're smart to send your son to a good public school. He's going to be ahead of the game, way ahead, when he's an adult."

"I'm glad you say that; that's what I want from his education, but there's been a change. My son got into Coldwater, and so did Eli."

"I can't begin to know where this is going, but I'm getting a really bad feeling."

"Well, sir, I can't pretend that I don't know that you have a strained relationship with Greg. I don't know all the causes but I can guess. Greg worked with us at the Studio and he didn't do a good job with the classics division. We had to let him go. In spite of that, the fact is, we're still friends, not as friendly as our sons, but our wives are close, my second wife, that is. Ethan, my son, I had with my first wife. I'm not digressing to no purpose, sir, I want to draw a picture for you, a social picture, if you will. As I said, my son and your grandson were accepted at Coldwater. It's a great school."

"Ten percent of the kids at Harvard, Yale, and Princeton are geniuses, no question. The rest are shits. And not just the legacies. Legacies or no, they're shits. The same for Coldwater. It's a school for weaklings. It's a school that trains the children of the rich to be greedy nervous shits, that's what it is. It's a fucking cruise liner. Teachers in this world used to have authority, Mr. Mill, but at Coldwater they've been made into the entertainment directors on a cruise ship. Don't tell me about that school. I know the people there, I know who went there, and I know whose children go there now. My son asked me to pay for Eli's tuition and I told him absolutely not. He should go to public school with Mexicans, Africans, Koreans, Armenians. He should be down on the street with real people whose parents have real jobs or don't have jobs, so that when he's forty, and the world is in ruins around him, he'll feel in himself that he's a man among men, and he'll know who to trust and who to avoid, and he's not going to get that kind of real social education in a fucking hothouse incubation tray where the kids drive new Hummers and will be all in a tizzy when the world collapses because they can't get room service and people aren't smiling at them all the time. Why do you care? What are you, a social worker? You're here from the school hoping that if I pay for my grandson I'll buy them a hockey rink so my grandson can hire some farmer's kid from Manitoba to play in his place?"

"It's not like that, sir."

"Well, what way is it like, then, Mr. Mill?"

Griffin took a breath, and in that parenthesis he wrote his destiny, he wrote the loss of the moment for his one big move, he wrote a forced retirement because he was getting older and they could promote someone younger or hire someone from outside who could do just as good a job for a lot less money. He wrote bankruptcy. He wrote his death.

"No, sir, but just because you fucked Marilyn Monroe doesn't give you the right to throw your grandson into the ocean and hope he learns to swim."

"You're rude and disgusting. I didn't fuck her, I made love to her."

"He's your grandson and he deserves a great education. He's had eight years at public school and he's learned whatever he needs to know about the real Los Angeles and the real America. He'll always have that."

"And what are you to him, you molesting him? Is that what this is about? You're not blood. Does your son live with you or his mother?"

"His mother."

"Did she remarry?"

"No."

"How much time does your son spend with you?"

"Saturdays and Sundays."

"Every week?"

"When I'm in town."

"So what the fuck is this about? I guess if you were molesting the kid you'd pay for his education yourself, unless you're broke. Are you broke?"

"Of course not."

"A lot of people are broke these days. My son is broke."

"Yes, sir, and he wants his son to have a chance that he has failed to provide."

"Let me tell you what I've learned about life. A son who knows his father is a demented, deranged loser and makes a break from him grows up to be a stronger man than someone whose loser father manages to scrape together enough material to give the kid the illusion that his father actually knows something about the ways of the world and how to survive. Eli's mother, no saint herself, believe me, pays the rent because his father is washed up, and he's not even forty-five. If my grandson goes to public high school he'll come to learn that his father's failure to provide is a crime against nature, because his father had every chance, and he will make himself rich, or a leader in whatever he chooses even if money isn't the point, to avenge the shame of his father's sins. My father was a loser and a degenerate gambler, plain and simple. I made sixty-five movies, Mr. Mill, *sixty-five*, and do you know why? I had to knock on doors to get a quarter that people owed my father. That's why I made sixty-five movies and that's why I made love to Marilyn Monroe, because I understood life and I knew she was in pain. I hold myself responsible for her suicide, because I let her go. That's my pain. My grandson, who I happen to know is a very bright and capable boy, a good-looking kid with some real inner fiber, will go to public high school, and when it's time for college I'll tell him if he goes to Berkeley I'll support him, but if he's bound for the Ivies, I'll pay his tuition, room and board, and for his books, but if he wants spending money he'll have to get a college job. I'd like to see Eli become a doctor. Not because it would make me proud—well, maybe—but it would mean the lifting of the curse on this family and someone would actually make a difference in the world instead of serving up distraction, which is the real name and purpose of our business, Mr. Mill. And besides, in twenty years, when he's out of medical school, the ocean will have risen those few inches that mean Greenland melted and we'll be in hell, and in hell you get burned, and when you get burned you need a doctor. So get out of my office."

Griffin stood up, went to Warren Swaine's desk, put his face close to the old man's, and whispered, "You're just doing this to punish Greg, you stupid selfish fuck. If you know so much about what a child needs, why can't Greg make a living? I know why. You were too busy fucking Marilyn Monroe to teach your son to swim."

"You think you know what you're talking about, Mr. Mill? You think I'm the one to call a sick fucker? Is that it? Do you think your generation is better than mine? Do you think you know my son? Do you think you know what I'm protecting my grandson from? You have no idea. None! Nothing! You don't know any"—he stopped shouting and whispered the second syllable—". . . thing." He held up a hand, asking for a time out from his rage. With a voice dry with what Griffin at first mistook as pity, Swaine croaked out, "You don't know a thing about my son."

Swaine's breathing slowed behind a look of puzzled contemplation, as though his whole spiritual battle was like a tongue trying to find a psychotically annoying nearly invisible thread of celery between the teeth, if such a thread was also his soul. Ferocious but weak from agony, Swaine reached a palsied hand to a file drawer on the side of his desk. Griffin thought, *He's going for the heart medicine* and moved quickly around the desk, and then, as though innocent of what he was doing, he braced his leg against the drawer and looked into Swaine's eyes. Lying to him, Griffin asked, "Warren, are you all right?"

Swaine fought for the drawer but Griffin's knee held it closed, and the dying man didn't have the power that Griffin knew would return if he could only get to the medicine in the drawer that Griffin was blocking. "Should I get help?" But he meant to say, *If you live, and you don't pay your grandson's tuition, then my son Ethan won't go to Coldwater and I won't meet Phil Ginsberg and I won't survive the end of the world.*

Warren Swaine fell forward, his nose hitting the desk. Griffin touched the back of Swaine's neck and, finding no pulse, shouted, "Help!" and ran for the handsome butler, who called for a private ambulance, using his speed dial, and if the ambulance was on speed dial, with Swaine's weak heart they were prepared for an attack, which would deflect suspicion about Griffin, if there was going to be any, and there would be. They ran back to the office, where Swaine was sitting up, his nose bleeding, the drawer open. The butler said, "Oh, thank God, Warren. Griffin thought you were dying." Swaine raised his right arm and pointed a finger at Griffin, and, after a guttural squawk that sounded enough like *him* not to sound like anything else, settled in his chair and fell forward again, this time dead. The drawer was open but Griffin couldn't see inside. The butler saw and closed it, before touching his dead boss. Though the paramedics found a dead man they still used electricity to try and start his heart again, but in respect for the old man, and his Oscars on the desk, they were gentle with the body.

The butler called Swaine's daughter and said, "It's Chris Tryon at your father's, and I have some bad news." Tryon told her the truth simply. "Your father just passed away. He was having a meeting and his heart stopped. It was over quickly. The ambulance came in twelve minutes, by the way, but it was too late. I think he died peacefully."

From Tryon's side of the conversation, Griffin understood that Swaine's daughter would tell her brothers and sisters, including Greg.

Tryon didn't even mention Griffin's name or the sequence of events, because they didn't matter to the woman, but then he called Swaine's lawyer.

"He was having a meeting when he collapsed. . . . Griffin Mill." To Griffin, "Toby Redd would like to talk to you."

Everyone knew Swaine's lawyer, who treated the world with an indiscriminate familiarity that always made Griffin feel that he had been mistaken for someone else.

"So you were having a meeting?"

"We'd just started."

"What about?"

Griffin looked at the posters on the wall, and two of them were for films that had been made at the Studio when Griffin was five. He grabbed one title. "I was here to ask him if he would let us develop it for a remake."

"He must have loved that."

"He seemed pleased, yes."

"He was a character. Old school. To die knowing that he was still wanted."

"Yes."

"That's the way we all want to go."

"After a full life, of course."

"So you brought him comfort."

"I hope so."

"Or the shock that anybody still cared was enough to kill him."

"I hope not."

"I assume you don't want it in the public record that you were there when he died."

"There's no reason, is there?"

"I don't think so," said Redd.

Griffin left the office and sat in a chair under an umbrella by the pool, waiting for Greg Swaine, while Chris Tryon talked to other people on the phone.

"I'm so sorry," said Griffin, as soon as Greg walked into the backyard. He could have added a few more words, but any embellishments to the simplicity of sympathy would be noticed by Greg like a gaudy monogram on a handkerchief offered to wipe away a tear. In response, Greg had no obligation greater than saying "Thank you," and then he asked Griffin to stay where he was while he went into the office to see his father's body. Griffin timed him, to set a mark against which he could measure someone else the next time this happened. After thirty-five minutes, Greg came out. Griffin assumed he'd called his sister, or his wife, or doctor, or lawyer, or all of them. Greg was now an orphan.

"I never got to say good-bye."

"I'm sorry."

"And you were here why?"

"To see if he thought any of his old films might be worth a remake."

"He must have liked that."

"I think he did."

"So he died the way he wanted."

"At work?"

"Yeah. He always wanted to be carried out feet first."

"And having lived a full life."

"Did he say anything before he died?"

"Nothing, really."

"Chris said my dad raised his arm, pointed at you, and said *him*."

"I think he was just pointing in front of himself and there I was."

"No, he said my father pointed at you and said *him*."

"I don't know."

"Chris does."

"I thought it was more of a religious moment, actually. He could have been looking into the distance and he could have said *heaven*. It could have been that."

"You think?"

"It could have been. It sounded like this. It was sort of like *hwhimmnn*. It wasn't one syllable, he drew it out. It was the end of his breath, Greg. It could have been *him*, it could have been *heaven*, it could have been nothing. Or maybe he wanted to finish business. He knew he was dying, Greg. I think he was upset that he was being taken away from me."

"Why did he point?"

"Because he couldn't stand up. Maybe he was reaching to me, for me to give him a hand. Maybe he was saying, Please, God, don't take me away in the middle of a meeting; I haven't finished talking to himmm." Griffin pointed, to make his point.

"Finish business. That'd be my father. Not even to give himself enough time to die in a spiritual way."

"I wouldn't know. Active death, active life, why die in contemplation?"

"How is that spiritual? I mean with closure, with peace, with his family around him, after he'd made peace with us and peace with himself. Maybe this was his punishment, to die with a stranger, no offense."

"But this way he went quickly, without pain."

49

"The heart attack was painful."

"It was over in three minutes."

"I hope you're right. But between us, fuck him. That's what I have to tell you. Fuck him. He wouldn't even give me his death. He took that away from me; he even took his death away from me. I'll never have a chance to prove myself a man to my own father"—a sentiment he was to repeat to everyone, even the foreign investors he took to dinner. "Still, fuck him, because now that he's dead he's going to give me what he wanted to keep from me. He's only leaving me a million dollars, but the first check I write is to Coldwater. Eli's going to get the education he deserves."

Griffin wanted to see inside the drawer he had blocked, but Chris Tryon was sitting in the dead man's chair, talking on the phone with the caterers for Swaine's memorial service. There was the body floating under the words, "Vegetarian, yes."

This was all because of Griffin's second murder.

Four

Duncan Tillinghast, just forty, Coldwater's headmaster, was one of those ambitious guys Griffin was seeing more of around the private schools, not the older breed of stout enthusiastic gatekeepers, living impressions of autonomy who worked for the parents and also for the protection of their class, which today, like the Orthodox Jew's fear of the name of God, no one would dare pronounce. Los Angeles didn't have a network of good private schools until California killed the property tax. The public schools in the bad parts of town got worse, but even in the rich parts of town, like Beverly Hills—where there wasn't a threat of the forced busing in of gangbangers—the doctors, lawyers, real estate developers, television producers, and comedy writers surrendered the shells of their old public schools to the Persians, Russians, and Asians, hard-working immigrants like most of their own grandparents, whose offense was to remind them of their own immutable vulgarity.

The baby-boom wealthy took over the old private schools or built them fresh and—to prove to themselves that they did have class—named their children Ashley, Ashleigh, Brent, Brett, Brandon, Max, Jason, Jordan, Justin, Eli, and Ethan. The whites made fun of the names of the blacks, LaShrelle, Vonique, LaTwana, Kawanse, Kobe, and Shaquille, but the names of their cowboys, Caesars, prophets, and Argonauts were not as interesting.

Almost nothing of the authority of the cloister and seminary, foundation of the New England academies, remained. The younger headmasters, like Tillinghast, with advanced degrees from elite universities, would have been on the track for academic glory if the best universities weren't cutting back on hires, just like Boeing. Instead of cursing fate while teaching part time at three community colleges, where they might actually be of service to humanity and bring a few grapes from the vine of their Dartmouth knowledge to students who could barely afford the fees, who were the first in the families to go to college, who were never going to make more than—what?—at best $60,000 a year, the Duncan Tillinghasts of America dove into the private schools, where a headmaster could make $200,000 a year, live rent free in a nice house, and sit on the boards of a few of the companies run by trustees of the school, who needed a reliable vote from a well-regarded educator for the usual moral laundry.

Tillinghast knew that a morning visit from a parent whose son had yet to enter the school was only about money, so his opinion of Griffin was good. Griffin was bored by the sexless vigor of triathletes like Tillinghast, especially those who finished midpack but still kept pictures of themselves on the wall. June didn't think that runners were sexy, she didn't trust a man sexually if he didn't have on a few pounds of gratuitous meat. Griffin liked her in bed more than Lisa.

"So," said Tillinghast, "how can I help you?"

"I called you to help the school."

"That's always welcome. What did you have in mind?"

"I know it's probably odd for someone to make a significant contribution before his son even starts the academic year, but I knew that I'd be giving you money someday, so I thought, Why not put that money in place while my children—I have a daughter too, at Children's Lincoln—"

"Wonderful school," said Tillinghast, pointlessly interrupting Griffin.

"—can take advantage of what that money will—you know—buy."

"Most people don't think ahead like that; the school is grateful. How much?"

"It's not just how much but for what."

"You already have a program in mind that you'd like to support?"

"I want to give some money for the new media center."

"Of course, being in the entertainment industry yourself. We're grateful for whatever you can do to help get the center off the ground. How much are you thinking about giving to help out?"

"What's your budget for the center?"

"About a million."

"I'm giving you seven hundred and fifty thousand dollars."

Tillinghast had expected fifteen or twenty thousand, but he had learned from running not to waste energy with a cake and candles for every personal best.

"I'd have to talk to the board, but I think that puts your name on the building."

"I hadn't thought that far. It's probably a bit corrupt of me to give money to a school that's already rich, but on the other hand, seven hundred and fifty thousand can't save the public schools, and at least here I know how the money will be spent."

"I don't know what kind of supervision of the money you expect or want to have. Do you have any restrictions on the gift?"

"Like what?"

"Approval of architect? I don't know if we can give that to you."

"Keep it simple, is all I ask. Nothing fancy. Save the money for what's inside."

"Phillip Ginsberg is going to be very grateful."

"He's part of this?"

"He's been pushing for it."

"More power to him."

"Will this be cash or a transfer of stock?"

"Transfer of stock."

"Are you making a pledge over a few years or will this be a one-time gift?"

"One-time. Let's get the paperwork in order and try to make this happen quickly."

Yes! thought Griffin. That should make some noise in Mr. Ginsberg's ear.

Which it did. The call came to Griffin's car while he was driving back to the Studio. Ginsberg didn't introduce himself. "I don't even know you, Griffin, and I can't believe what you did. That's fantastic, just fantastic. Why? I mean your son just started, I mean he hasn't even started, he just got in and look at this; why?"

"This must be Phillip Ginsberg."

"I can't thank you enough. It's the most beautiful thing, the most beautiful gift, the most outrageous generosity. I'm really humbled by this; really, Griffin."

"As I told Duncan Tillinghast, my son is probably going to end up in the business so why not give him the advantage from the start? I don't mean the open door but technical knowledge, so he has something to trade on other than his last name."

"Wow, that's all. Wow."

"You have a son there, right?"

"Squire. He loves it. And is he going to be jealous, because the media center won't be complete until he's already at Columbia or Williams."

"Can't we speed things up?"

"Anything is possible. You'll put your name on the building, right?"

"I hadn't thought about it."

"No, Mill, now you're lying to me. If I'm on the board for reasons that aren't all pure, you didn't give three quarters of a million dollars for your son to learn how to focus a camera. What's your bad motive in this? You don't do anything for one reason only; neither do I. We've been around too long."

"Are you suspicious of everyone's motives?"

"What are you, an idiot? I'll answer the question over lunch."

"Any day."

"On my boat, Sunday afternoon, bring Ethan. I'll bring Squire. He's a good boy."

They said good-bye, and Griffin pulled the car to a side street and parked, to get away from the traffic. He wept, big sentimental happy-ending tears, because he had taken a ridiculously big risk, and though he couldn't be sure that he would ever make a hundred million dollars, he knew, with the confidence that the sun would rise in the morning, that everyone who ever made a hundred million dollars took a risk like his and felt as alive. Even his tears were a sign of progress, a sign of hope, a prophecy of vast success.

Thank you, God. Thank you.

Although he did wonder how Ginsberg had known his son's name, and then thought, No, of course, he got it from Tillinghast. He was ready to have a warm thought for Ginsberg, for the generosity to his son, not to take his dad away from him on a Sunday afternoon, but considering the massive strategic attack he had launched to put himself into position to be invited for an afternoon on Ginsberg's yacht, he forced himself to keep in mind always that every step of his life with Ginsberg was business, business only.

...

That night it was Lisa's turn to read a book to Willa, and Griffin waited for her in the bedroom, naked and cross-legged on the carpet, behind the candle.

"I can't fuck you, Lisa. I know I can't and I don't want to try, but I'd like to hold you tonight, and give you whatever you need to come. Just out of love. I was confused. You told me you were ready to leave me, and then you asked me to think about myself in a way that I hadn't before. You made me stronger. And today, it all paid off, I spoke to Phil Ginsberg."

"So you gave some money to the school."

"And it got his attention."

"How much did you give?"

"We gave the school seven hundred and fifty thousand dollars." Why, Griffin had a second to wonder before Lisa hit him, do we sometimes, maybe even usually, have to hear ourselves say things above a whisper to understand our biggest mistakes?

She punched him on his ear and kicked him in the balls, screaming, "You are one big motherfucking thief! Twenty thousand would have done the trick, you stupid fuckhead. That's *our* money, you asshole. That's *ours*, not yours, *ours*! And you didn't tell me how fucking much money you were going to give. That's theft! You stole from me, and that means you stole from Willa. Put your clothes on. You're not going to touch me. You're never going to touch me again. I thought I was scared of divorce, but right now I'm more scared of you. I'll take whatever I can of what's left for me to take, but I want a divorce. You're out of your mind. Sleep in Ethan's room, but you are not sleeping in my bed. Do you understand? You are not sleeping with me ever again. Idiot."

"I know what I'm doing," said Griffin, refusing to touch himself where she hurt him, refusing to let her know how much it hurt. "I'm not going to say anymore about this, but I know what I'm doing."

"Put your clothes on and get out of this room."

"If I do that, it will only make Willa anxious."

"Anxious. What a weaselly shitty word. Anxious! You can't even say scared. If you were a man, a mature man, you would say, 'I don't want to leave this room at night because if I do, and our daughter sees me sleeping on her brother's bed, it's going to scare her, so let's work this out,' or, better, 'I'm staying here. I made the right decision about the money so just shut the fuck up and watch me.' That's what a man would say, a real man, not a fifty-two-year-old Hollywood boy man with his shirt-tails out and gel in his hair. If you did that, I'd have to shut up; I'd have to calm down; I'd have to accept your leadership and guidance, and so would our daughter. You talk too much. Real men don't talk so much. There isn't a real man in all of Hollywood, not even the grips and the teamsters. This fucking circus. I hate it!"

"Okay. Fine. Trust me. Just let me do what I'm doing and trust me."

"It's too late to say that, Griffin. It doesn't work; I told you what to say. Stay here. Never mind. Go to sleep."

. . .

Both June and Lisa asked Griffin why he was bringing only Ethan on the boat, but Ginsberg surely knew about his family, and if he had wanted to entertain Griffin's daughters, he would have invited them.

57

June knew that Griffin was lying about something and that he needed Ethan as a prop.

"These aren't good people, Ethan, they have bad values."

"This is an afternoon on a boat. I think I'm safe."

"That's how corruption begins. You get used to luxury and then you expect it."

"I think it's good for Dad's business."

"Is that what he says?"

"Mr. Ginsberg has a son at Coldwater. I think it would be good for Dad to bring me along, so Squire and I can hang out."

"I don't like this. That's all I'm going to say."

"You think Dad is a bad person."

"No. I'm saying that your father has to make a living in a business of bad people."

"That sounds like you're just being careful, because you don't want to say what you really think, which is that Dad is bad. Do you think Daddy is bad?"

She could say, He's my eternal husband and I will give you the strength to remind him by the example of your moral gravity of his responsibility by his own example to make certain that his son becomes a competent moral adult, and that a casual afternoon in the orbit of the predatory rich can't change that moral alignment so finely tuned by his mother.

Instead, to offer her own example of restraint, as a packet of energy she could attach to Ethan and let him deliver to his father, she said, "Business, not just Hollywood, forces men to live split between the office and the home—or homes, in your father's case—and not until they're deep into the world of work do they learn the cost of all that money they take home."

"You didn't answer my question. Do you think my father is bad?"

"I think that show business is often bad and even the best men help launch awful poisons into the world."

"You're still not answering my question, Mom. Do you think my father is bad?"

"He has a pure soul. We all have pure souls."

"So if he has a pure soul, then no matter what business he does with this guy, with Ginsberg, his soul won't get dirty."

"That's right," she said, lying. Griffin's soul was already crapped up. Nobody who fucks a woman into pregnancy and then leaves his wife, who also gets pregnant, can easily run himself through any milk bath of purification and come out all warm and puffy without a painful struggle of a magnitude Griffin had never approached. Griffin's eagerness to comply with the men-only invitation smelled to June like the sacrifice of his daughters, since the Sunday afternoon he gave over to Ginsberg stole his attention from the girls, when they both needed him. Inattention, willful distraction; these are sins.

"It's just an afternoon."

"Keep your eyes open. Remember everything. I want to know what it's like."

. . .

Sunday night, when Ethan came home, he told her.

"We got down to the marina and this crew guy met us at the gate to the dock and took us to the boat. It's ninety-five feet long, made in Italy. It looks like a dagger. There's a big area for sitting in the back, and the bridge where the boat is steered from is up on top. Inside it was amazing; they have a complete gym and a game room, and a big-screen video room.

"Squire was okay. I guess we're supposed to get along because both of our parents are divorced. He said that probably my father isn't gay, although you never know. I said I knew and he said, No, you don't, you never know. I said, Are you? and he said he wasn't and his father being gay used to sort of make him sick but his therapist told him that's because of his father leaving his mother. And his rabbi is a lesbian. He's inviting me to his bar mitzvah. And he said his mother is kind of weird and a lot of people think she's ridiculous, but a lot of women in Hollywood love her and he feels really protective of her, and he doesn't let his father say anything bad about her. And he said his father is really rich but that was obvious. I liked him, anyway. He didn't try to buy me with anything or make any big promises to me the way some rich kids do; he sort of treated the whole thing like the boat belonged to someone else and he knew his way around it.

"There were a few other guests on the boat, but Dad and Squire's father spent most of their time at the back of the boat, talking, and the others kept away from them. Ginsberg's friendly, but everyone waits to see what he's going to do and then they all do it unless he tells them not to.

"I got to steer the boat and Squire said he's gotten to steer a G-Five, and I asked him what that was, and he said, A Gulfstream 5; it's their highest number and it's really fast and you can take it to London if you stop for gas in Canada. He's been all over on it. I was kind of jealous of that. Steering the boat was really cool, and we went out far. The food was good. I don't know."

. . .

Griffin didn't care about the boat, he didn't want the boat. While Ginsberg showed him the heavy insulation in the engine room and the redundancies built into the navigation system, Griffin wondered if he himself had lost millions in the burst of the tech bubble because he didn't connect the meaning of money with the world of stuff you can touch. Maybe Ginsberg wanted money and made so much because he wanted what you can buy with it. *Am I insufficiently materialistic for grand ambition?*

"This is great, Phil, really great," said Griffin.

"I have a bigger boat, which I keep in the Caribbean in the winter and either the Med or Nantucket in the summer. It's a hundred and sixty feet long."

"That's big."

"There's bigger."

"Do you need it?"

"A boat that size?"

"Two boats that size."

"You pull into Virgin Gorda in my boat, and there's only three or four other boats that long. You invite the owners over for a drink, and it's great. You meet your cousins by money, which is better than blood. Money makes a better affinity group than family."

"The truth is, I'm surprised it matters to you. I thought you were in it for the power."

"Cleopatra had her royal barge."

They sat outside as the boat went up the shore toward Malibu. "All of Los Angeles is over there," said Ginsberg, "millions of people, and look around you, there's fifty boats out here. This is where you get away and clear the cobwebs. It's also great for sex. Everybody wants to get away. You don't like your job, do you?"

"It's a great job."

"Are you going to waste my time with diplomacy?"

"It's a great job and I'm tired of it."

"You've lost a lot of money. Your stock is down. Your options are worthless. Your gift to Coldwater was more than someone with your portfolio should have given away."

"It got me on the boat, Phil."

"Did you pay three quarters of a million dollars for a meeting with me?"

"No. I wanted to help the school."

"I want that to be the last lie you ever tell me. If you ever lie again, whatever we're doing, you're out. Tell me the truth."

"I wanted to meet you and I wanted to prove that I was a little crazy, so you'd take me on as a partner."

"A *partner?*" Ginsberg pressed so much incredulity into the small word that it spilled out the sides, like an overstuffed burrito. "Who are you, Griffin? Development girl to Stella Baal? You're the tea boy for a couple of producers. A few years ago your options were worth some decent change but what do you have left? Seven? Six? You were nuts to drop three quarters of a million dollars. I have three quarters of a *billion.* You want a job with me?"

"Yes. You're smart, but you don't have a billion yet. And you want more than one, don't you?"

"And to make four billion dollars you think I need a straight partner and you're the only one willing to take on the job? You think I'm too queer for big business? You think you're an original because you came up with that idea? You think you're the first?"

"I think I'm the best," said Griffin, the sentence delivered like the losing audition for a one-line role.

"You're too old to be the best. The best are proven by the time they're thirty-five. I stopped flying commercial jets when I was thirty-two. I have no frequent flier mileage, Griffin, none. Think of that! I don't want it because I don't want to waste my time thinking about how the airlines make it hard to use. Frequent flier mileage: that's for guys with careers, that's for guys with jobs. I had fifty million dollars, not miles, by the time I was thirty-four. You're the guy who knows how many miles he's earned, aren't you? You're the guy who checks his mileage statement, you're the guy who uses a credit card that earns you airline miles for every dollar you spend, and you're the guy who chose his telephone company because it gives you miles on your airline of choice. The only thing to buy at a discount is stock. Stock. That's you, stock stuck in a stupid job, like the old public stocks. You're pilloried in your stupid job; you all are. And even if you were running the studio I'd say the same thing. I've said it to Stella. It's a waste of time what you do, president of production, vice president of production, making movies, worrying about how your career rides on the opening weekend box office of a collectively made fantasy you hope is timed to the public's changing taste in diversion. Pegging your *careeeeer* to the fortunes of someone else, a director, a movie star; you're wasting your time. It's like patting yourself on the back for buying a case of twenty-five-dollar wine, storing it in a locker you rent in a temperature- and humidity-controlled warehouse and then drinking it fifteen years later, when the same bottle would cost you a hundred and ten dollars, and believing that this validation of your analysis of the possibility of profit in strong tannins somehow proves you know something worth knowing about life. The ones who play that game are sentimental intellectuals who cry themselves to sleep because they're not sure if their lives have meaning."

"Yes," said Griffin, thinking of Greg Swaine. "Exactly. I agree. And that's why I'm here."

"You're here because you're fucked up, that's why you're here. Three quarters of a million, and listen to this: You're going to make good on that pledge, whether I give you a job or not."

. . .

In the overtones of Griffin's submission to Ginsberg's attack, more than in the words that drifted through the curtain of sound from the engine and the wind, Ethan heard the collapse of his father's confidence, and this he would not tell his mother. There would be nothing she could do about it except worry. On the way home, he asked his father, "Are you going to work for him?"

"Why do you say that?"

"I heard you talking."

"What did you hear?"

"That he thinks the movie business is a waste of time unless you own the studio."

"No. Unless you own the company that owns the studio."

"Does he?"

"Not yet. You need billions for that, and he only has millions."

"But more than you."

"Much more."

"Why does anyone keep working if they have so much money?"

"After a while it's not the money."

"What is it?"

"A big game. A club. A chance to make a difference in the world. A chance to have enough money to throw it away on charity."

"Do you have enough money for that?"

"Money you give to charity is never thrown away."

"But you just said it was."

"I was wrong. I made a mistake." But Griffin was talking about Phil Ginsberg and $750,000 and his own profound stupidity, punishment for murder. And he was thinking that he should have said to Ginsberg, Phil, you're yakking away about the price of all the toys on this boat, and then you mock the guy who puts down a few cases of wine, and for the life of me, Phil, I don't see the difference. What is it about the guy who cellars his wine that makes you so insecure? Was your father a wine bore? What did he do, set down wine that turned out not to be worth the trouble? Or do you not know the difference? And mind you, Phil, I'm not saying that knowing wine is by itself an achievement or not, I'm saying that you put a lot of energy into dismissing something that's not worth thinking about. No wonder you're not what you want to be.

Griffin felt refreshed by this unexpressed rant. He was starting to feel immunized against the worst of Ginsberg's facile bullying.

Five

When Griffin drove up to the Studio gate the next morning, he saw Walter Stuckel, head of security, in the guards' booth, crowded with five more guards than normal. Griffin had last seen Stuckel at the gate the second week of September 2001 and wondered if there was a new terrorist threat.

Stuckel came to Griffin and said, "I'm sorry to be the one to tell you this, Griffin, but you've been barred from the lot."

It was all so obvious, one of those millisecond flashes of complete understanding. Ginsberg had called Stella and told her that Griffin was leaving the studio to work for him; otherwise she would have called Griffin at home as soon as she'd heard the rumor. "Walter, can I park in the lot and make a few calls?"

"No. I'm sorry. You have to leave the lot. You're not an employee of the Studio anymore. I'm sorry. And this is really awful and I wish they'd tell you this yourself, but you have to return tomorrow night's Laker tickets. I hate having to do this. I've known you a long time. You've done a lot for this place, but that's the thing about this business, no one remembers."

Well, of course they remember, thought Griffin. Ginsberg remembers something Stella did to offend him, and Stella remembers it differently and I'm the one she's punishing. She remembers probably every particle of whatever cluster of lint she thinks Ginsberg has turned into whatever it is he's using me for as a weapon against her. And the Studio really should take away my seats. I don't work here anymore and everyone will know I've quit/been fired and they'll wonder what I'm doing in the Studio's seats.

"I'm sorry," said Stuckel.

"You already said that," said Griffin.

"I mean it. I like you. We've known each other a long time. You can pull around the booth."

Griffin made a large U-turn around the guards' booth, all of them watching him, amused, he was sure, at the fall of a big shot. He could have said, *I was fired because I took another job, a really good job*, but of course he didn't.

He drove a few blocks to a 7-Eleven parking lot. He had to call his lawyer but he owed his son the game, and before facing any more of the day's obligatory nightmares, he called his doctor's office and asked the receptionist if the doctor used a ticket broker when he couldn't get friends at the studios or agencies to get him good seats, and she had the number, he called, and paid six hundred dollars for the two best seats available. All this took four minutes, which tickled him, and then the tickle disappointed him, because being entertained by the speed of technology is something Phil Ginsberg never bothered with, unless he could find a way to turn it into money.

Tickets assured, he called Rick Mellen Jr., his lawyer. Mellen came on the line without a pleasantry.

"It makes me sick that you didn't call me before you made this decision about Ginsberg. I actually don't know if we can continue to work together if you're going to keep something this important from me, because it makes me look like a summer intern to tell people I didn't know."

"It's going to be great, Rick. The studio business is over for me."

"Griffin, it's not past him to steal you from the Studio as part of a three-dimensional chess game, a move that nobody really understands because the game he's playing is on too many levels. He steals you to create an empty space on one part of the board, which he fills with a fresh knight or bishop brought in from another studio, which means that when the replacement is moved, there's yet another space on the board, and a piece is lost; but the real purpose of his move is to clear out some pieces below, between two teams, while he's really just using this battle as a way to distract the players on a higher level."

"Fine, so to continue your thought, since I'm not off the board I've been press-ganged into his navy. And even if I'm not a bishop anymore—which is what I am at the Studio, an adviser to the queen—I was doomed there anyway. And if my army wins, if I don't die, I'll get a bigger prize than I would have with Stella. I like Stella and I've learned from her, I've even learned my limits here, but the limits don't have to transfer with me. Some of them come with the office. And if he's really smart enough to guess who Stella will hire in my place, and what that will do to the company he or she comes from, then it means I'm working with a master of the universe, and how great is that?"

"So you move from one queen to another."

"You're fired." Mellen thought Griffin was joking, but he meant it. He called Stella.

"I should have been given a chance to talk to you."

"Why? Obviously, you've been wanting to leave for a while, but you didn't talk to me about it. You had bad feelings about working with me, but you didn't say what they were. You didn't trust me, and I've done nothing for you to make you not trust me. If it was money, you would have told me and I would have found it for you. You're too valuable for me to lose. You're great at figuring out what's wrong with a story, Griffin. Obviously you decided that our story, yours and mine, didn't have a third act, but instead of asking me for my notes on the plot, Griffin sits on his unhappy emotions, Griffin keeps his secrets as always, and the only one who suffers is Griffin. It doesn't hurt me. If I got bent out of shape by the luxury problems of overpaid executives who feel unfulfilled because we make product instead of cinema, I'd have no staff and lose my way. My rule is, Your inner life belongs to you until too much of it spills over into the work. And I mean too much. We all bring our personal problems to the job; that's life. And I think in a creative business like ours, some honest depravity is good; it keeps you sensitive, and that helps with the artists and with the scripts. Phil's an evil man, but I'm sure he thinks I'm an evil woman. He's wrong. I'm right. Tell Rick Mellen to call business affairs and we'll settle your contract. Good luck and make a lot of money, because otherwise there is no good reason to leave me without having given me a chance to work this out."

"I fired Rick Mellen. I have to find someone else."

"That's for you to deal with, isn't it? Why are you telling me this?"

"I'm sorry, Stella."

"Disingenuous bullshit. It's too early for you to say that. Good-bye."

. . .

He called Ginsberg from the car.

"You're mad at me, aren't you?" said his new boss.

"First of all I thought you didn't want me, and second of all we haven't agreed on terms. And third of all, I made a mistake and I shouldn't have given the school the money just to send you a message. I feel like the people who survive jumping from the Golden Gate Bridge; they all say that on the way down they realize how stupid they'd been."

"So that's why they lived. They wanted to live. Regret is an underestimated restorative. Maybe the dead jumpers went down smiling; maybe they comprehended the full measure of their awful lives with the clarity of twenty Buddhas and were only sorry that they'd waited so long; maybe they were happy about ending it all, and that's why they died. The water was one final baptism or, if you prefer, *mikvah*, although you need to go down three times in a ritual bath, right?"

"I don't know, Phil."

"Anton, look it up." Anton would be one of Ginsberg's assistants, listening on the line, taking notes.

"This should have been my decision."

"No, it was my decision. It was my decision to hire you. It was my decision to bring this attention to my business, because your coming to me will be news. It was also my decision to fuck over Stella Baal because she fucked over me."

"When?"

"Seven years ago."

"What did she do?"

"I remember the pain. The reason doesn't matter, especially to you. Next: the press. They'll be all over us. I already released your statement. And by the way, yes, three times fully immersed for ritual cleaning in a ritual bath. You'll miss your friends at the Studio, but after so many years in production, you couldn't pass up the opportunity for a new perspective on the entertainment industry. I said that Griffin Mill has always impressed me with his vision, and while we have no specific plans yet, we believe that the digital communications revolution cannot be stopped and we're looking to the future. It's going to be an adventure for both of us. I almost gave that word to you, but I like *adventure* so I kept it for myself. There you go. Come on over. Let's get to work."

He told Lisa the news without telling her that Phil had called Stella.

"How much longer do you stay at the Studio?"

"I'm gone. Stella told me to pack up and leave. She wouldn't even let me get my address book. I said good-bye to the secretaries, and here I am."

"That's not fair. You made so much money for them. It's not fair. What are we going to do?"

"Everything is going to be fine."

"How do you know that? Don't give the money to the school."

"I made a pledge."

"And you made a pledge to me when we got married to protect me, and giving away three quarters of a million dollars, Griffin—that doesn't protect me when the economy is shaky and you're getting old in a job for younger men and you can't afford your life. I said I would help you but that didn't mean I'd stand behind any stupid thing you wanted to do. I'm scared, Griffin. I'm really scared."

"I love you."

"Not really." And she hung up.

• • •

Then he called June.

"I just wanted to let you know so you don't read about it in the trades—"

She interrupted him. "I don't read the trades."

"I start working with Phil Ginsberg tomorrow."

"So you're going to make a lot of money."

"I hope so."

"What does that mean? Can you still pay for two houses and all the tuition?"

"You could have said, Good luck."

"I'm sorry for worrying about the children, Griffin. But other than that, to be fair, I didn't think you could do this. I worried that in the last few years you gave up the fight. And I've been sad for you."

Griffin almost said, "I trust you more than I trust Lisa." He wondered what she was wearing.

"Griffin, are you there?"

"I'm here. I was just smiling at what you said."

"I still love you, you know."

"Really? I was so horrible to you."

"So what else is new about men? Do you ever love me?"

"Yeah."

"Not yes? Just yeah? It hurts."

"I know that."

"No, you don't. Last night—" She stopped. She wanted to tell him about Goth night, she wanted to tell him about the clothes she wears at night, sometimes.

She wanted to tell him how much the other men she met left her hating herself. They started out well, could play sexually together so she believed they belonged in each other's lives. There were two men of promise, with artful houses, good jobs, relaxed in the world, patient, who described themselves to her as ethical hedonists, a path in life they presented as though they were Columbus landing on the shore of a new philosophy. June agreed at first, but when such a man used the word pleasure, he meant more than pleasure, he meant "the use of you." It took these two men to teach her that an ethical hedonist could never be a real friend. She wanted a husband who would leave the curtains open and the lights on when they made love in a great hotel room. She knew a lot of people were kinky and she loved them for their kinkiness, but they still walked away from her. And then they called her crazy.

Lost in this, she heard Griffin call her back to the moment. "Last night? June? What happened last night?"

"Ethan figured this out on Sunday, on the boat. I'll tell Jessa."

"Thank you."

"Jessa is lonely without you."

"I don't know what to say. This is my life now."

"Maybe I'm wrong about wishing you the best."

"What else can I do?"

"You can understand fidelity at a deeper level, that's what you can do. You can find a way to be faithful to me even while you're married to Lisa."

"Which would mean being unfaithful to Lisa."

"No. It just means you remember that I'm the mother of your children, it means you remember that we shared a bed, and it means you remember that you loved me."

"I'm sorry I hurt you."

"And you still hurt me, which hurts your children. That's what I mean by fidelity. Find a way to stop hurting me. I'm not an evil person."

"I never said you were." In the past twenty minutes, two women had declared themselves not evil. He didn't know what to make of this.

"I'm a complete person."

"Yes, you are."

"I'm a good person."

"I know that."

"I'm a loving person."

"You always were."

"Really bad things have happened to me."

"I know that."

"And you were a part of the two worst things that ever happened to me, David's murder and the divorce."

"I can't turn back the clock." *And I can't unkill your old boyfriend.*

"Why not?"

Six

The next morning, Griffin drove to Ginsberg's office in Beverly Hills, at the corner of Wilshire Boulevard and Beverly Drive. The office, a large suite but not the entire floor, had been designed by a naval architect without a nautical theme, but everything fit together comfortably, and everything was soft on the eyes. The cabinets were cherry and ash, warm-looking, with gently rounded corners. Griffin said his name to the receptionist, and in less than the count of five Ginsberg opened the door.

"Is your wife," Phil Ginsberg asked Griffin, "a toaster or a trophy?"

"What's the better answer?"

Ginsberg held the door for Griffin and led him to his office.

"A toaster is one of those very efficient women who live between Beverly Hills and Pacific Palisades. They're not especially beautiful, they're even a little hard to look at, but their efficiency and dependability make them socially compelling. You can't imagine them talking dirty on the phone. They tend to have thick hair, I don't know why, although a few have dead-mouse hair. And their sons have large heads and shiny hair. It's freaky. All of them. Shiny black hair and big running shoes with the laces undone, like they have swollen feet. And their husbands almost never leave them; why should they?

They're like a good toaster, and you never get rid of a good toaster; they do what they're supposed to do and never break.

"A trophy is obvious, we know what that is. But trophies tarnish. That's the problem with them. These trophy wives, they're not dependable. And think about a trophy case in someone's den, not a teenager but someone your age. There it is, home-run king of the high school. And that includes the industry awards. Every time you let an award impress a guest, you're bouncing a check on your soul, because when you look at a trophy all it does is remind you of the past. No reserve for the future. A credit line is more impressive. Toasters remind you of—well, toast. Breakfast. Jam. Toast and jam. It makes you think of Saturday morning and a lovely weekend. When a man leaves a toaster for a trophy, he never gets another toaster. Your first wife, was she a trophy or a toaster?"

"I don't think of her that way."

"How could you? It's a new concept. But you were the last person to see her husband before he was murdered. She came to you wrapped in the glamour of her little tragedy. She's kind of a tragic figure all around, yes? Her first husband dies, her second husband leaves her for the mother of his new child. That's not the stuff of toasters, Griffin. That's not how a guy like you would treat an appliance. Is Lisa a trophy? Do you think you'll leave Lisa?"

"I don't think so." Griffin knew better than to ask Ginsberg how he knew so much about him. Any good private investigator would have found the story in a lazy afternoon. He wasn't sure of the significance of Ginsberg's mistake in calling Kahane June's husband instead of boyfriend.

"There you go, she's your toaster. Was your first wife beautiful?"

Now they were in Ginsberg's office, the famous office without a desk, just chairs and a single telephone.

"I thought so."

"Very beautiful?"

"Nice to look at."

"Is she still good looking?"

"Better looking."

"That's the first good answer you've given me. I don't care about your wives, I just want to know how you talk about them. I want to know how you answer rude questions."

"Do I pass?"

"Who's better in bed, June or Lisa?"

If he said *That's private*, he would convict himself of pious modesty and Ginsberg would never trust him. He could have said that Lisa kissed well and held her kisses longer, that Lisa's skin was softer and her perfume always smelled rich, but that June gave a better blow job, liked sex more, just the rolling around in bed and trying things, and laughing, and games; he could have said to Ginsberg, *She's a bit like you, Phil, sometimes June has the behind in mind.* "If I thought you wanted to know so you could choose one of them to sleep with, Phil, I'd be happy to tell you."

"Good enough. Now let's talk about us. I've rented an office for you, and you have a secretary named Alicia. I want you to sit in your office and I want you to think. There's a chair and a phone. I want you to think about things that I can't even imagine. I want you to look at your life, your own life, as the life of the world. I'm not going to give you any analogies because I want you to start fresh. Look for a story. That's what you did for twenty-five years, and you're good at it. You've got that mythic structure in your head and you know how to make things work according to the rules, which everyone is supposed to know but doesn't. Look for mistakes. Look for bruised fruit, bruised businesses. When you find them, tell me about them. We'll make a better one. And don't come back to me tomorrow, that'd be a bad sign. Let it all sink in. Take your time. That's what I did."

"And now you're stuck. You're worried that you've reached the limit of your vision."

"I told you, I want four billion. I've got friends with that kind of money. You'd think that after seven hundred and fifty million there's no real difference because there's not much to buy that you can't afford, but there always is. With the really big money you can buy an industry that needs a little work, fix it up, sell it, and make another billion. Then you do it again. And there are toys. That's when you can buy a Boeing 767 if you want one. With that kind of money all the borders disappear, you never flash a passport, your bags are never searched. There's a beautiful silence around you. Everyone smiles, because they know you have a billion. I've got seven hundred and fifty million dollars, but when I'm with the billionaires, I feel small. Do you know that a man with four billion dollars can buy a battleship? He can buy ten fighter jets and make war on Guatemala if he wants to. The money: you can't imagine what four billion dollars can do. I'm not looking for ten billion; some people have that much but I don't think I'll get there, though you never know. But four billion, that's in reach. If I make a billion, I can make four, I know it. And if you make this work, you'll get your taste of it. We haven't discussed money yet. I work on the bonus system, but a big bonus. No salary."

"Listen to me, Phil, just listen. I made one point five million dollars a year, plus benefits, plus a travel allowance, plus an expense account."

"And now you make nothing. That's a good impetus to get to work, don't you think?"

"I can't live on nothing."

"You have no choice. You can't go back to Stella, I burned that bridge already."

"She said she'd welcome me back."

"If I thought you believed her I'd fire you for gullibility. You know you can't go back. And who else is going to take you if you quit after three weeks with me? Do you think they won't call me and get my side of the story? I'd have to say something awful about you, about your nosebleeds at my altitude. I'd have to protect myself at the expense of your reputation. Don't do this to yourself."

"Do what?"

"Torture yourself because you have no control. Look at the deal I'm giving you. All I want you to do is walk with me and think. Isn't that why you gave seven hundred and fifty thousand to Coldwater, to get next to me? Here you are. And don't look so shocked. I know you think I know everything, but if I did, I'd have my battleship by now. Make the best of this, Mr. Mill. I promise that if we do the thing I want to do, you will have enough money for your own jet and the island of your dreams. That's what you want, isn't it? Tell the truth. Forty acres on an atoll in the South Pacific?"

"Yes. How did you know?"

"You were at a dinner party three months ago and told a friend of mine that you think the world is coming to an end and you want a private island somewhere. I think you're wrong, we've just had a bad couple of thousand years, but we'll muddle through, at least until our great-grandchildren have children. And then, fuck it, it's their problem. Get the private island now, but with enough high ground to still have room for the farm after the ocean rises, and leave it in trust for them if that makes you feel better. Until then, while I favor Oregon ranch land a hundred miles inland, with hydroponic farming and enough well water, a private island is a lot of fun for its own sake, and if you want that island, stay with me on my terms and you can have it. Your office is in a dull little building on Bundy, with a view of the parking lot. You don't want to be there long, so get to work. Alicia is waiting."

. . .

The building was the color of snail meat, and Griffin's name was misspelled: GRYPHON MILLER, Suite 204, no elevator, up the stairs. The black steel door was locked, and after a few hard knocks, and a Hello? that stayed in his throat like heartburn, Alicia, who never told him her last name, let him in. He felt sorry for her, could not control this first impression, and knew she could see his opinion in his face. She was probably fifty, probably twice divorced, probably lived in Marina del Rey, probably worked out five times a week, and the last three men she dated were themselves too damaged to see any hope for healing and love with her. She had long blond hair, to the small of her back, too much a conversation piece—like a rich man on a camping trip showing off a twenty-thousand-dollar watch—the only trick she could do.

"I'm Griffin, and you must be Alicia."

"That indeed is who I am. Yes yes yes. Come on in. I've got everything fixed up the way I was told, and this is my office and in there is yours, and you'll see that there's no desk, just a rocking chair and a little side table. There's no computer. And no phone."

"He said I'd have a phone."

"They want you to think, and then you'll get a phone."

"They? Who is they?"

"Did I say they? I meant he. Mr. G. He said you have to wait before you get a phone."

"Then I'll use my cell phone."

"And then you'll be fired. That's why you have to give me your cell phone while you're working."

"I'm not going to do that."

"Call Mr. Ginsberg and tell him so yourself. I'm sure he's eager for the interruption."

THE RETURN OF THE PLAYER

Griffin gave her the phone while trying to keep a smile that said, *This is silly, but I'm not going to play the game by fighting it.*

"Mr. Mill, Mr. Ginsberg told me you're a brilliant man but you need some encouragement to discover your real genius, and that kind of encouragement only confidence can give you, of the know-thyself variety, which demands a fair amount of quiet time, as you've been at the mercy of the phone for your entire career in Hollywood, though the law is just as bad, if not worse. Lawyers can't hide in screening rooms. On the other hand, the law has a much broader peak. Make partner, do the right dance steps, and grow rich. Be brilliant and make yourself a dependable career. Not like this wonderful crazy business of ours, hey?"

Griffin sat in the rocking chair. The pegs of the chair's rockers were pulling out of the frame, and Griffin had to knock them into place with the heel of his palm while Alicia watched, unreadable.

"Maybe you could get me another chair?"

"No can do."

"Or some glue?"

"Don't have it."

"There's a Staples or an Office Depot somewhere within fifteen seconds of this place."

"What you have is what you get, Mr. Mill. That's what I was told."

"Am I allowed to buy my own chair or my own glue?"

"Is there anything about that in your contract?"

"I don't have a contract."

"It's up to you."

Instead of adding another volley to this stupid conversation, Griffin sat in the chair, rocked, and kept his eyes on Alicia without saying a word. She stayed there, waiting for the word. They kept this up for fifteen minutes, until he said, "I guess that's all then, thank you."

81

"I'll be up front. Next week, or thereabouts, you can use my computer. Good thoughts!" And then she closed the door and he wanted to crawl on his knees and beg forgiveness, for what, he couldn't have said, not the murder, not adultery, not the waste of seven hundred and fifty thousand dollars. No, he knew. He wanted to apologize for looking at the pouches under her eyes and thinking *pouches.*

God knows who had this office before me, thought Griffin, or if Ginsberg owned the building and kept the suite, with Alicia, ready for whatever sicko game he wanted to play with any fly dumb enough to challenge the web. It was the office of someone returned from ten years as a hostage and now writing an unsellable memoir, or the office of a compulsive gambler who used to be an accountant, lost his practice for double billing, and keeps an office with the last few bucks he had before final suicidal destitution or just alcoholic dissolution into the mist of the city and then, six years later, a drug-and-alcohol counseling degree from LA City College and a few gigs speaking to union workers caught drinking on the job, and then that fails, and then who the fuck cares. It was a depressing ugly one-window box of a room in an architectural tumor.

What trick had his life played on him now? What a mess. This lunatic homosexual boss of his was going to torture him to death by reminding him of how little he understood the world, how close one could come to heroic wealth and then fail because of hesitation, because of a sentimental reliance on salvation by careful balance on the path between work and life. Fuck life, says money, fuck life.

He regretted leaving the Studio. He missed the routine business of the movies, missed his humble place on the assembly line where the collective grinding away of a story to the lowest gear could pull the price of ten million tickets from the pockets of America and, in exchange, relieve ten million Americans of nothing more than their daily woe.

He knocked on the inside of his own door to alert his weird secretary that he wanted to come out to the reception area. She opened the door an inch.

"Hi there. You must need the phone or the bathroom key."

"I need to use the phone."

"Isn't it a little too soon to be making calls, Mr. Mill? Shouldn't you give yourself more time to think? Genius needs patience; inspiration comes cheap. You know what Einstein said."

"That if time goes forward, it should go backward."

"That genius is ten percent *inspiration* and ninety percent *perspiration*. I love that sentiment, Mr. Mill."

"That was Thomas Edison, wasn't it?"

"No, it was Einstein."

"I don't think so," said Griffin.

"That's your opinion, and it's a free country."

"Actually, you're right," said Griffin, following an instinct for caution when stuck in a debate with this particularly American confusion of assertion with accuracy.

"You're a little hasty there with the concession, but I'll let it go."

"I need to talk to my wife," said Griffin.

"I'm sure you do."

"Now. I'd like to talk to her now. May I have my phone back? We talk a few times a day and she hasn't heard from me yet."

"You can call in an hour."

"Yes, I'm sure you think that's the best way to protect your job, but I want to protect my marriage."

"And if you're working in a crummy office without a phone, desk, or your own washroom, my-oh-my, that has to put enormous pressure on a marriage that is probably already shaky, since you just switched jobs."

"May I have my phone back for just a few minutes?"

"If I start to horse-trade with you on day one, particularly about the only thing of yours that I can honestly say is under my control, by order of the Jew who writes our checks—well, my checks; you're not getting paid, as I understand things—I put my livelihood at risk. Let me see, should I do that for someone I have known for only a few hours? Waiting for an answer . . . oh, here it comes now. *Ring-a-ling-ling.* Nope. No can do. Sit here and work."

"What if I have to use the bathroom?"

"Hold it in for an hour or just piss in the corner."

"I wouldn't do that."

"Then you're going to have to hold it in, aren't you? Hmm?"

The pegs squealed, but the long rockers held. He pushed with his toes, let his hands relax in his lap, tipped backward to the edge of giddiness, and rolled forward slowly, afraid of falling on his face. Who doesn't love a rocking chair? he thought. Since Ginsberg chose everything, he probably picked out this chair himself. Griffin saw deeper into the man's genius, or he wanted to believe, with the selection of this particular noisy rocking chair, that Phil Ginsberg completed another section of his intricate scaffold.

So he rocked for an hour, looking for patterns in the noises he made with the chair, finding music that way, pretending he was a six-year-old boy in his grandpa's rocking chair on the porch with a grand view of blue foothills, edging the rocker close to the tail of a big sleepy ol' coon dog, Big Nig, just for the pleasure of seeing that ol' hound dog barely suffer the pain as he resettled himself on the other side of the porch, good ol' dog. What dreams fill the days of a mountain child with ambition to see what manner of men live beyond the foothills, a dreamer who wants to join those men but still reap the gain of such a high vantage point, so broad and privileged a view, where even the big dogs know better than to complain about his sometimes casual pleasure at their expense?

An hour in this reverie, and then he asked for the phone.

"You need to go to the bathroom."

He took the phone to the bathroom and closed a stall. He called Lisa, not to frighten her with his remorse, because he owed her a show of gravity, but to hear her voice.

"I was just thinking of you," he said.

"Griffin, I'm too angry with you to talk about fixing this."

"I love you," he said, the sound of the maimed pride in his voice equal to the look of chastising bewilderment in the eyes of a big dog whose tail has been cracked by a rocking chair.

"Of course you say that. A: You don't want to lose me because you don't want to be embarrassed. B: You wish you hadn't left Stella. I can hear it in your voice, the little wimpy-boy voice. Why don't you just say, *Lisa, I'm sawee, I'm vewy sawee.*"

"Are you making fun of your daughter?"

"I'm making fun of you."

"Things are going to work out."

"Then I have nothing to worry about and I'm sorry, I'm verrreeee sorreee, in advance, for ever doubting you. I'm at school."

"I'll see you later."

Griffin now had to pee, and this was a good thing, he thought, because he wouldn't make himself a liar to Alicia.

When she closed the phone, Lisa felt her husband's fear of Ginsberg infecting her with more sickening images of the end of life as she knew it. She tried to scourge the devil of vanity, who dodged her swipes at him and showed her more of the beautiful privileges she'd lose after the divorce.

Seven

And time, as they say, passed, and time is a day, and a day passed. At home, Lisa was cold and Willa was quiet, but if Lisa had pulled a scarf from her neck to unveil a snake tattoo and then after dinner bummed a cigarette from Willa, Griffin would not have noticed, since his consciousness still sloshed around in his head to the pulse of the rocking chair.

On the second morning, Griffin surrendered his mobile phone to Alicia before she could ask for it and then, without saying hello, he once again sat in his chair and rocked. He thought about Bill Gates. Bill Gates grew up in the heart of a provincial aristocracy. His parents had high social position in Seattle's small world of banking and law. The infant Bill Gates rocked in his crib, rolling on his back, head to feet and back to head again. The rocking scared his mother. Nothing would stop him. No one had ever seen a child with such a strong will. When he was five his mother took him to a psychiatrist, who tested Bill, pronounced him a genius, and said his mother would have to learn to live with him, because Bill would always win.

Computers, obviously, thought Griffin. Revelation one. Depressing, though. What's left to make money from in computers? He trusted the rocking chair. The rocking chair will tell me. Bill Gates, the rocking dervish of money, the boy genius who conned IBM into renting the operating code from him instead of buying it. If they had said, "Sorry, Bill, your Microsoft Disk Operating System works well with our new personal computers, but we can't let you lease the code to anyone who builds a computer, because anyone with the code can build a machine to run the code and then why would they want an IBM except for the myth of the brand?" Had they told him to sell his code outright or they'd move on, he would have sold and taken his ten million dollars, if that, and considered himself a most fortunate fellow. He was like George Lucas, who kept the merchandise rights for *Star Wars* because Fox never imagined that he understood everything about children. And if the negotiators for Fox had said to George, "We'll have the merchandise rights and give you a small piece of the action," George would have counted himself a fortunate fellow if the royalties from the toys made him a few million dollars over the years, since it would have been unimaginable to expect Fox to give him the right to make four billion dollars for himself, any more than Bill Gates would have cursed IBM's greed for seeing through his insane bid to lease the software to 93 percent of the world's computers and make him the richest man who ever lived. They didn't understand that he was a once-in-three-millenniums avatar who understood all that was important to know, not some sort of easily manipulated high school whiz-kid Harvard dropout with filthy shirts and dirty hair, who smelled, sprayed when he talked, and looked like nothing with a face that showed no character; he was a rocker, he loved fast cars, he went to private school.

Griffin drew energy from this reverie, a bashful appreciation for Gates's achievement. He rocked for the morning, he rocked through lunch, he rocked for the afternoon, through nausea into emptiness. He felt himself everywhere and nowhere, smart and dumb, lucky and cursed, and then blessed, the opposite of cursed, blessed, because the universe in all its ugly twisting had delivered that colony of cells known as Griffin Mill into a room with nothing but a squeaking chair, and the noise of the rocker floated on the silence of eternity, not death but time without life, and for the first time ever he knew absolute confidence, a feeling as though he had already achieved his goals; he was reading the last page of the story or the caption under the photograph: GRIFFIN WINS. He stopped rocking, to get up and tell Alicia, Three days after His death, Christ pushed back the cover to the tomb, and after three days in the tomb of this office, I'm ready for my phone.

He knocked on the inside of his door to let Alicia know he was coming out, not to scare her, but she didn't answer. He opened the door slowly. She was gone from her desk. He came around to her side of the desk to see if she'd left a note. On the computer screen was a picture of June in a swimming pool, her face rising through the surface of the water, thick hair floating around her shoulders, her smile kissing the camera and, through the camera, Jessa, the photographer. Under the picture was a statement.

JUNEBUG4PLAY: 42. I know better than to look here, or really anywhere for that matter, for love. Instead I look for just really good companionship. Love follows or it doesn't. And sometimes we don't want love, we just want release. Like sometimes I just want the release of a good run down a slope in Deer Valley (love the snow there, love the service, hate the prices), sometimes I just need to jog an extra mile in the morning, sometimes I just need good cause to scream and hope the neighbors don't mind. And sometimes I don't care what the neighbors think. But I am a single Mom, so I have to say that, but I'm also free most weekends, so I have to say that too. If you're a man with a sexy phone voice, a man who understands what's going on in the world and can tell me about it, a man who can make me laugh, and a man who lives not too far from where I live (Los Angeles), let's talk. Let's even . . . chat?

Why is this here? What is Alicia or Ginsberg trying to tell me?
But this revelation follows my rocking.

I am supposed to look at this picture and think about money. Or is Ginsberg just fucking with my head because I crossed his path years ago, getting in the way of something he wanted, and now am I being sealed up in a forgotten corner of his wine cellar, built on the foundations of an old mission catacomb? Or something like that.

And Alicia is gone because it's six o'clock and her day is over, if it ever begins.

He left the picture on the computer, locked the office door, and, when he was in the garage, walked slowly back to the office for another set of dim reasons and turned the computer off. Before going back to the car, he sat in the chair and rocked twelve times. He wanted to see June naked again. He thought of the shape of her nipples in the swimsuit, how she must have chosen that picture for the way her nipples advertised the thing the statement didn't need to tell Mr. Single Dad, that she wasn't asking for much yet, just a little hope, and that she'd trade the delusion of misplaced hope for the man who could see that the homey author of the statement loved cock.

He called Lisa from the car and reminded her that he was stopping at June's to take Ethan to the Lakers game. Lisa wanted to tell him to come home, because the signal vibrations of the universe, passing through Griffin, warned her that June held a new fascination for him. She blamed herself, not knowing about the Internet ad, because now that Lisa was trying to find a way to leave Griffin, she worried that the threat of her possible moving out would add something to June's luster, since an abandoned Griffin would finally and compassionately understand the enormity of June's pain. And June the first wife had two children with him, twice the number of children he had with Lisa the second wife, twice the responsibility, that much more to love. She said, "Can you come home first? Willa had a hard day. She was awful when I picked her up at school."

"I can't. I'm sorry, there's not enough time. I'll put her to bed."

. . .

Griffin called June to tell her he was coming over and she asked him why because now it was her turn for suspicion, and he heard Ethan shout out, "The game, Mom!" It was everyone's turn to have everyone else's emotions, it was that kind of day, the little network of Griffin's family sharing a duplication of the same feelings, a re-dundancy like the backup navigation systems on Ginsberg's yacht. On the one hand, thought Griffin, we hate the sameness of the com-mercial world, the same chain stores, the same fashions, the same music and movies, but on the other hand we're the same animal liv-ing in the same social system, so what is everyone complaining about? Give us something different, isolate us in an experience we don't yet already know, and we freak out. He felt the pulse of the rocking chair in the thought. It wasn't original but he didn't want an original thought, he wanted to think the most obvious common thought that no one else had figured out to be the lid on a big bucket of money. Bucket? Fountain. Fountain? Ocean.

. . .

Ethan stood on the front step of the house in his purple-and-gold Lakers jacket, so excited to be with his father that even he couldn't hide from himself the pathetic quality of his eagerness to spend time with his dad, who should never have left his mother. I am with my father now, a whole four hours not mandated by a custody agreement.

Griffin felt sad for Ethan, sad for Jessa, sad for June, sad for Lisa, sad for Willa, sad for himself. We're all alive and this is life? This is it? Right turns on red light, homework, some kind of accommodation with death, some kind of theology to overcome envy, some kind of gesture in the direction of making the world better, a little charity, and, other than that, trying not to let your bad feelings spoil someone else's day or—not anything so remote as a day—a minute, a moment. A good meal, sure, the appropriate wine, yes, but is that all there is?

June asked Griffin to talk to her for a few minutes, and they left the children on the sidewalk while they walked to the front door.

She was worried about Ethan, about the Internet, about pornography. Griffin felt a swoon coming on. It couldn't be a simple accident that the first thing his ex-wife wanted to tell him was about the Internet, when the only thing he could think of looking at her was that he'd seen her on the Internet, and while she told him, he looked at her T-shirt, at the unexcited nipples making a slight impression through the bra and the shirt. But he had just seen them on Alicia's computer, so he was thinking about them, which made him excited to be with June, so that she had to ask if he'd heard what she just said.

"Yes, you're worried about Ethan looking at porn."

"Ethan and Eli. They know how to delete the history of the sites they visit, and the cookies, but I'm sure they're looking at porn."

"Why?"

"Because they shut the door and I don't hear the sound of a video game, but when I open the door the video game is right there, and I think they have a way to switch from the Internet to the game by touching one of the function keys. Something's not right. They're guilty about something. Is this how Dylan Klebold's mother felt the night before Columbine?" June could not remember such a calm chat with Griffin when the subject was her fears for their children. She couldn't understand why he seemed happy to be talking to her. She wanted to keep talking, to test his patience with her. She continued. "It hit me at the time of the shooting that nobody said anything about it being a Dylan who led the attack. He was named for Bob Dylan; they wanted Bob Dylan to be their son's astral guardian. Bob Dylan didn't have to be asked, but if you name your kid Dylan you hope for certain spiritual qualities."

June wished that Lisa could hear this conversation, because she wouldn't have slept that night, because Griffin could never talk so freely with Lisa about something from the news.

"But you were never a Dylan fan," said Griffin.

"He's romantic, but he's not sexy. I need sex."

She meant, *in the music I like,* but the thought came out stuck to the same deep truth about her that Griffin had found in her picture on the Internet. She added, "You know what I mean."

"So what music is giving you the sex you like?"

Griffin asked this so impersonally that June guessed the impersonal reason. "This is something you need to help you with work?"

"Yes, work. It's important."

"I'll think about what you need."

"Thank you."

"If you think about what I need."

Griffin thought about her nipples in the bathing suit, and her beautiful hair, and drops of water on her cheeks, and the smile she gave her daughter. And spanking June the way she liked.

"Well, what you need now is to install one of those programs that tracks keystrokes so you can see where Ethan is going on the Internet. The program runs invisibly, and then, after a few weeks, we can go back and see what he and Eli are up to. Give them time to look around; don't bust them after one session. I'll get the program and you can install it while he's at school, and if that's the day he goes to school loaded with nail bombs, then we'll know that next time you suspect him of planning a massacre, trust your intuition."

She punched his arm in play. "You're evil."

"I never said I wasn't."

He walked to the car, sorry he didn't tell her to fuck someone, just for the fun of it, because she deserved some pleasure. He wanted to tell her to fuck a stranger and then call him later and tell him about it. They used to talk dirty together; when he traveled he even packed a bottle of sex lube in his bag and waited for her to tell him when to put it on.

He had to pay for parking six blocks from the Staples Center. Ethan had never walked so far from the car to the game; their tickets to the front row had always come with VIP parking close to the entrance. "You lost your house seats, huh?" Ethan asked, in a tone of surprising sympathy.

"I'll get them back."

"Don't do it for me, Dad. It doesn't matter."

"Everything matters in Hollywood."

"What was it like when Eli's grandpa died?"

"I think he was surprised to die. He wasn't ready. He was rich and he had a lot of nice things and he had a few girlfriends too."

"Eli told me he didn't like Greg. And Greg didn't like him either."

"So this is a discussion about fathers and sons." That was an insulting thing to say; Griffin tried to take it back. "That came out wrong. I mean, if you're worried about it, I love you." Right, I love you so much I killed for you.

The seats were off to the side and twenty rows back, and except for the nights that Griffin had joined friends from companies that kept skyboxes, he had never sat so high above the floor. He was used to sitting either in the Studio's floor seats, across from Jack Nicholson, or in the first row behind.

And there was Phil Ginsberg, next to Squire, sitting in the Studio's seats, given away only with the written permission of Stella Baal herself. Ginsberg turned around while Griffin was looking at him and summoned him with a wave. Squire didn't turn around to see who his father was talking to.

"Wait here," said Griffin to Ethan, "I just want to say hello." Griffin walked down the steps to the end of the level and was picked up by a camera that put the image on the big screens above the floor. The steps ended at a rail. To get to the next level of seats, Griffin would have had to walk back up to the entrance tunnel and take a flight of stairs down to the lower level and be turned back by the guards. No one would let him climb over this rail to get closer to Ginsberg. Everyone in the arena was looking at the screens, because Griffin had been caught, it seemed, trying to get past security and push his way to the movie stars or, worse, the floor, where he might do something dreadful, unimaginable, nasty, and fun to watch.

One minute to game and the teams were coming out to the floor.

Griffin told the security guard that he had been asked to come down by Mr. Ginsberg over there, but Ginsberg had turned his attention to the players on the court and was pointing something out to Squire.

Griffin, in close-up, asked the guard to ask Mr. Ginsberg, and the guard said that Mr. Ginsberg didn't have the authority to invite someone to the floor who didn't have a ticket on the floor. Griffin said, "Well, if Jack called me down, you would," which was stupid to say because of course the guard said, "But Mr. Nicholson hasn't called you down, and he never does; he's a Lakers fan and he knows the rules."

Griffin stumbled as he walked back to his now-embarrassed son, who was ashamed of his father for trying so stupidly and unnecessarily to catch Squire's dad's attention, when Squire's dad knew that Griffin was there but didn't want to talk to him. Griffin wished he had no children, so he could go to another city, get drunk in the lobby bar of an airport hotel, cry in front of strangers, take a cab to a biker bar in the ugly part of town, tell a Hells Angel to fuck his mother, and be stomped to death, quickly.

Eight

On the way to Swaine's memorial, Griffin turned on his car's GPS, to find a way up the canyon to the green fields he'd seen from Swaine's terrace. At the bottom of the canyon, with the map's parameters set to put the car in the center of a one-mile radius, the map showed him all the Brentwood streets he'd known for years. When he reached the top of the canyon and could see the fields through gaps in an oleander hedge at the beginning of Swaine's estate, he saw the riding rings, the children on ponies, and the big dogs. The map on his GPS screen did not show the canyon or the fields, just the next ridge of houses on Mandeville as though a mile closer. All he could say to himself was *bizarre*, and for this he was grateful for his worm-eaten vocabulary. If he knew too many words, the evidence of something large would scare him.

He gave the car to the valet and went inside.

There was a long white tent set on the lawn, with a few hundred chairs, and white roses wrapped around the poles holding up the tent. There were two bars, and waiters passing trays, and Sinatra on the sound system. Griffin was getting tired of Sinatra; the songs were pretty, some of them, and even deep, some of them, at least the songs of loss and failure, but so much about Sinatra alarmed him, Sinatra's popularity and the rise of Las Vegas was one of the reasons Griffin believed the world was coming to a chaotic end, but on the other hand no one killed a Rat Packer to impress Jodie Foster—or who would it have been then, Annette Funicello?—and no one named for Dino or Sammy ever bloodied a high school library.

The door to Warren Swaine's office was open, and before the memorial service started, Griffin wanted to look inside the drawer in Warren Swaine's desk to see if he had really killed the man by denying him his medicine. Of course, after a week someone could have cleaned everything out, but Griffin thought this was something Greg and his sister would want to do, and he thought it might be awhile before they got through everything and packed it away. They were probably just waiting until the memorial service was over before tearing the house apart like the set of a movie that had wrapped. That's what I would do, thought Griffin. The office had a bathroom, so there was no need to make up a reason for being there. He asked directions from a waiter, in case Tryon was watching him.

The trophies on the desk were gone. There weren't any papers on the desk. Griffin calculated the angle to the window and whether he'd be seen from outside if he should cross behind the desk, knock a book from the shelf, pick it up, and, as he rose, steady himself on the desk and quickly open the drawer. The toilet in the bathroom flushed, he heard the sink run, and then the door opened, and it was Stella.

"Oh, Griffin, it's so good to see you," and she gave him an all-is-forgotten hug that he might have expected a year later, if they'd run into each other in Burma. "I shouldn't have tossed you out. I should have fought for you. The first morning meeting without you, I knew I'd made a mistake. It's just I got caught in a thing with Ginsberg. He does that to me. That's what I thought was going on; you don't understand that he's using you against me."

"I went to him first. It was my move."

"You think so."

"I know it."

"That's how he works, that's how the guy does business."

"I wanted to leave the Studio. And if it's any comfort, Stella, I knew I could never do as good a job as you do."

"But I need you. We're a team. You're the reason I looked good. Without you, I don't know what to do."

"For real?"

"I'm telling you the truth. And now it's probably too late. I miss you. Everyone misses you."

This was too close, she'd said too much, and now they ate the silence, until she whispered, "I sucked Warren Swaine's cock, right here in this room. I was 25. He was already old. It was fun. And I'll tell you the truth, I think a few of the guys here were there before me. He understood sex. Now the only ones who still understand sex are the homosexuals, don't you think?"

"I haven't slept with any," said Griffin.

"Never?" She asked this with the same surprise she'd have shown if he said he'd never eaten Chinese food, and he didn't know if she meant something in Griffin's aura seemed open to fucking a guy, or just generally, that a man of the world should know the world.

"You mean Phil gave you the job without testing you?"

"He tested me."

"With your clothes on?"

"He asked me which of my wives was better in bed."

"June, of course."

"And I say that I told Ginsberg, *I'll only tell you if you want to fuck one of them.*"

"You didn't."

"Yes, basically, that's what I told him. You can ask."

He sat down at the desk and opened the drawer that he had held closed with his knee against the dying Swaine, delighting Stella with a naughtiness she had never suspected.

"Are you going through his desk?"

"If he left the secret formula for a long career, I'll split it with you."

The drawer was empty.

He heard Chris Tryon's voice. "What are you doing? Are you stealing something at a funeral?"

But Griffin had Stella as a shield, she was included in Tryon's accusation. She was younger than him and better at life, and she knew what to say. She told the truth. "We were looking to see if he'd left the secret of his success."

"You shouldn't be here. But if you want to know, his children cleaned the drawers yesterday. If they found anything like that, they didn't tell me." Griffin wasn't satisfied with this, because Tryon kept his eyes locked on Griffin's when he said this, because Tryon knew something, because Tryon believed, so Griffin thought, that Griffin had not said everything about the moments surrounding Swaine's death.

"We're going, we're going," Stella said to Tryon, pulling Griffin out of the chair like she owned him in an inaccessibly sexy way, part fun, part destructive, and her freedom to grab him with such contempt for Tryon, after Griffin had fucked around with the dead man's stuff, proved to Griffin once again that Stella deserved her high job and that, in some people, arrogance is humility.

As they passed the window overlooking the canyon with the three riding rings and the polo field, Griffin asked her, "Do you see that canyon?"

"Yes."

"It's not on the map. It's not even on GPS. That should be Mandeville, but it's not. How does that work? The satellites don't show that canyon."

"What are you talking about?"

"Do the rich have their own maps of the world that are different from the ones you and I get? They do, don't they? My God, Stella, that valley over there, it isn't registered on the satellite map or the regular maps. How long has it been a secret? What other places are like that? This is freaking me out. What else don't we know about the rich?"

"Don't assume that you and I have the same maps to the world. Leave it alone."

. . .

The service, or whatever they were calling it, started without introduction when a minister took to the lectern beside a table with Swaine's awards surrounded by photographs of him from childhood to three weeks ago. There were no pictures of Swaine with his family, only movie stars. A minister. Griffin always assumed that the Swaines were Jews.

"We are here not to mourn Warren Swaine but to celebrate him." Griffin turned his eyes to the green fields of the unmapped canyon, and then those fields, along with whatever was said about Warren Swaine, disappeared into the boring glare that sprays through the city's silver overcast, an unbearable illusion that the speed of light is infinite, bringing the news of everything at once, blinding us.

Swaine is dead, I killed him, I'm almost broke, I don't know what I'm doing, I'm afraid all the time, I have no friends, the globe of the rich is larger than anyone knows.

. . .

While Griffin tried to turn confusion into transcendence, Willa needed new shoes and Lisa took her to the Nordstrom's in The Grove, which everyone agreed was the most pleasant mall in the world. Lisa left the car with the valet instead of driving into the parking structure, but still she worried about having to drive in long lines in garages, searching for a parking space, once she got divorced, and hated herself again for that kind of pathetic worry. They crossed the fake village square, and Willa wanted ice cream or a *boba*, and Lisa said no. Lisa felt tugged by a devil who said, It will build your daughter's character if you refuse to bribe her for good behavior while you are buying her the shoes she wants, as if those shoes aren't or shouldn't be enough of a bribe for her to promise good behavior in the store.

"I want ice cream, Mom."

"It's going to spoil your appetite."

"Just a little?"

"You mean buy a cup and throw it away after three spoons?"

"Yeah."

"That's wasteful, Willa."

"You don't like me."

"I do like you."

"Ooh like me but ooh doan lummee."

"I love you, Willa."

"Nah really."

"I love you enough to buy you shoes."

"Big deal. Ooh supposa buy me shooze. Ooh my mutha."

Willa needed party shoes, one pair; running shoes, one pair; regular walk-around shoes, two pairs. Lisa asked the salesman to first show her the party shoes, thinking Willa would soften after she'd made her choice, but when the salesman returned with a stack of boxes and offered Willa a pair of red sequin shoes with green sequin buckles, she shook her head and refused even to say *no*. Lisa told Willa to speak up.

"I know what she's saying," said the salesman, Ted, with a practiced wink at Willa, to add in code, *Let a professional do his job. This is how I make a living, your frustration is my meat.*

"What's your name?"

"Willa," said Lisa.

"No. Doan tellum."

"Willa, that's a pretty name. I know two dogs named Willa. Two different friends called their dogs Willa."

"I ahn not a dog!" cried Willa.

"Dogs don't wear shoes," said the salesman, opening another box of shoes, the same style as the first but with the colors switched, green shoe and red buckle. He reached for Willa's right foot.

"No, thass uglee. It's the same as before, just different. Green where the red was and red where the green was. Itsa same shooze. I want all red."

"No promise but maybe also no problem-o," said Ted. "I got a million of 'em."

"You hear what he said, Willa? He's got a million more shoes," said Lisa. Ted opened up three more boxes, but the styles were all variations on the first pair, no sequins, different colors.

The girl pushed them away. "Ai ohn like deez shooze. Ai ohn like ennyovum."

"I'll see what else we have," said Ted.

"No," said Lisa, stopping him. "She has to choose one of these. Willa, choose one of these shoes or I'll choose for you."

"Don't waste your money," said Willa, without any resonance of her flapping tongue.

Lisa grabbed her daughter's wrist. "Willa, just choose one of these fucking shoes, now!"

The surprise of her mother's vehemence and the force of her grip flushed Willa's tongue down her throat. "Nohn. I ohn wannum. An ooh seh fuck! Ooh seh fuck!"

"Ma'am," said the salesman, wanting to calm Lisa, "it's shoes; she can come back, it's not that important."

"I don't want to come back. We'll take these," she said.

"No! I ohn wannum!" screamed her daughter, picking up one of the discarded shoes, the red shoe with the green buckle, throwing it at her mother but missing her, and sending it into a baby carriage being pushed by a five-year-old whose mother was looking at baby shoes. The baby, fat like a big marzipan pear, wailed, her nose red where the shoe smacked her, bleeding.

As the baby's cry snapped the mother's attention, the five-year-old said, "She threw it," and when the mother understood what had happened, when she saw the shoe sitting on her baby's shoulder, she screamed at Lisa, "What did your daughter do to my baby?"

"Now see what you've done?" said Lisa to Willa, and then to the mother, "This has not been my day. I'm sorry. Willa, get the shoe. I'll pay for these, and then we're going." She picked up the green shoes with the red buckles.

Willa said, "No. I hey deeze shooze!"

"You hurt my baby and you're going to leave?" screamed the woman, which frightened the baby more. "She's bleeding. Susanna, are you all right? Susanna?" Susanna cried and the woman turned to Lisa again. "I'm going to have you arrested."

Lisa turned to Willa. "This is your goddamn fault."

"Fuck ooh," said Willa.

Lisa slapped her daughter's face with a flat open hand, and then watched herself hit Willa again, this time with a closed fist, knocking Willa to the floor, and she would have punched Willa again if the salesman had not pulled the screaming girl to safety.

"I'm okay," said Lisa, "I'm okay. We can go home now, we can go home." She knew she was in trouble, for tearing such a large hole in the fabulous banality of a department store, for doing this to her daughter.

Willa lay on the floor, quiet, staring at the ceiling. Her left eye was swollen shut, and her ear was hot. She heard the rising wails of baby Susanna, baby Susanna's five-year-old brother, and the children's mother, like a Dixieland funeral band, discordant music of grief but not without its own exuberant pleasure.

The floor manager and two security guards ran to the shoe department and grabbed Lisa's arms and forced her to the door where shoe salesmen go to "see if we have this style in your size."

At the same time, the mother of the baby in the carriage called 911 and told the police she'd been attacked.

Two hours later, with Willa in Griffin's lap, refusing to speak but gobbling the fifth Krispy Kreme donut the store's office staff had given the little girl as a bribe against tears, he called Rick Mellen to hire him again, and Mellen advised Griffin to cooperate, because so long as the social workers didn't know that Griffin was well known in town, the press would never hear of it.

"Kids are boiled alive in ammonia every day, Griff," said Mellen. "What's this? A slap in the face of a child who's throwing things in public and they call out the marines?"

"It was more than a slap in the face, Rick. She gave her a black eye."

"That changes things. Lisa's a superb mother, as sweet as a superb Sauterne, you two are superb parents, but if the ink on a newspaper ever carries the story, you'll be stained for the rest of your life. Cooperate and keep it very low key. Blame yourself, tell them switching jobs put the marriage under a lot of pressure, and then ask the social worker for any help she can give you: referrals to a family therapist or to self-help groups for families that suffer domestic violence. Just say that, don't say more. And it was the first time, yes?"

"Yes."

"How do you know?"

"Willa would have told me."

"They say children sometimes carry this stuff secretly."

"I wouldn't know."

"You better sound more convincing when the social worker asks you that question. But not so convincing that it feels like you're too convincing, because then she'll doubt you."

"How do I do that?"

"I don't know. But I never hit my kids, and neither did my wives."

Griffin called June and told her that Lisa had hit Willa and Willa was now in protective custody.

"I'll bring the kids to your house."

"Why?"

"Because you're their father, she's their mother, in her way, and Willa is their sister, and you all need our support."

"I don't know what to do."

"You don't have to know anything. I'm taking care of this. You just stay with Lisa and be as loving and forgiving as you're able."

. . .

Lisa waited with the police for the social worker, who talked to Willa first, alone, and then with Griffin, and then with Lisa, and then with Griffin again. The social worker, Maya Hernandez, showed more compassion for the family's distress than Griffin expected; she asked her questions in a soft voice, with none of the prosecutor's smug satisfaction that Griffin would have looked for in an audition of an actress reading the same lines. She was in her twenties, and sharp. Griffin wondered if she had ever thought about working at a studio or an agency. The agencies could use more of these Latinas, he thought.

"Willa hurt another child, and then your wife slapped her. So this isn't just a simple case of a mom getting kind of exasperated, is it? There's a pattern here, of violence."

"This is the first time."

"I hope that's true. Sometimes parents lose control, and we don't want anyone's life ruined if your wife just lost control this one time."

"Thank you. May I see her?"

"She's kind of incoherent right now. What I'm going to do now, Mr. Mill, is to take your child into protective custody."

"Why can't you leave my daughter with me?"

"Because your wife hasn't done enough to warrant an arrest, but we can't release your daughter into your custody until we can be certain of her safety at home."

"What if I take my daughter to a hotel, or send my wife to a hotel, and promise not to let her see Willa without the supervision of a social worker?"

"So you're telling me that your daughter is not safe with your wife without someone else in the room?"

"No. Lisa has never once hit Willa. This was a horrible mistake, but these things happen, don't they, even in the most stable families sometimes, and I'm only saying that if you'd let me take Willa I'd guarantee that, at least until you've had a chance to get to know us better, I'll keep the two apart." If Griffin could take Willa home, he could hire the most expensive litigator in the world by tomorrow morning, who would end up suing Nordstrom's for having overreacted or something, or maybe a private detective would discover a history of pedophilia in the shoe salesman, or a drug rap against one of the security guards. Griffin didn't know, but he wasn't a lawyer, and a lawyer could save his life right now, save his job; this was just awful, all of it, poor Willa to be slapped like that in public; the public part of this was half of what made it so awful, not that hitting her in private would be any better.

Griffin could not follow his own thoughts, and Willa, crying, screaming, kicking, went with Maya Hernandez to spend the night in a dorm with the daughters of crack whores, who might, he considered, think their children equally terrorized by the forced company of the beaten daughter of a rich guy.

. . .

They drove home, Griffin settling into the perpetual traffic jam, choosing the slowest lanes, following buses, anything to keep them in suspended animation. Lisa stared at the road.

"What if we had a hundred million dollars?" asked Griffin. "Would that make a difference to you? Would it help you, would you be happier, less angry, less frustrated? If I had a hundred million and you could sue me for divorce and take half of that, would you? Would you, Lisa?"

"A hundred million dollars. I could afford the best child care for my daughter, I could stay at the best mental hospital in America or Switzerland, they could unfreeze Jung's brain for me, I could live in Switzerland and nurses in white uniforms would help me settle into a long deck chair and wrap me in blankets and bring me herb tea, and I would wear a silk scarf tied over my head and knotted under my chin, like Audrey Hepburn, and my sunglasses would be like hers too, cat's eyes with diamonds, and my daughter would visit me a few times a year, and she would pity me, and I would cry in her arms, and this would not destroy her because she would have had the most expensive therapy money can buy, she would have worked through her rage at me, would have recognized that when I committed myself to the Swiss clinic I cut myself off from the world I loved to protect what I loved more than the world, to protect my daughter, and you would have also had therapy and with guidance you would have explored your feminine side, your motherly nurturing side, and Willa would later tell her own children that her father was her father and also her mother, and her mother was her mother and also her sad and crazy aunt, and that's what I would do if we had a hundred million dollars."

"You're not going to hurt Willa. You love her and you're only saying this because you have awful feelings and you're afraid of them."

"No, I'm going to hurt her again. You don't know how I felt after I hit her, the feeling of peace; that's what I haven't told anyone. I haven't told anyone about the silence. I understand child molesters and the priests who rape altar boys, because the release of the tension is better than heroin, better than any drug I've ever had, and it only lasted for a few seconds but there's nothing I've ever tasted like this, Griffin, and I'm scared of wanting it again, of hitting her again or worse, just so I can have that feeling, even if it means I will never see her again or will go to jail."

"You should tell this to Teri Barr."

"But I can't, Griffin. The law says she has to inform Child Protective Services if I make a credible threat against a child, against anyone. This is not a little daydream about a relief from the car pool, this comes up from the deep, and Teri knows me and she will believe me, and she will have to call Maya Hernandez, who will be only too happy to lock me up, take Wills away from us, and even go after you with the power of the law. And don't think the friends who protected us so far will help out if I'm locked up again."

"What do you want me to do?" he asked, hoping she would know but sure of her answer.

"I need you home. Be with me. Watch me. Don't let me leave the house. Don't let me get in my car and drive to June's house. Don't let me get anywhere near your daughter, if you love her."

"Of course I love her."

Lisa slammed the side of her head into the window. "I'm so bad. I'm so bad. I'm the worst mother who ever lived. I'm so bad."

Griffin tried to calm her.

"Don't do this to yourself, sweetie."

"I'm so bad."

"Just hold on."

"I should die."

"No, no, no. This is all going to work out."

"If I die. Only if I die."

"We need you, Lisa. Willa and I both need you. We love you."

"No. You don't. You're just saying that."

"No, baby. I'm not." He stretched his arm to hold her and keep her away from the door. He turned to a side street, parked, and grabbed Lisa's hair, pulling her head hard against the seat. "Listen to me, Lisa, are you listening to me? Shut the fuck up. You shut up now. You listen to me. I'm trying to figure something out and you're getting in my way. Stop complaining."

"You're hurting me."

"Just shut up. Listen to me. Everything in my life is pointing to a few things. I'm not the smartest person in the world. Phil Ginsberg is a lot smarter than I am, but he gave me a mandate and I'm trying to make sense of it. It's like all this drama in my family is what everyone is going through; there's nothing special about my problems, and there's nothing special about your problems either, Lisa, nothing."

"Let go of my hair."

"No. I will not let go of your hair. I will hold your head back like this so you can't move and you have to listen me. And I'm not being jungle boss. I'm trying to understand something without the interruptions that come from your special place of grief. I don't give a shit about your special place of grief. I'm trying to understand your common place of grief. The planet is dying. That's why the world expressed Hollywood out of itself a hundred years ago. It needed to hypnotize itself at twenty-four frames a second. Physics cracked the atom, biology cracked the genome, and Hollywood cracked the story. It's all the same thing. The journey of the hero is about the champion, about the guy who fights his father and beats his nemesis and gets a new name and cleans the stable and brings fire to the people and gets the princess, and that's the lottery ticket fantasy, it's your personal Jesus; it's why Joseph Campbell hated the Jews because the funny thing about having so many Jews in the movie business is that their religion doesn't have the formula for the journey of the hero. Moses dies before he brings the tribe across the river; that's not a really satisfying movie ending. Moses has a sister and a brother, and he's married and has kids who don't amount to much. That's just life; that's not a movie. That's why the structure of Greek legends makes good movies and the structure of Jewish legends makes mediocre television miniseries. And all of Greek theater comes from a period that lasted about as long as the time from the invention of sound to September 2001. Seventy years, eighty years. And then it ended. The movies had their run and now the movies are over. The planet is dying, what do people want? I'm not looking for a movie story right now—that's escape—and I'm not trying to isolate your story so people can identify with it. I spent twenty-five years learning how to do that, moving the same blocks of stuff around to fit the day's fashion, and giving them a slight twist. It takes amazing strength to manage this, strength *and* genius, if you know the detective is going to find the killer, and if you know that Darth Vader is going to die just as he dies in every movie unless he's the horror-movie villain. I learned why Freddy the slasher killer is a hero. I learned the rules of the road on making a character sympathetic but Phil Ginsberg took me out of the movies and asked me to look at my life like it's a movie, and I'm trying to take notes on it to see how to make money out of it. Are you confused?"

"Let go of my hair!"

"No. You're not whining about yourself now, you're in real pain. Good. There's no point to a moral lesson anymore because what good will it do you? I don't mean short run, I mean long. Yeah, honesty, patience, sure sure sure, do unto others or don't do unto others; I got that one and I break that one. We know the moral lessons already. They're just a drug. They're antidepressants. And when the moral lessons of the movies can't blunt the pain or give you energy because you're too poor or hungry or scared or trapped—so trapped that the Journey of the Hero is the story of how your oppressors won King of the Hill—you can't be helped by anything except violence in the real world, but it's the kind of violence the movies lay off on the villain, mass violence."

"You're being violent with me now. And you're hurting me."

"Of course I'm hurting you. I'm the villain. It's the Emerald City. I'm running for mayor. Did you ever consider that Superman and Dorothy are brother and sister? They both come from over the rainbow, they both land in Kansas, and what does it mean that Oz and Kryptonite are both green?"

"Griffin?"

"Yes, Lisa."

"Who was David Kahane?"

That question, now? "He was June's boyfriend before I met her. You know the story. He died; he was murdered."

"Even Elixa thought it was strange that this is the second time you've been the last person to see a man before he died."

"Warren Swaine had a heart attack, he wasn't murdered."

"But it's not nothing, is it? I've never been the last person to see anyone before he died. You never talk about David Kahane."

"David Kahane was just a small part of the story of how I met June. I guess I didn't want you to—I don't know, I guess not feel a lot of sympathy for June, since I was leaving her for you and since she'd had a boyfriend murdered."

"So my affair with you was like having a boyfriend murdered?"

"I'm not saying that."

"But I am. I'm saying that. Divorce is murder, or adultery is murder. That's why it's in the Ten Commandments."

"Well," said Griffin, "that's just one god's opinion."

"Did you kill him?"

He didn't hesitate. "Yes. Yes. Yes. I killed David Kahane."

"Why?"

"I thought he was someone else. I thought he was threatening my life."

"How?"

"There was this writer sending me postcards."

"Postcards?"

"I killed him by mistake. I thought he was someone else, but the other guy never figured out what I was doing and went away."

"I don't understand. But you really killed him?"

"I choked him to death. In a parking lot. In Pasadena. He died easily." There it was, out.

Lisa was quiet, lovingly quiet, he thought, marrying him in her silence. "Do you think that's why I hit Willa? Can you do the math? Do you think I hit Willa because you killed David Kahane and the violence continued through you to me to Willa?"

"Yes, I do."

"Did you kill Greg's father?"

"Swaine had a heart attack after I yelled at him. He was reaching for his medicine. I wouldn't let him have it. If I had and he'd lived, Greg would never have had the money to send Eli to Coldwater and I couldn't have approached Ginsberg the way I did."

"Did you marry June out of guilt?"

"I loved her."

"You can love and be guilty, Griffin, that's adultery. Did you marry June because you were guilty?"

"There's no answer to that question. I loved her. She wasn't like anyone I knew. She was direct, she was honest, and she was amazing in bed."

"And I'm more direct and honest and worse in bed?"

"I love you more than I ever loved her."

"Because you're not sleeping with the woman whose boyfriend you killed."

"Maybe."

"You've never been this honest with me, Griffin."

"I'm tired of lying."

"You're going to make a lot of money now, Griffin."

"Because I told you I killed a man?"

"When you killed David Kahane, did your life get better?"

"I took command of my career."

"Why do you trust me not to tell anyone?"

"Because you won't."

"Why are you so sure I won't tell anyone my husband is guilty of one murder and one manslaughter?"

"Because you've always suspected that there was something in my life I wouldn't talk about. Because you love me and you love Willa, and because you've done enough damage. That's why you could ask me what you finally were ready to hear."

"That makes me an accomplice to murder, doesn't it?"

"I don't know the answer to that question."

"Am I Lady Macbeth?"

"No. You're Lisa Kaplan Mill. And you've had a terrible few days. And I love you."

"Then why are you impotent?"

"I think because I'm so upset about money."

"And because you don't like to make love to me. Because I'm getting old."

"No."

"I can't believe I married a murderer."

"You said you weren't going to hold that against me."

"I said I wasn't going to tell anybody that I married a murderer. I didn't say I wouldn't remind myself about it."

"And you hit our daughter," said Griffin. "You gave her a black eye, I didn't. And now she's been taken from you by the law. Don't think something in your daughter isn't dead because of you."

"Killer, are you going to kill me too?"

"I don't think so. I don't think I have to and I don't think it's a good idea because unless I kill Willa she'll have a horrible time if her mother is dead, although I think you'd like me to kill you because you're too afraid of suicide. You want someone to take that out of your hands."

Griffin left the curb and turned onto the main boulevard from the side street. There was nothing to say, nothing new.

Why, Griffin asked himself, can't I make my life into the Journey of the Hero? Why can't I find my comic spirit guides and a shapeshifter or two to help me integrate my light and dark shadows?

It was the idle brain chatter of a man without meaningful employment.

"What are you thinking about?" asked Lisa. He heard a change in her voice, as though after months of silence, a year in a meditation cave, she admitted to herself that all the ways in which she had held her various selves together in the past were a web of self-protective lies and was finally letting go of the central unifying bad idea left unexamined since childhood.

"I'm thinking about everyone in my immediate existence, and what's fucking them up, and why. And instead of trying to solve their problems with a two-hour movie, I want to know what they want. June is a nice person, she's good looking, she likes to fuck, she looks like she can cuddle, why can't she find someone?"

"It's just hard for people to connect, Griffin. And there are more women than men. It's really not very complicated. Everyone wants love. After you feed them, they want love. And when you feed them they want food from someone they love."

"Someone they love, or someone who loves them?"

"I think it's both."

"Why is there so much divorce?"

"Because each husband kills his first wife's boyfriend and can't live with the guilt anymore."

"I've lived with the guilt for a long time."

"And your career stalled, you lost your erections, and all the rest. We're going around in circles, Griffin. Figure out what you want."

Drained by the effort of her sympathy, she hit her head against the window again. Out of kindness, Griffin didn't try to stop her.

. . .

It was almost nine o'clock at night as he put the key into the front door. June, Jessa, and Ethan were in the house. June didn't have a key, but each child did. June had never been deeper into the house than the front door, but here she was, sitting at the dining room table, enjoying her triumph.

"Willa is their sister. You're their father. Lisa needs us. You need us."

Lisa waved a hand. "I just want to lie down. Can someone bring me some water? I'll be in the living room. This is very embarrassing. I'm sorry. I'm just really sorry. This shouldn't have happened. I don't know what happened."

June nodded to Jessa, who found a bottle of water.

In the living room, Lisa stretched out on the couch. June sat on the carpet and held Lisa's hand. Had they ever touched? Griffin wondered.

"I lost my mind," said Lisa. "I really didn't mean to hit her. I kept saying things that I was thinking. I called her a little fuck. I was thinking it, and then I said it. And then I was thinking about how I wanted to slap her for throwing her shoes away. One of them hit a baby in a carriage, and the mother screamed at Willa, which I would have done too, Willa said, "Fuck you," and then I saw myself slap her."

"We all go crazy sometimes," said June. Her compassion for Lisa surprised Griffin, who suspected, though he was wrong, that June's mercy came easily to her, now that the bitch who stole her husband had jumped head first into the pickle barrel. He worried that June might even tell the investigators how little she thought of Lisa's gifts as a mother, but nothing could stop this now, and he consoled himself with his memory of a message in a fortune cookie, that life cannot be grasped but only lived. And then he thought, It has come to this: I take comfort from fortune cookies.

He left the two women and took the children up the stairs to the bedrooms he had set aside for them. Then he pulled out the cot from under the bed in Willa's room, because June would sleep in the house tonight. He stayed with Jessa while she looked through the drawers in her room for clothing to wear in the morning. He made certain, or rather Lisa made certain, to keep up with the children's sizes as they grew, and he would tell that to a jury if this was bound for trial, because how evil can a woman be when she looks at children who aren't even hers and knows how much they've grown and buys them clothes that fit?

After he kissed Jessa good night, he opened Ethan's door.

"I've seen her do it before," said Ethan. "She's hit me a couple of times."

"You never told me."

"I was stealing from her and she found me."

"What were you stealing?"

"Money, from her purse."

"And why are you telling me this now?"

"Everything's falling apart. You should know the truth."

"Thank you for telling me. That's very mature of you. I appreciate it."

Griffin sat on the bed and put a hand on his son's cheek. There was nothing to say, so he didn't, but let the sounds of Los Angeles at night, like surf without a pause between waves, punish him with premonitions of disaster. He counted to one hundred, for something to do, something he could control, and went downstairs.

In the living room, June had covered Lisa with a comforter and turned off the lights. She met Griffin in the dining room and turned off the lights there too. They sat at the table in the dark.

"How is she?" asked Griffin.

"She hates herself and wants to die."

"Is she suicidal?"

"You have to get Willa back tomorrow."

"Is Lisa in any shape to be interviewed by the social workers?"

"She'll have to be. Who's her therapist?"

"Teri Barr."

June took this as terrible news. "Teri Barr is a society whore. She buys tickets when her patients are on the board of charity dinner committees, and she ends up at the head table."

"What's wrong with that?"

"The reason you don't understand what's wrong with a therapist getting involved in her patients' public social lives is part of why Willa is in protective custody."

"I still don't understand."

"Because a therapist who uses her clients to get famous so she can get more clients can't be a good therapist."

"Whatever. Call her now." Griffin said *whatever* just to fuck with June, because she hated the word and its contempt for discussion. She said the word came from Hollywood the way swine flu came from some pigpen in Cambodia. *Whatever* was the attitude of Hollywood after her husband knocked up another woman and ran off with her while June was pregnant.

Barr's office machine answered; he hoped she checked it at night. After the beep, Griffin said, "It's Griffin Mill. Lisa hit Willa in Nordstrom's this afternoon, the one in The Grove, and now Willa is in protective custody and Lisa is catatonic on the living room couch. This is a matter of life and death." He left all his numbers: mobile phone, car phone—which was different from his mobile phone— his two home numbers, the one he gave out for work and his private number (which he almost never gave out because he couldn't remember it), and June's phone numbers, home and mobile, in case he was at her house with the children.

June said that she would drive the kids to school. "You wait here with Lisa for her therapist to call. And get a lawyer." This was all so practical and simple.

"We're doomed," said Griffin. "This new job, with Ginsberg— he'll dump me now and I'll never have lunch in this town again."

"Do you want lunch again or do you want to get out of Hollywood or do you want to save your daughter? Make up your mind and stop feeling sorry for yourself. Everything is going to work out, better than all right."

"That's no help. That's what the limo drivers say to every nominee on the way to the Oscars: 'I always bring back a winner.' Four out of five are liars."

"I'm not lying." She said this without defending herself. "I know that this has been a horrible day, and I know that tomorrow won't be easy, and your life will be hard for a long time after, but this will end in joy for all of us." She didn't know why she said this, but she believed herself as though the vessel for an angel. A man and a woman, they've had sex in the past, and children, and in a house filled with panic and grief they stand together as guardians, and they think about sex again, how pleasant they felt together, naked. "I'm going to sleep," said June, and she walked up the stairs slowly, for Griffin to watch her. She kept her hands open, her fingers relaxed.

Griffin stayed downstairs and poured a shot of tequila, worried that he was imitating a magazine image but drank it anyway, and then on the way to bed he passed through the living room and put a hand on Lisa's forehead. Believing her to be asleep, he kissed her cheek and walked upstairs, thinking of Pooh thumping behind Christopher Robin. He could be that little boy now, that would make him happy, Christopher Robin going back up the stairs, back in time like Merlin, back to the moment he could change it all and then forget.

. . .

Lisa had only pretended to sleep when June tucked the comforter around her. Then Griffin kissed her and still she pretended to sleep. With her eyes closed she listened to Griffin settle into bed the children of his first wife, who was sleeping in the guest room on the same floor. She thought this through without indignation. It was just a fact. Her husband's first wife was going to sleep on the same floor of the house as her husband. And her husband's gentle first wife had nursed the violent second wife with tenderness. But if the social workers took the second wife away, then the first wife might be living in the second wife's house with the first wife's children and also the second wife's daughter, while the second wife was in jail for child abuse, and when the law released her back into the world she would have to register with the local police as a known danger to children. If she committed suicide, her daughter would never recover. But if she were dead, she wouldn't know.

Nine

How far am I from the ways of normal life? Griffin asked himself, when he woke up from an already bad sleep. His phone rang at six-thirty. He hoped for Teri Barr, loopy she might be but Lisa trusted her, and I need this bullshit settled so I can make a living. Instead, one of Phil Ginsberg's "glow boys," another twenty-five-year-old, about as likely to survive his job as the Pakistani peasants who clean the inside of nuclear reactors with no more protection against radiation than a Bob Marley T-shirt taken in trade for hash.

"Mr. Ginsberg calling for Mr. Mill?"

"I'm here," said Griffin, sitting up and putting his feet on the floor, to let his throat clear of sleep.

Ginsberg was on the line. "Why didn't you call me from Nordstrom's? What gives you the illusion that you can hide anything from me?"

"This is a family matter."

"I literally do not understand the meaning of those words. I know that some people bow to the idea of family like it's the Shroud of Turin, like there's work and there's family. A family matter? What the fuck is a family matter? I've already called the mayor's office, and he's already on the city child services people. What do you think this is? Did you suppose I'd be cool about having a man with an abusive wife working so close to me? Do you think that? Do you think Gunther Hitt would be cool with this?"

"Who is Gunther Hitt?"

"Do you need to know?"

"I'm just asking, since you said his name."

"If Gunther Hitt wanted the world to know his name, he'd say so. But ten billion dollars buys some privacy these days. And what the fuck difference does that make to you, since you don't even earn a salary?"

"That was your choice."

"You took the job, Griffin; I don't have to go into that now. You're a hidden man, Griffin, there's more to you than anybody knows. I have to figure out why you didn't tell me what happened at Nordstrom's."

"I would have told you this morning once I had more information."

"What more information do you need? Your wife went bonzo in the shoe department. Willa hurt a baby, your wife hurt Willa, the cops came with the social workers, your wife failed the evaluation, and Willa was stuck in a home last night. Is there anything else I should know?"

"That's pretty much it."

"Pretty much? Has she hurt the children before?"

"She may have been rough with my son, who lives with my first wife."

"May have been? Jesus fucking Christ. May have been?"

"He said she was."

"When?"

"When did he say this or when was she rough?"

"Yes."

"He told me last night, and I think it happened in the last year."

"Was it reported?"

"No."

"All right. We can't try to hide from this, but we don't have to go public. We'll do a year of therapy for your wife and the same for Willa, and she can come home tonight. And no visits from the social workers."

Ginsberg said nothing more, and hung up the phone.

Why even ask Phil Ginsberg how the story of Griffin's messy evening came to him so quickly and how he could put in the fix before dawn? Griffin assumed that with $750 million, a man could hire a squadron of detectives to follow another man every day until the end of time. The rich might own a network of spy satellites and hire them to follow . . . what . . . ? Griffin pushed his speculation into a fog that only wealth could penetrate, because the fog was wealth itself and what could stop the masters of the known universe, a few thousand people on a planet with six billion, reaching down from the demicentibillionaires to the ordinary billionaires, from owning networks of observation, independent of government, for their mutual protection? He went to the bookshelf in the den and once again looked to Candace for a hint. He opened *Sharing His Closet.*

· · ·

The awfulest part of the divorce was the way that my husband and the father of our beautiful child wanted full custody. Oh the things he prepared to say about me in court! And perhaps maybe he might be right, I said to myself then and to be truthfully honest, he still might be right. Rabbi Cyndee, my very own spiritual counselor who brought me back to my ancient path, taught me that in a valley of the shadow of death, there really is evil but not to fear that evil, and Teri Barr, my wonderflu therapist, refused to let me feel so high and mighty and superior to Phil, as a human in the family of humans, and as a parent to a child both of us cared for and love. I know I had the inclination to be a bit cuckoo at times, disorderly in my daily habits, missing appointments with friends, just for lunch or whatever, not remembering doctor's appointments for Squire, not remembering evening social engagements that I should have put on my calendar, so more than a few times Phil, keeper of his own calendar, thank you, was ready to go to an important Hollywood party and I had completely put such things out of my mind, and why, I don't know, because I loved those parties, who wouldn't?

Teri Barr helped me to see things from Phil's perspective, of course because she was in his pay but also because the fact is it was probably a little bit true, otherwise if they had forced me to believe something not to be true then I would have gone insane enough for shock treatments. It takes two to tango and there we were, a family of three. Phil was so brutal in the custody fight because he can not lose and he could not share, and because he can not have his and our son Squire be under the control of a woman, since he did not really understand women and wanted total control of eveyrthing in his

life, everything that was his. I think he preferred the sexual company of men just because
of this, that he could not understand women and
their needs but being a man he knew what men
wanted, or maybe he didn't understand anybody
but himself and so he could only know what he
wanted and did not care for the other, and a man
would know what he wanted and he could give a
man what he wanted for himself and be done with
him. I think when Phil sucks another man he really
is just sucking himself. This is why Phil has
never had a boyfriend, but only a series of pathetic spongers, some not even cute. Every few
months, so Squire told me, Phil was trailing yet
another young man, and when I met them, they all
had the same look in their eyes, like they believed that they were secretly engaged to him,
and that they had a reason to be proud of themselves, for something about them no one else
knew, like Phil was going to fly with them to
Barcelona or Amsterdam and marry them, like they
had actually achieved something permanent instead of being what they were, this week's ca-
bana boy in Phil Ginsberg's endless summer. Now
you may say, Candace, what makes this really so
different than the lifestyle of someone straight
like say Donald Trump, who just beds whomever
he cares to, and I suppose maybe it's just the
same with a different orientation, but I wasn't
married to Donald Trump (not my type anyway, although I think he's a good Dad). But if Donald

Trump uses women the way Phil uses men, well then, it's the same thing. I will admit this is my secret pleasure, that no matter how rich he is, no one will likely ever love him for who he is without his millions and millions. And I admit I may just be saying this because if he is rich and happy and has everything he wants, and if he sees love as just another thing that people use as a consolation prize when they don't have all the money in the world, then I would be really miserable. I admit that.

Rabbi Cyndee says the difference between a rabbi and a therapist is that the rabbi can tell me what to do. She tells me that I shouldn't see it all from Phil's POV, as they say in the movies. She tells me that I have a right to my own righteous anger. I am learning this.

. . .

Teri Barr called at breakfast. "Hello, Griffin. How can I help? I'll tell you. I'd like to talk to Lisa alone. I'd like you to set up a comfortable chair for her in a room that is not her bedroom, a downstairs room, a den with doors that close if you have one, and make sure the cordless phone is charged so the battery doesn't wear out, and then place her in that chair; cover her feet with a warm throw if you know where she keeps them, but don't ask for it if you don't find it; and then bring her a glass of water, and a box of tissues, or even folded toilet paper if you don't know where she keeps the tissues. Then I'd like you to close the door and give me time to talk to her alone. She's a very wounded woman."

Griffin took Lisa to the library room, carrying her blanket, set her in the Eames chair and ottoman, covered her feet with the blanket, found the tissues in the powder room, and brought two bottles of Fiji Water from the refrigerator. Then he went into the kitchen and, putting the phone on mute, lifted the receiver to hear the conversation.

Lisa told Teri how scared she was that her daughter would hate her forever.

"You say that now, honey."

"But it's true. You hate me for this too, don't you?"

"Of course not."

"No, yes, you do, you hate me now because you don't usually deal with people who beat their children. You deal with rich kids who make porno, but you don't deal with this kind of abuse."

"I work with troubled people. I don't put the troubles on a scale. If you're feeling alone, it doesn't matter if you're living in a thirty-million-dollar architectural masterpiece across three lots on Broad Beach or a favela, a slum, in Rio de Janeiro. A problem is a problem."

"What I did was a little bit worse than shoplifting, don't you think?"

"If you'd been caught shoplifting on camera, and you were still an actress and your career was important, this still wouldn't be the worst thing in the world."

"Now you're making me feel like shit because I don't have an acting career."

"What I just said was clumsy. That proves I'm human, doesn't it?"

"I guess."

"You more than guess, Lisa. Lisa knows. Does it bother Lisa that Teri is human?"

"It bothers me that my human daughter is going to hate me forever." Lisa cried again, pulsing five shrieks in a row between each awful sucking in of air through the tears in which she was drowning. Teri stayed quiet until Lisa asked, "Are you there?"

"Oh, Lisa, I'm always here."

"And you don't think Willa is going to hate me?"

"Have you ever hit a puppy?" asked Teri. "If you hit them all the time they run away, but if you hit them one day and love them the next, and you feed them, trust me—studies prove this time and again—they come back."

"But she's my daughter. She's not a dog."

"But you don't love her as deeply as you'd like. She knows that. Subconsciously she probably has known it for a while, and now your actions affirmed her suspicions. So that's liberating! It's all out in the open! You should celebrate this! You can only go up from here."

"Unless I hit her again."

"But you won't."

"How can you be so sure?"

"Because the next time she needs shoes at Nordstrom's, you'll send her with the nanny."

. . .

Jessa Mill knew her father did not smile when he saw her porky face. This did not bother her, because Lisa admired and understood her. She knew she was freely given much of the love Lisa should have given to her own daughter, because Lisa hated or resented Willa as the whining souvenir of the lustful mistake she'd made with Griffin. Jessa appreciated Lisa's interest in her but did not care about her, never worried about her, had no opinion of her life or death, though she did worry about Willa, because Willa's torments affected June. And then she only thought about any of them when their stupidity, like a tow truck, dragged the wrecks of their lives noisily into her private silent garden and blocked her view of an inner world none of them could imagine.

When Griffin and Lisa, on the way to court early in the morning, drove Jessa to school, she could have told them not to bother talking, because she knew everything they could possibly say to her, but without interruption she let them ramble on as though in the dress rehearsal for what they would say to her later. She always wanted to ask adults to come back to her when they had their lines memorized.

They told her how some people have very bad days that don't reflect on the full picture of their lives, and that everyone is going to be stronger for having this experience, and that her sister Willa was going to be stronger after she had the time to work through the process of healing, which all of us will help her with, because we love her.

Lisa thought Jessa even more of a special child for accepting her apology for causing so much pain in the family, and then tried to imagine Willa in Jessa's position, and how she'd want to reduce all of this to *good* versus *bad,* and that no matter how patiently everything was explained, Willa would just come back with the verdict that hitting someone is bad and whoever hits is not good. When Lisa banged her head against the passenger window, Jessa, from the backseat, leaned forward to put her hand on Lisa's cheek and stopped her. Jessa knew what to say and what to do, and knew she knew, just as she knew that her father and his wife praised her and thanked her with such ridiculous enthusiasm because they misinterpreted her indifference as forgiveness.

. . .

At the same time, June and Ethan picked up Eli Swaine for the drive to their school in the Valley, but from the moment Eli threw his massive book bag across the backseat, June saw him watching her as he had been for the last few weeks. She told him she was sorry about his grandfather's death and asked how his father was doing.

Eli said he didn't really know his grandfather very well, and that considering how much his own father felt hated by Warren, he seemed pretty upset. Ethan said, "Well, his father died," and Eli said, "I guess." June thought Eli's casual answers weren't real, that something else was on his mind and his answers were so cold because he wasn't really listening to the questions, that a computer virus had made the first interspecies jump between the electronic and the organic, and his ad blocker was disabled and he couldn't understand June's questions because of the distraction of an infinite stream of pornographic windows popping into his brain.

Leaving him alone with the confusion of a grief that didn't match whatever she thought was appropriate, she stopped talking, but today neither of the boys was talking, either. For a few days, she had sensed a new high wall between them, a reinforced barricade, which she at first assigned to teenage hormones, but this morning, because the agony of the previous fifteen hours had made her sensitive to every shift in the normal flow of the familiar, when June looked in the rearview mirror at Eli in the backseat, the expression he returned told her that he knew more about her than she did about him. He refused to look away; worse, she saw that it wasn't she who was looking at Eli, it was Eli looking at her; she had not brought her eyes to the mirror because she was curious about him but because, when she checked the traffic behind her, she saw him staring at her. And the boys said nothing to each other, which June might have interpreted as Ethan's only defense against the pain in the house, but even Ethan seemed absorbed by something larger, or something someplace else. When she looked into the rearview mirror, Eli was still looking at her. She saw that he wanted to fuck her.

Ten

G riffin signed their names at the reception desk after the receptionist would not announce him unless he signed. The room with twenty hard plastic chairs had posters of baby animals on the walls, and a few battered plastic building blocks, and a construction of stiff twisted wires running through little disks and balls made of painted wood. It was meant to stimulate the brains of children, and Griffin, needing stimulation, rolled the blocks up and down the arches, or through the loops, with Lisa beside him, until the door opened to the deep obscure scary world of public interference in the troubled, helpless family.

Maya Hernandez asked how each of them was and Lisa answered, "I'm not very good, actually. I'm sorry, I don't know what else to say." And Griffin said, "We're both really upset about this, and we miss our daughter." He wanted to add, Do you think the brain-stimulating wire-and-balls thing over there can help an adult man's brain after five minutes of playing with it?

Hernandez said that first they would have to complete their evaluation. There was no mention of Ginsberg's connections to the mayor, or the mayor's call to whomever called Maya's boss or even Maya directly, and Griffin wondered if Ginsberg had told him the truth about his political power or had made up the story about helping him as a test of his credulity.

"I'd like to talk to Lisa alone," said Hernandez, putting a hand on Griffin's arm for assurance and leading Lisa into the world past the door. Griffin sat on the floor beside the toy and pushed wood over wire, trying to remember what such toys felt like when he was a kid, what it meant to have so much concentrated imagination for the thing in front of you and no concern for anything beyond—not even memory, really.

In Hernandez's office, Lisa prayed silently to the kind God of Los Angeles, the Higher Power of Twelve Steps, bodhisattva of moral inventory and making amends, the Kali of yoga and Ein Sof of Kaballah, the great hybrid Lord Prius of the Bodhi Tree. She did not know that June, on her own path, was also finding her own religion—or making her own religion—but she would have told Maya Hernandez if she had known, so she was lucky not to bring this up, since Hernandez was interested only in the concrete.

Hernandez asked, "Let me ask this first. Was your violence at Nordstrom's in place of violence against your husband?"

"I don't think so."

"He just changed jobs, though, didn't he?"

"How do you know?"

"Willa told us."

"Griffin just switched jobs, to a better job than the one he had. We're all very excited about it."

"Your husband is rich?"

"In comparison to his new boss, no, but by the way the world measures things, yes, he's rich."

"What kind of car does he drive?"

"A BMW convertible."

"How much did it cost?"

"He leases it, but the car costs about eighty-five thousand . . . dollars."

"What kind of car do you drive?"

"A BMW station wagon."

"Do you drink?"

"Wine a few times a week."

"And your husband?"

"About the same. Maybe a little more. Normal."

Hernandez stopped asking questions. Lisa smiled, stopped smiling, smiled again, made herself look open by silently letting out as much breath as she could, and concentrated on relaxing her forehead and chin.

Hernandez told her to wait and left the room.

Griffin came in two minutes later and told Lisa that Hernandez was getting Willa.

"Did she tell you what we talked about?" Lisa asked him.

"Not really. No. But I guess you passed the test; otherwise we wouldn't be taking Willa home now."

Then the door opened.

"Jesus Christ!" said Griffin, out of control, because Willa had a black eye, the left side of her face was bruised purple, and he had not until now understood why the social worker wanted to keep the little girl from her dangerous mother.

Willa held Hernandez's hand and did not offer herself to her mother for the hug her mother wanted to give her. Griffin got on his knees and offered his open arms to Willa, who shook her head, no.

"I'm so sorry about what happened yesterday," said Lisa. "I would do anything to turn back the clock."

"Why did you hit me?"

"I was being selfish about the time you were taking to make a choice about the shoes that you would have to wear. That was stupid of me. Look at where my anger got me, and you still don't have your shoes."

"I want red shoes. They didn't have any red shoes."

"Yes, they did, honey. The shoe you threw at the baby was a red shoe."

"With green buckles. I want all red."

"Then the next time we go shopping, I'll call the store first to find out if they have red shoes in your size and we won't go unless they do."

"Promise?"

"That's such a promise. I love you too much and I'm so sorry this happened." Lisa wasn't certain if she really did love this little girl, but she was absolutely certain that her anger at Willa was really her anger at Griffin for not being faithful to June, and anger at herself for being such a slime that year, but here was the flesh of her flesh, hurt to the soul by her mother's frustration with her father and her own weakness, and for this alone, kindness to a damaged child, Lisa opened her arms and said, "Baby, let me kiss you."

Willa stood beside Hernandez, more like a shy four-year-old than twelve, and said nothing. Griffin could hear a tantrum advancing through his daughter's faster breath, like a Panzer division hidden by a sandstorm. If the situation exploded, would Hernandez risk the loss of her promotion from the mayor's office for this dirty favor, out of respect for the purpose of her job, to save children from depraved parents?

Lisa bent down to Willa's eye level and tried again. "Willa, I'm really sorry about what happened last night. I'm sorry that they took you away from me, but they did what they thought was right. And they wouldn't have given you back to me if they didn't think it was right." Lisa felt more comfortable telling this lie to her child than trying to prove to Hernandez that she was no longer a threat to her daughter's safety. "I love you, Willa, and I will work very hard to prove to you that I will never hurt you again."

"You might."

"I don't think so."

"Why did you hit me?"

"She won't," said Griffin.

"I was angry and tired," said Lisa.

"What will you do when you get angry and tired again?"

"I'll count to ten, I'll have a glass of water, and I'll catch my breath."

"That's what she'll do," said Griffin.

"What if I make her angry to eleven?"

"I'll count to twenty, love," said Lisa.

"Where are you going to geh the water?"

"There's always water around."

"Where are ooh going to geh the glass?"

"She'll have a bottle," said Griffin.

"What if ooh can't get a bottle?"

"I'm going to remember to bring a bottle of water with me wherever I go," said Lisa.

"What if you already drank it aw?"

"I'll get another bottle."

"And what if oo drinn tha baha an then oo geh angry again and I doh wan any uhva shooze?"

"If that happens, if I bring two bottles and drink them both before I get angry, and then if I get angry, you're going to remember this conversation and you're going to remind me, and that will calm me down, but I won't get angry again like that."

"Buh wha if ooh geh too anghee to cah daown?"

"She won't," said Griffin.

"Ooh seh dat naow. S'eezee to seh dah naow. Wha' abouw layduh if she forgeh? She'll hit me ageh. Ooh'll huht me, mommee. Ooh'll huht me an my fee-ings."

"No, I won't, I promise. Let me hug you. Let me show you how much I love you."

"Oh, rye, so ooh ca' huht me ageh? Fuh ooh."

And for another night, Willa was taken away from the uncertain care of her mother. As they drove home, Griffin's phone rang. It was Ginsberg.

"Do you want me to quit?"

"If I wanted you to quit would I have used this big a favor from the mayor? The social workers have been assured that the family has the means at hand to get the best private help available, and in the end that's what's going to be best for the little girl. And we'll settle as quickly as possible with the woman whose baby got hurt. So you're into me for a shitload of money and favors, Griffin, but I will not have your wife's violence become a news story with my name in it anywhere. I told you: I don't want to be embarrassed."

"I don't know what to say."

"If you did know what to say, you fucking bimbo, *I'd* be working for *you.* I almost took you off the list for Squire's bar mitzvah."

"Do what you think is best."

"I want you at that bar mitzvah. It's next Saturday."

"I'll be there."

"I raised a million and a half dollars for the mayor's campaign. That's a slap in the face of my honor, my own honor, Griffin, so this is personal for me, you've got me on your side now, because I gave him a guarantee, Griffin, I promised him your family was a good family. Did Gunther Hitt call?"

"No."

"He probably knows about this. It's just the sort of attention getter he hates. If I were him, I'd avoid you too. But I'm not. I'm me, and I say, Willa should come home today."

"Thank you," said Griffin. "You don't know what it will mean to me to have her home tonight."

"Did I say she *would* be home tonight? Reality check, Griffin: I wish I could do that for you, but I can't. I need the mayor more than he needs me, because he wants to be governor, and he might even be president, and you don't sacrifice the value of that kind of relationship just for something negligible like your own honor, or even something noble like keeping a kid from a foster home, especially if the kid's not yours. You understand."

Griffin might have said that he had been in Hollywood too long to tell Ginsberg, "But I just heard you say that she was coming home tonight, I just heard you tell me that I am going to get a call telling me where to go to meet her." He knew this wasn't just Hollywood, and he took that as sour comfort.

. . .

At home, June met Griffin and Lisa with a pot of tea. Griffin told her, "I don't know what a psychiatric evaluation is exactly, but Lisa and I have to get one or take one to prove that we can be trusted to have Willa back. I know you well enough, and I know that you wouldn't want Willa to spend any more time in protective custody. I think you can ask to take care of her here."

"Of course I'll do that," said June, impressing Griffin with her gratitude for this call to service, not knowing that this was an answer to her prayers.

"I really appreciate it, June. I know how hard this must be for you."

"We're all one family, Griffin. We're showing our children how to take care of the people who matter to them." Knowing none of the details of Griffin's problems with his new boss but seeing his misery, she put a hand on his shoulder and said, "I know this is hard for you, but everything is going to work out, first of all for Willa, then for Lisa, then for Ethan and Jessa, and then for you."

In her own bed in her own house Lisa stared into her life to look for all the patterns that might open a passage to that tangle of reasons to explain what had brought her to this place, a daughter taken from her for the daughter's safety.

What did she see? Frustrated dreams of permanent social achievement and a long history of living on the fringes of whatever passed for the local elite, and now, with Griffin quitting the Studio to serve as the lapdog to an evil pansy—to use her father's favorite word—who was already driving her husband crazy, she was certain that the new job would last about five months and then her husband would be off the merry-go-round forever and would have to find a job in an industry where people actually worked for a living. She hit her daughter in Nordstrom's because the sparkly red shoes were for a party whose invitation was about to be withdrawn.

They'll keep you away from me for six years, Willa, and they'll be right. I'm not safe for you. Even if I don't hit you again I'll find another way to cause you pain; maybe I'll manufacture such a brilliant presentation of repentance that the world will think me cured, but in full view of everyone, I'll destroy you, you'll hear undertones of mockery and diminishment, I'll confuse you and breed termites in your confidence, you won't be able to pick a dress from the closet without hearing my disapproval for the choice.

June came to her. "I know you're a good mother. I don't know what happened at the mall, but I know you. Your intentions are good. I know Willa needs to be with people who love her and know her.

We'd like to take her into our house. Would you let us? They may set restrictions on your right to visit her. I may have to guarantee that I won't let you see her without permission or supervision. I'll do whatever I'm told."

"Well, June, I guess I have to say, I wouldn't want you to do anything less."

Lisa closed her eyes and cried, feeling her face strain to release something she had never known before, and in the middle of the tears she remembered an acting-class exercise to re-create just this emotion of a self-replenishing grief and she thought, If I were in that class now the teacher would have applauded, but I couldn't cry then because I didn't really know how. This is the worst thing that has ever happened to me. I should go back to acting class.

She cried harder, not so much for her daughter as for the years she had wasted making herself look beautiful for auditions when she had nothing great to share with the world, no inexhaustible well of pure emotion, so that the world and all the multitudes who need comfort could recognize themselves in her expression of what she had survived and learn hope from her survival. For years she saw her limited beauty become mere prettiness, so much like the mere prettiness of so many women in Los Angeles that the mirror might as well have been a photograph of fifty thousand other girls like her, with small well-shaped features but neither amusing nor lively, just attractive enough to turn heads at traffic lights, and only for a moment, never a second look.

June wanted to hug Lisa, something she had never done, no, not even shaken her hand, but she let her sister-in-marriage cry, and keep on crying, because the right time would be so obvious that Lisa would reach for her first.

The phone rang. Griffin made a pointless apology and picked it up in the kitchen. It was Gunther Hitt.

"Is this a bad time?" Hitt asked.

"Can I call you back later?" asked Griffin.

"Do I sound far away?"

"No."

"I mean, do I sound like I'm not in my office in New York?"

"Connections are always good now."

"I'm on a four-hundred-sixty-six-foot boat and I'm looking at Sardinia, Griffin. Sardinia is just a shadow against the stars, Griffin, a sleeping elephant beneath a billion distant lights, powdered sugar on infinity, and it's one of those insane nights when there's not a cloud in the sky, and you can see the whole Milky Way, and you feel like you're both the most insignificant piece of an incomprehensible universe and also that the whole shebang was made just for you. The boat is mine, and it only sleeps sixteen, plus crew. Four hundred sixty-six feet, a bowling alley on gimbals, and a private submarine for twelve that can stay down at thirteen hundred feet for a week. This is life today for some of us. The brand names don't matter, the thread count doesn't matter, it's the freedom from time that matters. Why do rich Americans buy themselves hospitals? We don't do that in Europe. I have all the time in the world, Griffin; don't you want that too?"

"I think I do."

"Well, how are you going to get there from where you are? No one I know who has a billion dollars was ever anyone's whipping boy."

"Is that what I am?"

"I can't hear you."

But of course he could. "Is that what you think I am, Phil's whipping boy?"

"I can't hear you."

"I haven't been working for Phil long enough to be whipped."

"Does it bother you that I'm insulting you, Griffin?"

"I wish you weren't."

"I want to be your friend. You know movie stars."

"Not that many."

"I want them on my boat."

"What do you want from me?"

"We believe in you, Griffin. More than you believe in yourself. Think about that: The masters of the universe believe in you."

"I thought you said you're the most insignificant creatures in the whole shebang."

"I don't really believe that, Griffin. You have no idea what ten billion dollars is like. That's two dollars and fifty cents for every year since the world began. If dollars were days, a billion days is two million seven hundred and forty years. A million days is only two *thousand* seven hundred and forty years. You don't know what a few extra decimal places taste like. There are wines, Griffin—my God, you don't know what they do for you—from vineyards that stopped selling to the public about forty popes ago. I own a Rembrandt, a self-portrait, Rembrandt and Saskia, naked, he has a hard-on, she has cum on her big Dutch tits; Griffin, he sold it to a rich Jew, I bought it from Picasso. The provenance of this painting is without blemish and the painting has never been publicly cataloged, like a lot of the most amazing pieces of this world, Griff, and I paid for it using the interest of the interest of the interest. A hundred and twenty-five million dollars. I had more money an hour after I signed the check for that painting than I did when I bought it. I can do whatever I want. And I am by no means the richest man in the world, not even close, Griffin, not even close. You work a long time at Wal-Mart to make ten dollars an hour; the Waltons have a hundred billion dollars. Shit! That's a lot of money. If the wage-slave Hottentots knew what we had, boy, they'd eat us alive."

"Are you asking me to leave Phil and work for you?"

"Would you do it if he asked?" said Ginsberg, in sudden ambush from his muted phone. The fucker had been listening on the line. That Griffin wasn't surprised, that he didn't miss a step in the dance, convinced him, finally, of whatever merit these men saw in him.

"If he offered more money," said Griffin. "I'm not stupid."

"You mean money at all, Griffin. Gunther, are you going to offer him more money?"

"Not yet. Good night."

"Phil, are you still on?" asked Griffin.

"Get to work."

"But what is my job?"

Phil asked, "What do you get if you cross an elephant and a rhinoceros?"

"An 'ell-if-er-I-know," said Griffin. "I have three children. Each one of them taught me that joke."

The German went on. "Look for an opportunity. I'm the Queen of Spain and you're one of the guys who followed Columbus. We know there's something out there now, but we don't know what because we haven't explored it all. You're the man who understands story. The MBAs are useless now, and most of the big ideas have been taken. Murdoch owns television in China, for fuck's sake. He got the satellite rights to the biggest country in the world. The Internet has been strip-mined; we can't buy a film studio and make enough on the investment to justify the risk and the hassle. It's too late to invent the car. The real estate is gone, and even if I had a million acres in Wyoming, the value at this point is sentimental. We thought about buying the Ukraine, but they're too crooked there for business. We don't want to dick around finding overlooked value in small companies, join the boards of directors, and make decisions about things we don't understand or have the patience to learn about."

"But Phil told me to look for bruised fruit."

"That's because Phil has seven hundred and fifty million dollars. All he can afford is bruised fruit. Seven hundred and fifty million and you think you're rich, Phil."

"I never say that," said Ginsberg, "but it reminds me of a joke. An old Jew walks down the street when a brick falls off a building and hits him on the head, smashing his skull. He's lying there on the sidewalk and the paramedic arrives, checks his pulse, and asks him, "Are you comfortable?" The old Jew shrugs and says, "I make a living.""

"This is all too grim, Griffin. We started out looking for what's left, and we realized, as I said to Phil, that we're like writers stuck at the end of an endless second act, with no idea of what comes next because we fucked something up at the beginning of the story."

"No. You're at the *beginning* of the second act, that's your problem. The third act is easy. You put your lessons to the test, and you win. The problem is you don't know what kind of story you're telling. You're still trying to write rags-to-riches, but you're doing it as destroy-the-monster."

"That's why we hired you."

"And I'm not the only one you've hired, am I?"

"Of course not."

"You've hired other men for their own areas of knowledge."

"Of course."

"And what you want from them is to look at the world and see what new stories can be told with money."

"Right."

"So I don't have to do anything except whatever I want. Meet people, travel around, read magazines, channel surf."

"I can't promise you a Rembrandt, but I bet you that a flight of Picasso erotic drawings would look really pretty on the walls of your town house in Paris. Secret Picassos, Griffin; bulls fucking women,

Griffin; think of it, all the secrets money can buy. Drink that secret papal wine and fuck a flight of Rhodes Scholar supermodels all turned on by your portfolio of secret Picassos. If you figure this out, you make your money and then you're done."

"This is just a thought, but isn't it possible that the story is over and what you have, your immense financial reward, fulfills all the themes established in the first act, the challenges in the second, and the triumph in the third, and your problem now is you don't know the credits are rolling and the ushers are sweeping up the popcorn? Or isn't it possible that out there on your yacht, Gunther, you're not James Bond, you're Thunderball?"

"Then why are we still talking?"

"You'd know better than I. I know you each want more dough. I know that seven or eight hundred million isn't enough for you, Phil, and obviously ten billion doesn't give you, Gunther, enough altitude if the market collapses for five years and world currency inflates and ten billion dollars becomes nine hundred million. These are not the problems of the common man. If this were a script I'd say you had character problems, because there's no reason to root for you. You know what I mean?"

"I hired the same designer as they use in the Bond films," said Gunther. "He's pretty smart, Phil. Griffin, you're pretty smart."

"I'll be right back," said Ginsberg, putting Griffin on hold.

"Have you ever heard of the Telluride Group?" Gunther asked.

"Of course I have."

"That means you know what it does. So, what does it do?"

"It's a convention for the world's richest people in communications technology. They meet in July."

"Would you like to join us this year?"

Watching Lisa's face, Griffin could not think of anything but that after all this had passed, and Willa was home, and June restored to her own house, his wife, his second wife, would never look young again. With this on his mind, instead of opportunity, Griffin said, "Yeah, sure." It was too careless and casual a way of accepting, and if Griffin wasn't so exhausted from trying to hold his life together, if all his defenses, all the decoration on his personality hadn't been washed away by June's tears, Lisa's tears, and Willa's tears, he might have shown some enthusiasm, but at this moment, the way he favored his child over his dreams of wealth gave Griffin hope for the recovery of his soul, whatever that means.

"We'd like to have you," said Hitt.

"I don't know if I can come."

"What are you worrying about? Are you worrying about Willa? It's all taken care of. Maya Hernandez is dropping her at June's house in an hour and a half. Isn't that what you want?"

"Are you sure?"

"Griffin, what do you think?"

Jessa came into the kitchen for a hug, and Griffin put his arm around her shoulders. Of the three, because he had moved out of the house before she was born, he knew her the least.

"I'll call you tomorrow," said Griffin, hanging up. He looked down at the stranger with the pudgy red face. "I love you, Jessa." Everything is wrong, he thought, nothing is real, not even this, and he hugged the little girl to convince himself that something in his universe had mass. Now the little girl, proto-punk and all that, smarter than her parents, wise, avatar of a new generation that the future, if perspective and posterity survive, will recognize as the pivot of history that everything since the discovery of Hispaniola had waited for, dreamed of, slaughtered, and died for, all those Thermidors, Year Zeroes, Long Marches, reconciliations of VHS and Beta, Bluetooth, Woodstocks, Entebbes, and parades of assassins, broadbands, WiFi, Grand Theft Auto, the American refusal to ratify the Kyoto Accords,

Bob Dylan's ads for Victoria's Secret, the Chechen murder of school-children, and the two elections stolen by George Bush.

The little girl, future leader of the Instant Messengers of Death, grabbed her father's waist and held him tight, squeezing him harder than she had ever held him, because she knew that at this moment he needed her, and because everyone wants that—love, strong arms holding tight—so that even as frustration and longing scream for release or escape, a voice that might be conscience cries, *Surrender to this, yield to this, make it so, make it love.* She needed her daddy as much as he needed her.

June took Lisa's hand. "I have to go home and meet Willa. Thee must get to bed, Lisa." It was a measure of the insanity of the house that no one heard June's leaking home-brewed Mormonism so bizarrely twist her language.

. . .

Willa wanted to sleep in Jessa's room, and Jessa said no because she—well, because if your father leaves your mother for the mother of your half-sister, a mother who then hits your half-sister, the catalyst for the chain reaction that burned a hole in your family can sleep alone.

Ethan heard Willa crying and went to June, who was cleaning up in the kitchen. June went to the girls and took them into the guest room.

"This is a king-size bed, and that's big enough for all three of us. We'll sleep together tonight. Get into bed now and leave room for me in the middle. I still have a few things to do. Whichever one of you doesn't want to share the bed with me sleeps alone."

The girls, refusing to talk to each other, took their sides of the bed. June thanked them and went downstairs and told Griffin what she was doing. She had thought of putting on her dressing gown first, but the unhappiness of the girls called her to modesty.

Griffin thanked her for being so helpful. His mind was blank.

. . .

In bed, June puts an arm around each girl, and each sees how far or close the other comes to a breast, and then Willa rolls closer, then Jessa, and for bilateral peace June directs the flow of her love symmetrically. She makes herself still and imagines the serenity of a marble Gothic princess on the lid of a sarcophagus, in virgin white, arms by her side, palms up, and then adjusts this, a Gothic queen on the lid of a sarcophagus wide enough for a carving of the drowned mother holding her also martyred daughters in her arms, martyred— yes, martyred, better than drowned, burned—to defend the holy name of the Jesus who preached to the tribes of America during his forty days of resurrection, after he left the apostles, the story told by Moroni to Joseph Smith. Why a Gothic tomb for an American queen? June asked this of herself, and wanted to ask, What is this? Why am I here? What happened? How can I get out? Who can I ask for help?

A marble dead Mormon queen and her two marble dead children have dead marble ears, and what could she hear from a dead marble mouth?

Eleven

It was late Saturday afternoon, and the long gray line of the 405 Freeway, as he drove along Mulholland on the way to Squire's bar mitzvah, stood out to Griffin in a way he'd never noticed, like the unmapped canyons and riding rings of Brentwood, with the significance of a monument secretly erected, a road but also something else, its meaning known only to the builders. If civil or geological disaster ever pushed the city beyond the limits of social cohesion, the 405 leading to the 5 would be the only useful route of escape from the west side of Los Angeles. Griffin filled his gas tanks whenever they dropped to half full, enough fuel to get him past Bakersfield into farm country, where he could survive on irrigation water by pumping it through the water purifiers he kept in the trunks of his cars, and eat whatever fruits or vegetables were in season. Escaping east on the 10, toward the desert, would be insane. Going south toward San Diego was pointless; no fresh water there. He didn't have a boat to go west. The 101 through Santa Barbara might be worth trying but a few dozen survivalists, or billionaires in Montecito with private armies, could blow up a hillside and block the road. He thought often about learning to ride a motorcycle, because the roads would be hopelessly jammed, with frightened fuckheads and their shotguns, and he knew that his fantasies of escape were of the same kind as the fantasy of having a conscious reaction to a nuclear attack on the city. As though anyone would have the time to say *Whoa, Nelly!* before the blast killed them. Maybe underneath the freeways, the builders had secretly hidden tunnels with a few camouflage entrances, so that those in the know would have a safe fast route ahead of the deranged mob.

The synagogue—Reform—shared a driveway and parking garage with Milken High School.

"Did they really name a high school for Michael Milken?" Griffin asked Lisa, as they left the parking garage. Milken High, on a ridge at the top of Mulholland Drive with a wide view of the Valley, was down a slight hill from the synagogue's sanctuary, brick buildings linked by covered walkways with half-assed arches between the columns, offering an impression of the memory of the idea of cloistered Christian devotion, the arches flattened as though rejected by heaven.

"It's not for Michael Milken, it was his brother Lowell, the brother's family, that built the high school."

"Oh, sure," said Griffin. "That makes everything better."

"Who is Michael Milken?" asked Ethan.

"He did hard time for stock fraud and built this high school, or his family did, to clear his name."

"At least he didn't rape any boys in confessionals," said Lisa. "The synagogues haven't paid out a billion dollars to settle sex-abuse claims."

"Every tribe has its way of bringing on shame."

"It isn't comparable, Griffin."

"I didn't say it was," said Griffin, "but it's not unexpected. Michael Corleone is at a baptism when his hit men are wiping out the Barzinis and the Tartaglias."

"And that was an insult to Italians and only a movie," she said.

"*The Sopranos.* I'd like to see a show about corrupt Jews that was true to Jewish corruption the way *The Sopranos* is true to small-time mafia. The thing about Jewish corruption that would make an interesting show is the way it's manipulated by the goyim. Jews still want the approval of the country club, and then the country club throws the Jews away once they've figured out the scam to make the right goyim rich. That's what happened to Michael Milken, which is why Milken High could also be called Milken Martyr. He made the right people rich and then they threw him to the dogs. He paid the largest fine in history, half a billion. Terrible, what he suffered; they made him take off his toupee. Then he had cancer, but that was like a lucky break, reputation wise, you know? And he's still alive and he's still rich. I don't know, maybe corrupt Jews aren't dramatically interesting. Or maybe the Jews have an authenticity that can't be faked, like a hard-on can't be faked, without chemicals. Sorry, Ethan, I'm being vulgar. Let's go in."

• • •

Jessa had been invited to Sonia's house that night. Sonia's older sister was having a birthday party, and June asked Jessa if she would take Willa, and Jessa said it was all right with her but she should call the mom, so June called the mom, and it was fine with the mom; the party was for her older daughter, fifteen, a sophomore at Rossmore, the girls' school. "Drop off at seven, pick up at eleven-thirty." The address was Los Feliz.

June checked the Calendar section for movies at the Arclight, so she could drop the girls off, see a film, and then pick them up. *Wedding Crashers* was playing so she could see that and submerge herself in comedy, which was the only kind of movie she liked anymore.

• • •

Griffin didn't recognize as many people at the bar mitzvah as he had expected to. He couldn't discern, yet, any differences between the Ginsbergs and the Netters, but the patterns in the small crowd were familiar. Prosperity shined everywhere, in gold, in tans, in thick black hair, in big watches, scarves, silk, and the tribal noise, the remains of ululation, of cousins calling to each other from twenty feet away. Griffin saw them, the trim skeptical men and their two categories of wives, all of them brilliantly educated, some of them successful professionals themselves, others still drifting on the messy alibi supplied by their genuinely screwed-up relationship with their genuinely screwed-up mothers, but all of them, pediatric endocrinologists, failed Tibetan wool importers, soccer moms and private school committee volunteers, recognizing each other's clan by a signal from within an unfakable right for their chaotic anxieties and complaints to take up space around them. And sprinkled in the crowd was another sign of the tribe—Griffin had seen this before at the fiestas of rich Jewish families—the depressed sister with that look of earnest disappointment reworked as spiritual criticism that comes from a breakdown in every system in her life except the trust fund.

Griffin wondered how many of the blood relatives, from Toledo or Boston or wherever, knew that two of the men just now threading past the blood-cousin clots were billionaires. And how many of them were expecting movie stars because of the mother and father's connections and were going to be disappointed, since the stars almost never came out for these things. Ginsberg wouldn't waste his favors on family.

In the back of the crowd, almost against the wall, a line of women gathered to kiss, hug, or just touch a woman with the most frightening face-lift Griffin had ever seen. She was only in her forties, but a vulture of a plastic surgeon, a sadist who deserved prison, had sold this woman on a step into body modification way beyond transexualism into trans-speciesism.

"That's Candace," said Lisa.

Griffin wanted to hit himself on the head to adjust the picture. You see actresses you love, movie stars, powerfully talented, panicked by the injustice of the punishment for age lines, who go to the wrong plastic surgeon and destroy their careers more completely than death by making themselves look like female impersonators of who they used to be, their lips puffed as though attacked by swarms of bees from an organic hive, eyelids stapled deep into the sockets, beach-ball bosoms, and forehead frozen with Botox into an emotional unintelligibility useful for the championship of the World Series of Poker. No, what happened to Candace Netter Ginsberg, or what she had chosen to have happen, this was way, way On Beyond Zebra, this was supermarket tabloid-cover kidnappers from outer space meet Egyptian cat god, an Egyptian goddess made in their own image by the aliens from *Close Encounters of the Third Kind*, the squared chin and high cheeks and broad nose of a cat, with the tilted ovoid eye sockets and enlarged forehead of a true believer's idea of wise beings from ancient galaxies. The reconstruction had severed every nerve in her face, so that nothing moved, or even twitched, except her eyes and her jaw. She spoke as though her teeth were wired shut. This was everything that's wrong with everything. But . . . but . . . but . . . this creature was Candace Netter Ginsberg, and Griffin knew her and loved her from her book. She suffered and she told the truth. Inside all this monstrous deformation, Griffin saw the stunning, clear, and forgiving eyes of a dying sacrificial victim whose endurance of suffering would bring her torturers to repentance, if torturers have souls. Some of them do. No one who had read the book would wonder why the crowd of women wanted to touch her, or why they had kept the secret of her book from reaching their husbands, or why only to save her marriage would Lisa have broken the vow of secrecy. Seeing the agony and compassion in Candace Netter's eyes, Griffin felt within himself the corrosive damage his own spirit suffered for sustaining contempt and derision for so many women as they grew older. He wanted to hold Candace and cry with her; he wanted to tell Candace that he might look like a man but he was really a woman, that her book with all its misspellings had made him a woman, and that he would bring her optimism and cheer for teaching him to be a good mother to himself, a good mother with the lesson that life is not altogether hard or cruel or careless, no matter the accidents and holocausts. He wanted to tell her that her freakishness challenged all who looked at—well, *upon*, yes, who looked *upon* her—who looked upon her to see, instead of punished vanity and its scars, yes, to see within the lifted horrifying face an icon of the risen Christ, even if it was a little like the face of crucified Christ on a Mexican-restaurant bleeding-Jesus-crown-of-thorns hologram, with the three-dimensional eyes that follow you around the room. Griffin felt this powerful urge to shout praise for Jesus and tummy tucks, and only the Israeli flag at the entrance to the sanctuary, along with a hundred and fifty rich Jews, reminded him that rushing up to this stranger and babbling on about face-lifts and Jesus the son of God wouldn't be the coolest thing to do, given his bizarre relationship to the evil ex-husband, that and the imminent calling of Candace Netter's son, her only son, her beloved son, to the Torah.

"Do any other men know about her book?" Griffin asked Lisa.

"What book?" asked Ethan.

"Nothing," said Griffin. "It's between your mother and me."

"She's not my mother."

Griffin gripped his son's arm and said, "I need your help right now, and that wasn't helpful."

Ethan understood and apologized to Lisa. Lisa said, "It's okay. And thank you."

Then Ethan asked again about the book.

"She wrote a book about her life," said Griffin, telling the truth because now that he had seen this woman's eyes he didn't want to lie.

Lisa shook her head with guilt for having told him about *Sharing His Closet.* "I shouldn't have told you. You shouldn't have told Ethan."

"It's okay."

"Why is it okay?"

"Because it's done, that's why. Because I understand that book and now that I see her I understand who she is. Her secret is safe with me."

Ethan tugged on his father's arm. "What secret, Dad?"

"The secret of life," said Griffin.

"What's the secret of life?"

"It's a secret, my boy. Go play with your friends. Some of them are cute." He gave Ethan a loving nudge to join the boys and girls.

Lisa hugged Griffin's arm. "That was lovely. That was nice of you."

"I love him."

"You do? I'm never sure how you really feel about your children—any children."

"I didn't know how I felt until just now."

"Why? What's happening to you?"

"Everything. Thank you."

"What for? I've been nothing but a source of pain to you. I've brought you embarrassment, and I hurt your child."

"All of this is leading to something wonderful."

"You believe that?"

"I know it. And that's why I want to thank you."

"You've never been this—what's the word?—never been this sappy, Griffin. I've never seen you so sincere."

"You don't trust it."

"No. But that doesn't mean I can't; I just, right now, don't understand it. Sappiness is a shortcut to a real emotion without the work. I don't know how long you'll last this way before you turn on me. Hide from me."

"Is that what I do?"

"It's what men do, the ones I've known."

"Then men are shits. But that's what I'm learning from Candace."

They passed into the foyer of the sanctuary, where Griffin took a white yarmulke embroidered with the Dodgers' blue logo. Inside it was stamped in gold SQUIRE'S BAR MITZVAH. So far, this season, the team was losing.

Phil Ginsberg appeared from nowhere; behind him were brothers or cousins, with the same general outlines to their faces.

Phil introduced him first, to his brother, Dave, and the others, cousins: Stew, Alan, Paul, Gary. There were nods and palms and mazel tovs as Ginsberg introduced Griffin and Lisa, without first introducing himself to Lisa, so the brother and cousins assumed that they were already friends. Formalities over, Ginsberg put his arm over Lisa's shoulder and guided her away without apology to his family for leaving them, and Griffin had to follow, catching up with his boss and his wife as he heard Ginsberg say, ". . . must be so difficult for you."

"I don't know how to thank you," said Lisa.

"Really? You don't? I find that hard to believe."

"What can I do?"

"You can be a better mother, for one fucking thing, Lisa. You can fucking control yourself. You can pick up the phone after I've kept this bullshit out of the papers and you can call me and you can say, Thank you, Phil. You can do that."

"I don't have your number."

"What the fuck kind of stupid excuse is that? Listen to yourself."

"Yes, sir."

"You can help your husband by not getting in his way as long as he's working for me. That's what you can do to thank me. Do you understand what I'm saying? Listen to me, Lisa."

"Yes, sir."

"What am I saying?"

"To trust you."

"No. To do what I say. I don't care if you trust me. That's not the point. Now do you understand?"

"This is confusing."

"Your husband knows what I mean. Thanks for coming. It means a lot to me, and I'm sure it means a lot to Candace. I'll see you at the party."

"Thank you. Mazel tov."

"And thank you." Ginsberg turned to Griffin. "Why don't you guys a find a seat?"

He turned from them, and gave a hug to Chris Tryon, who had just come in the door. Tryon looked through Griffin as he put on the Dodger yarmulke.

Lisa took Griffin's hand, unaware of all that confused him at this moment, the connection between Ginsberg and Swaine's handsome butler. Had they always known each other? Had Tryon talked to Ginsberg about the visit?

They walked into the sanctuary and took seats in the middle of a row in a section to the right of the altar.

My whole life has hung upon a series of partial victories, Griffin thought, and I am down the slope from too many people who have conquered their own Everests. He watched the two billionaires taking their seats, and the way they looked at the synagogue, studying and measuring the purpose of the sanctuary's details. The seats fanned out almost 180 degrees from a raised platform. In most synagogues the Torahs were kept behind the closed heavy doors of the ark, but in this room eight Torahs dressed in embroidered covers and silver breastplates stood on the branches of a sculpted tree behind a sheer curtain, like expensive boots in a winter window display.

Griffin watched the billionaires sizing up the room. What did they see that he might also recognize? The seats were well padded and comfortable, with a Bible and prayer book in a shelf on the back of the next row. The building was from the early 1960s, it was an architecture of a timidly arranged theological eventfulness, ecumenically blending an impression of the General Assembly of the United Nations, good wood, pale colors, and the absorption of all echo, with an air of the numbing impatience in the room of a fur salon where husbands look at mink coats with their wives. Did the billionaires see through the idea of God? Griffin sensed in the billionaires a glowing disillusion with something most men had not the courage to give up; the billionaires surpassed the illusion of disillusion. Not for nothing are stocks called securities and hadn't all the securities collapsed, social security in the broadest and most specific of meanings and implications and analogies? What fool could still let the world's shocks surprise him? What fool could still admit disillusionment? It takes genius to meditate on the illusions of the world until no disillusion remains. The billionaires were angry, yes, but never indignant. Does Gunther Hitt, whoever he is, distract himself with the noise of shattering illusions? Corrupt evangelists, pedophile priests, messianic Jews, no weapons of mass destruction, stolen elections: How could anyone manage to survive in a dying world if he let the collapse of institutions distract him? Griffin knew he needed to search his heart for all remaining indignation, all gullibilities.

Was that his prayer? How can anyone be surprised by anything anymore, even by the surprise of this comprehension? How can a man make a fortune if political reality still surprises him? No wonder the movies can't grow an audience; don't just blame technology. DVD Netflix video on demand plasma screens satellite TV Internet video games blah-blah-blah. No. The myths are shrinking because the gods are dying. We know the stories: Aristotle to Freud to Joseph Campbell to classes on story structure. The formula of myth is like the formula for the atom bomb and, once published, destroys the illusion of story. All that remains is rage, the first stage of mourning; rage, then denial.

To master the world—that is, to make his fortune—Griffin knew he would have to eradicate within himself every molecule of belief that somewhere else someone else lives a blessed existence, an original existence, and with this thought a voice inside screamed at him to remember Candace Netter's eyes, to remember the illumination of compassion, the proof of singularity.

I need to shake up the order of my perceptions, I need to rattle all hierarchies, I need to fly to Spain and look at Guernica while really stoned and listening to the Back Street Boys on my iPod, over and over, and if someone asks me I'll tell him that I'm listening to Stravinsky; that'll put them off the scent of the truth.

He smiled at Lisa and patted her hand in her lap. She rested her cheek against his shoulder and held his arm, collapsing into him as though he had the strength he doubted, as though with good reason she trusted him to protect her. *How can I achieve what I want when I am too many things at once?*

Lisa whispered to Griffin that she was scared of everything.

"I'm here to protect you."

"For real?"

"Yes. You and my children."

"All of them?"

"All three."

"I need help."

"You're getting it."

"Phil Ginsberg scares me. Do you know what you're doing?"

"Not completely."

"He does."

"No, you're wrong. He doesn't. That's why he needs me."

The cantor, about thirty, walked down the aisle to the altar, playing the guitar on a strap around his neck. He wore a cordless microphone, and the sound came from speakers around the room. "Hi, I'm Cantor Aryeh. Here's a song that's easy to learn because it doesn't have any words. It was sung by the great Rabbi Nachman in the woods of Eastern Europe, and it goes like this. . . ."

He had shining black curls cut short on the sides but dropping long behind, almost a mullet but without the Sonny Bono bell-bottom width, and a face with a gleaming happiness that would have been contagious if it didn't shimmer with a maniacally forced piety straining to friendliness.

But then, thought Griffin, so what if that's what he's like, so what if his spirituality comes from artificial turf? He's trying to humble us by asking us to sing with our broken voices. He's not asking us to accept God, he's asking us to go *lalalalalalalalalala*. Why can't we? Maybe our movies would be better if we could all just start the day going *lalalalalala biddybiddybum. Biddybiddybum*. Silliness.

A few people joined him, none of the kids, not even Squire. No adult with any sense of his own depravity could find a place for himself in the cantor's summer-camp religion. And then a voice, Candace's, thin and rasping like a debarked terrier, joined the cantor, who dipped his guitar toward her in gratitude, and with that, the women who loved Candace rose in their seats and joined her full-throated, like partisans at a rally. That still small voice spoke again to Griffin: *Sing, you murderous motherfucker, sing!* Griffin turned to Lisa because he wanted to tell her that God had just spoken to him, that

God had even called him a motherfucker, but instead of speaking, he sang, *"Lalalalalala biddybiddybum."* Lisa smiled, even giggled, and joined him. Candace heard Griffin and Lisa and looked their way, for just a second, and might have looked harder, but the rabbi came out as the cantor finished the song.

The rabbi was a large woman in her mid-thirties, not the synagogue's senior rabbi, whom Griffin had seen here before and would have expected, because Phil Ginsberg doesn't fly with the junior pilot, but Rabbi Cyndee, who as Griffin knew from *Sharing His Closet* was close to Candace. Griffin saw the braided silver bands on the rabbi's right ring finger; she had been married to a woman in Massachusetts. The rabbi didn't have the same need as the cantor to will herself into spiritual frenzy; maybe it was enough for her to wear the robes and the yarmulke and stand there weighing 270 lesbian pounds, defying tradition and consciously demanding attention, that gave her religious authority. Even if the crowd wouldn't sing along with her, they wouldn't ignore her or disdain her, not even those who most hated religion, but then maybe, for her, religion didn't need God as Griffin had come to imagine God to be, which was—what?—distracted omniscience, erratic omnipotence.

So Griffin hummed along and read aloud every prayer, and read along with the transliteration of the Hebrew, trying to match repeated English letters with the repeated square letters, and felt himself elevated by the meaningless sounds in spite of the billionaire skepticism he wanted to inhale from the money in the room.

He didn't know much about Judaism, but neither did most of the Jews of Hollywood, and half of them were married to Christians or called themselves Buddhist. He couldn't understand how the Jews could control Hollywood and know so little about themselves. He couldn't understand how the Jews could dominate entertainment when their sacred text told such incomplete stories. Homer made sense as a movie guy. Shakespeare made sense as a movie guy. Moses didn't make sense as a movie guy, because the Jewish stories didn't follow the plot arcs that make money.

Rabbi Cyndee called the Netter and Ginsberg families to join her in front of the ark. Griffin always liked this part of the ceremony, the tableau of the generations, handing the scroll down from Sinai to Jerusalem to Babylonia to Spain to Warsaw to Beverly Hills, but in all those centuries, no one had stolen attention from the Torah and the bar mitzvah with the dreadful fascination devoted now to Candace's plastic surgery.

Oh, and the added drama! Divorced homosexual showbiz mogul takes ancient holy scroll from his mother and gives it to his ex-wife, who gives the scroll to her son. At that moment, the tender ritual overcame the morbid fascination with Candace's face and awoke distress in the hearts of every parent in the room who didn't have a tradition to pass along to their children. Griffin looked at Ethan, goofing around with the boys beside him and not paying attention to the service, and for a second wanted to kill him, but early violent death in a synagogue seemed like an extreme way of handling the problem of his empty patrimonial bequest.

Squire led a procession from the stage through the congregation, and the Jews who knew what to do reached out with their fingers, prayer books, or the fringes of their prayer shawls to touch the Torah and then kiss what had touched it. As the Torah passed their row, Lisa squeezed past Griffin to touch the embroidered tablets of the Ten Commandments. Phil Ginsberg followed his son, reaching out to shake hands and accept the mazel tovs, and when his eyes passed Griffin's there was no special recognition. Griffin worried, because no adjustment in Ginsberg's energy was not premeditated.

The parade returned to the altar, where Ginsberg's cousins un-dressed the Torah and set it on the pulpit. The rabbi announced the page number in the Bible. Griffin wanted to watch the boy read and see the reactions of his parents.

Squire read more than children usually do at Reform services, es-pecially rich kids, but Griffin could hear Squire's clear chanting sup-ported by Candace's love for him, and his love for her, and at the same time his respect for his father, not that specific bundle of contradic-tions who tormented Griffin so powerfully but the idea of a father whose son would earn respect by his own diligent work, as though retrospectively a father is better in the past for his son's own good actions in the present. Griffin felt like a billionaire with this thought, which opened the doors of the idea of the ark. You can struggle a long time in Hollywood to believe the simple emotion of an idea that you'd mock, in anyone's heart but your own. And then it comes to you that the movies that make the most money tell the most familiar story, and either you walk away from the game saying the hell with humanity's need for banality or you try and find the wisdom. He looked down at Lisa's Bible and read the section that Squire was chanting.

And YHWH spoke to Moses, saying, "Speak to the children of Israel, and you shall say to them: I am YHWH, your God. You shall not do like what is done in the land of Egypt, in which you lived; and you shall not do like what is done in the land of Canaan, to which I'm bringing you; and you shall not go by their laws. You shall do my judgments, and you shall observe my laws, to go by them. I am YHWH, your God. And you shall observe my laws and my judgments, which, when a human will do them, he'll live through them! I am YHWH.

Any man, to any close relative of his, you shall not come close to expose nu-dity. I am YHWH. You shall not expose your father's nudity and your mother's nudity. She is your mother. You shall not expose her nudity. You shall not expose your father's wife's nudity. It is your father's nudity. Your sister's nudity—your father's daughter or your mother's daughter, born home or born outside—you shall not expose their nudity. The nudity of your son's daughter or your daughter's daughter—you shall not expose their nudity because they are your nudity. The nudity of your father's wife's daughter, born of your father: she is your sister; you shall not expose her nudity. You shall not expose your father's sister's nudity. She is your father's close relative. You shall not expose your mother's sister's nudity. She is your mother's close relative. You shall not expose your father's brother's nudity; you shall not come close to his wife. She is your aunt. You shall not expose your daughter-in-law's nudity. She is your son's wife. You shall not expose her nudity. You shall not expose your brother's wife's nudity. It is your brother's nudity. You shall not expose the nudity of a woman and her daughter. You shall not take her son's daughter or her daughter's daughter to expose her nudity. They are close relatives. It is perversion. And you shall not take a woman to her sister to rival, to expose her nudity along with her in her lifetime. And you shall not come close to a woman during her menstrual impurity to expose her nudity. And you shall not give your intercourse of seed to your fellow's wife, to become impure by it. And you shall not give any of your seed for passing to the Moloch, and you shall not desecrate your God's name. I am YHWH. And you shall not lie with a male like lying with a woman. It is an offensive thing.

Brilliant, thought Griffin, show business, beautiful; he had seen a bar mitzvah boy make everyone in the synagogue happy that they'd been invited to the service.

After he finished reading, more cousins dressed the scroll again, one of them took it aside, and Squire returned to the pulpit to speak.

"Rabbi Cyndee, Cantor Aryeh, Mother and Father, honored guests. My Torah portion today is from the Book of Leviticus, chapter eighteen. In Hebrew, the Book of Leviticus, which is the third book of the Torah, the Five Books of Moses, which is called Vayikra. Vayikra in Hebrew means 'And He called,' after the first word in the first chapter of the book. Every week of the year, we read a different chapter in the Torah, and the chapter from which my reading comes this week is called Ockray Moat, which in Hebrew means, 'after death,' which is about what happens after the death of Aaron's two sons, who are killed by God for making the wrong kind of sacrifice. They were not sacrificing to an idol like the Golden Calf, they were sacrificing to God, but they made their sacrifices in the wrong way. This week, God tells Moses the rules that the Israelites must follow if they want to live holy lives and not be killed by God. I chose to have my bar mitzvah on this Saturday because I wanted to study these rules because my father is a homosexual and Rabbi Cyndee is a homosexual and I have teachers who are homosexuals and some of my parents' friends are homosexual and there are many people who work in the entertainment industry who are homosexual and many great people throughout human history have been homosexual including Michelangelo and Walt Whitman and Michael Stipe, the lead singer for REM.

"The Torah says you shall not lie with a man as with a woman, so that makes it look like the Torah is saying that a man shouldn't be homosexual. So the first thing I did when I studied this chapter with Rabbi Cyndee, and with my mom, and also with my dad, was to ask myself, Does God hate my father for who he is or what he does? Does God hate Rabbi Cyndee and her life partner Avivah? Since homosexuals were killed by the Nazis too, and had to wear pink triangles while the Jews had to wear yellow stars, I wondered what God really thought. Did God want the Nazis to kill the homosexuals but not the Jews?

"The Torah makes many distinctions between the different kinds of sexual relationships that are forbidden in a family, but there is one kind of sexual relationship that the Torah never mentions at all and that is a homosexual relationship between two women, and the only time two women are not allowed to have their nudity exposed together is in verse eighteen, 'and you shall not take a woman to her sister to rival, to expose her nudity along with her in her lifetime.' This means that a man can marry two sisters, in the way that Jacob married Rachel and Leah, who were sisters, but he cannot have sex with them at the same time because the Bible was written during the time of polygamy and many men had more than one wife and there is no rule in the Torah against a man having sex with more than one wife at a time. The next thing I looked at when I studied this section was what God says to Moses: 'And you shall not lie with a male like lying with a woman. It is an offensive thing.' Rabbi Cyndee asked me what was interesting about the first sentence, what makes it different from something clear like *you shall not murder,* and I said that the rule is a comparison. Does it mean that men can have one kind of sex but not other kinds of sex? Does it mean that a man cannot have sex with men and women? The other rules are so clear and this rule is not very clear; we think we know what it means but the closer you look the less you can understand what it means exactly. Then I looked at the next sentence, and I want to thank Lev Broder, my Hebrew instructor, for helping me with this. When the Bible says it is an offensive thing, the word in Hebrew for offensive is 'toh-eebay.' And the other time that word is used in the Bible is when Joseph warns his brothers, who are shepherds, that being a shepherd in Egypt is offensive, is 'toh-eebay.' This means that what might be something normal in one place is something that in other places is considered to be a bad thing, is offensive. This means that the Torah is telling us that in some places and some times, being homosexual is perfectly normal, like being a shepherd is being normal for the Jews in the time of Joseph and his brothers. This means that the people today who say that homosexuals are sinners who are going to hell don't know what they're talking about, and it also means that I don't have to choose between being a good Jew and loving my father or having Rabbi Cyndee as my rabbi.

"I want to thank everyone for coming today and celebrating my bar mitzvah with me. I want to thank Rabbi Cyndee and Cantor Aryeh, I want to thank my Hebrew tutor Lev Broder and all my teachers at religious school, and I want to thank my mother and father and also all my relatives who came here from as far away as Boston."

You could hear a pin.

It was past six o'clock and still an hour to sunset, but the windows, high on the walls, faced east, and the weak dissipating glare of the day penetrated the sanctuary with a mild ambience, until the rabbi nodded to the cantor, who pushed a switch hidden on the pulpit, dimming the lights, bringing the outside and inside into balance, scaring Griffin with the idea that the world had come from elsewhere and might disappear. The rabbi blessed Squire Ginsberg, and the president of the synagogue thanked him for his words of Torah and gave him a pewter Kiddush cup.

The cantor set on the pulpit a large silver candlestick holding a tall braided candle, beside a silver Kiddush goblet and a spice box on a solid stand. The rabbi waved her hands upward and the congregation stood. The cantor started another wordless melody but this one was more familiar to the congregation and more people joined in, and at the same time, without being told what to do, almost everyone put their arms around the people beside them. Griffin hadn't even been aware of the person beside him but now he had his left arm over a man and his right over Lisa, whose right arm was around Ethan, who had appeared without Griffin's seeing him leave the row with the teenagers.

Griffin caught the melody, which seemed modern, with a tilt into a minor key for a few bars and then out, the sort of borrowed plaintive cry that usually signaled to Griffin an unearned transformation of sorrow become wisdom. But where the tune might have relied too heavily on shtetl inflections for the sound of authenticity, the response of the congregation was genuine. The moment of fellowship and feeling woven into the brightening glow of the braided candle, and the unembarrassed pleasure in the supporting touch of strangers, proved to Griffin that in this humility and completion—a moment wet with melting wax, with wine, and with tears—whoever wrote the melody understood something of the fabric of the universe, and if none of the billionaires could hear what Griffin was hearing, if the sincerity annoyed them with its denial of anyone's superiority, perhaps, thought Griffin, I have an advantage right now. If the song was a prayer, the insight was a red bicycle.

And the ritual got better, lifted Griffin higher, as the melody changed to something almost every Jew in the room seemed to know, a song about the prophet Elijah. The cantor sang, and the rabbi explained that the candle lighting marks the end of the Sabbath and with this we return to the earthbound week, but we can keep the glow by remembering the candle. She curled her fingers to see the light's reflection in her fingernails to see for herself that she was substance and not just spirit, and then blessed the spice box and passed the box into the congregation, and then another box, and when the box came to Griffin he inhaled clove and cinnamon and other spices, and the rabbi said everyone should savor that smell for the week, and then she blessed the wine, and she drank from the goblet, and so did the cantor, and then Squire, and then she doused the braided candle in the wine.

The bar mitzvah was over. The linked arms separated. Griffin made sure to be the first to introduce himself to the man he'd been touching. "I'm Griffin Mill," he said.

"I know," the stranger said. "I pitched a story to you about five years ago. You don't remember me."

This was how Griffin had started his conversation with David Kahane the night he murdered him.

"No, I'm sorry. I don't remember your name."

"Andy Rosenman." Rosenman was a screenwriter. He was paid two hundred grand a week to fix broken scripts.

"Of course," said Griffin. "I'm a big fan."

"Thanks. You must be working with Phil."

"That's right. How'd you know?"

"Why else would you be here? See you at the party."

. . .

On the way out, Lisa said, "I'm a Jew, Griffin. I'm a Jewish woman and that makes Willa a Jew. We should get her a bat mitzvah, she should go to Hebrew school and become a Jew. I know you'll think it's a bad idea, but I don't know what else to do."

Griffin said he didn't know either, but he did know and it wasn't something he wanted, not against Willa, but for Lisa: He didn't want Lisa caught up in God; it scared him that Lisa might find God and then leave him, even if he never made enough money for a luxurious alimony.

. . .

June drove up the hill in Los Feliz. It was the most mysterious rich neighborhood in the city, grand palazzos and haciendas tucked into the folds of Griffith Park, an area approaching a hundred years of age now, nothing grossly remodeled, impossible to decipher, vibrations of wealthy bohemianism, silent-movie stars, brilliant decorating invisible from the street; she could imagine no place in the world more attractive to the Goths than Los Feliz, no place better for private playrooms, private dungeons, fake blood on the walls.

The sisters chattered about things so infinitesimally local that June couldn't remember a word as soon as it passed between them, and their sentences lost coherence.

She left them at the curb of a big Moorish villa on a double lot, with a wide driveway and a tennis court on the side, didn't need to come in and meet the mom now but would say hello when she came to pick them up. Other parents were dropping off their children, mostly girls.

She returned to the movie theater in Hollywood to see the comedy.

· · ·

As Griffin drove through the main gate at the Studio, Lisa asked him, "What would give you a better career, Griffin? If you had to choose between being a Jew or being gay, which would help you the most in Hollywood?"

"That's a good question, Lisa."

"I got it from Jessa. She asked me that."

"Really?"

"Jessa asked me about Phil Ginsberg. And you. She said, 'If Daddy is working for this guy who scares everybody, what does he need to do to be more like him, so he can scare people too, since I don't think Daddy is very scary?' She asked me that, Griffin, pretty much in those words. Would Daddy be more successful if he were homosexual or Jewish, since that's half of Hollywood anyway. Willa would never think of asking that kind of question. Willa just wants results, she's not interested in working for anything for herself. Do you know I love Jessa more than Willa? Have I ever told you that?"

"No."

"I do. Love her. I love her. She's the smartest in the family. Do you know that about her? She's the most dangerous because she watches us and she has her own ideas about us. Jessa is always thinking ahead. Am I horrible for having these feelings?"

"I think you're normal."

"Then normal is really fucked up."

"I didn't say it wasn't."

"Maybe we should be religious. Or maybe it's too late. Not for us, just as a style in the world. Maybe you had to find religion in the nineties. Don't listen to me. Let me know how I can help you."

"Actually, Lisa, that's all you have to say; all you have to say is that you want to know how to help me, and that helps me, really helps me."

Bales of hay and mounds of horse shit marked the path to the party's sound stage. Servers dressed as Ukrainian peasants carried trays with shots of vodka. "I like this," said Lisa. "This is the first thing that's given me hope in a long time, this on top of the bar mitzvah. When the world is weirder than your strangest thoughts, when the weirdness of the world makes this much noise, it seems possible to get through something as awful as beating your child in the shoe department in Nordstrom's at The Grove."

"I'm not ready to go in," said Griffin, refusing a drink. He guided them away from the path to the reception, to walk through the lot where he had spent so many years.

There were plaques beside the doors to the stages, honoring the movies that had been shot there. The stages were old now: the commemorated movies dated to the 1930s. The titles of the old movies were like miracles. Bogart and John Ford and Carole Lombard and Rin Tin Tin and Henry Fonda and James Cagney—they'd all walked here, done their jobs, and died. Some of those actors worked for fifty years. Griffin fought the banality of nostalgia, which made him quiet. Lisa missed his change of mood, in the darkness.

"Do you know what I mean? Do you feel it? Can you see that there's hope?" she asked.

"There's always hope. I don't know how much for us, but there's always hope."

"I love you, Griffin. I'm glad I married you. Right now, I'm glad I married you."

"Why?"

"Because you're just a man. And these days, that doesn't mean anything. Men are nothing. Remember that."

His cell phone rang; it was Ginsberg. "You're missing my son's party. Get over here now. Put your wife on the phone." Griffin gave the phone to Lisa.

"Listen, Phil, it's Lisa. We're taking a walk. We'll be there and we'll work the room if that's what you want, but right now we're just enjoying each other's company. It's been a shitty week, if you don't already know, and I need my husband and he needs me." She closed the phone.

"You're a goddess," said Griffin.

"No. Let's not go that far, we owe him something. He sees talent in you, Griffin. When someone powerful tells you that he sees something good in you, believe him."

"But what if his confidence in me is a trick?"

"On who?"

"I don't know."

"You can't get out of it, Griffin, so his intentions don't make any difference. They can't. Smile. He's bringing us together."

. . .

It was a half-moon Saturday night and everyone in the world was stuck in traffic. The traffic moved badly. June could only find a parking space on the roof, and in the lobby of the Arclight Theater she waited forever in the line at the ticket counter, where the process of buying a ticket for a specific seat was as involving as a consultation on the shape of a nose job.

In *Wedding Crashers,* two divorce lawyers crash weddings and fuck women made horny by the flowing purity of the basic emotions released at a good wedding, even by a good funeral. They each meet their true love at the grandest society wedding of the season, but, presenting themselves as other than who they really are, their self-imposed disguises are found out and both are banished from the kingdom. By the end, the two couples are united by the power of the true love that comes from meeting the soul intended by God for the best match to assure the best children for the best continuation of humanity.

Wedding Crashers made June laugh, but with the perfect construction of the story, building toward two inevitable weddings and the clarification of everyone's lives, the weight of each piece of that assembly pressed too hard on her, made her suffer for her social condition, aging divorcée defined by the comedy as the essence of incomplete. She started to cry, and then, as the credits rolled, she heard herself screaming at the crowd, "I saw the world straight and didn't betray myself. Why am I here alone tonight? Why is my husband with his second wife, at a party, dancing? I am not the whorish wife of the stuffy politician, I am not the obnoxious widowed crone! But they are throwing me away like a useless embarrassing hag!"

There were other women like her in the theater, and they rushed to her and held her and walked her outside; someone gave her a bottle of water; others held her hands, asked if she needed a ride home, held her while she sobbed into shoulders and breasts she had never felt before.

. . .

In the alley behind the bar-mitzvah-party sound stage, Hasids and milkmaids smoked cigarettes while a klezmer clarinetist played variations of "Take Me Out to the Ball Game." A milkmaid said, "The stage isn't open yet for the dinner. Everyone is in the front. Over there and make a left."

Griffin thanked her, ignored her directions, and went in anyway. The stage was now a vast set modeled on the shtetl in *Fiddler on the Roof*. An immense back-lighted transparency hid the stage's walls, a circular photograph of a Jewish village in the late nineteenth century, and into this scene the set designer had digitally added soaring Chagall fiddlers and lovers curving from earth to heaven and back toward earth to kiss, on either side of a forty-foot-high photograph of Squire Ginsberg in a Dodgers uniform, standing on the pitcher's mound.

The sound stage was quiet, the guests not yet admitted; the band, in homespun costume, was still assembling, the waiters, wearing vests and Trotsky caps, and the waitresses, wearing head scarves, still setting the tables. Griffin and Lisa crossed the room, now seeing the set as intended, the tables and dance floor in the village square, and they followed the road outside, where the friends and families of Ginsbergs and Netters were being entertained by jugglers, stilt walkers, magicians, all as a Polish duke might have hired for the wedding of his daughter to a Prussian king. Ginsberg came out of the crowd and whispered to Griffin, "Everyone knows this is desecration, but everyone loves it. Why, Griffin? Why do the rabbis permit this kind of travesty? I organized tonight so that you could answer the questions that I keep knocking my head against, and I'm getting tired of feeling stupid. Do you have a thought at all?"

"Maybe there's nothing wrong with it," said Griffin.

"Really? What an idea," said Ginsberg, and Griffin thought for the first time that Ginsberg was not mocking him.

Lisa said, "It's just people being silly. It's not the end of the world."

Ginsberg raised a hand. "Excuse me, but your husband is the expert on the end of the world. I'm surprised he has children, he's so scared of the world's end. I'm surprised he lets them live if he's so sure the world is ending."

"That's why I want my island."

"Ah-ha! But if you didn't have children, would you want an island, or would you just like to get out there and fuck around a lot until it all comes crashing down? Or are children your insurance against emptiness if the world doesn't die, and you know you want comfort in your old age, some kind of flattery or gratitude from the gene pool for keeping the enterprise of life alive, huh?"

"That's what life makes us do, whether we want to or not," said Lisa, starting to cry.

"Oh, look what I've done," said Ginsberg. "I'm sorry." He put his arm around Lisa, whispered something into her ear, a secret she should keep from Griffin, who put his hands in his pockets without thinking and, when he found them there, wished he owned a gun, but he wasn't sure who would get the first bullet, probably himself, he murmured just inside his throat. Ginsberg let go of Lisa and nudged her back to Griffin. She didn't like this but couldn't find a way to say so, and Griffin thought, *She is doing this for me. I should love her.*

"What did he tell you?"

"I couldn't hear him. I don't think he was saying anything. It was for you. He wanted you to see him that close to me. I think he wants you to feel jealous. I think he believes you need to feel some ordinary human emotions, simple emotions. The ones he's lost touch with."

"I think that's what he told you."

"You don't think I'm smart enough to figure out his plans for you?"

Chris Tryon was outside, smoking a cigarette with a man whose back was turned to Griffin. "I have to talk to someone," said Griffin.

"Who?"

"Him, over there. He worked for Warren Swaine, and I haven't seen him since the funeral. I want to see how he's doing."

"Everyone in Hollywood does fine with death, Griffin, don't you know that?"

"Is that true, Lisa?"

"I'm telling you. Hollywood isn't so different from the rest of the world, really, except nobody's death, outside of the family, takes long for everyone or anyone to forget. And even in the family, for a lot of people, a father dies, a mother dies, you get that news third on the agenda in a phone call. 'I want you to read a script, it's just right for you.' *I'd love to. Thanks. How are you?* 'Oh, my dad died yesterday. Tell me how you like the script.'"

"You're pretty funny sometimes," said Griffin. "I underestimate you. I'm sorry."

"You should be. Go to work now. Go. Fetch, get the money, boy; good boy, get the money."

Griffin made a little barking sound and walked to Tryon. He could hear the German accent of the man who was talking to him—it was Gunther Hitt—and now Griffin was frightened, but it was too late to turn back.

Hitt was younger than Griffin, maybe forty-five. He was a tall man with shiny skin, dark hair combed back, and large eyes that gleamed with amusement behind very German eyeglasses, half frames, gold.

Griffin saw Tryon signal Hitt to be quiet. "Hello, Chris, how are you doing?"

"I'm doing fine, Mr. Mill, just fine. Do you know Gunther Hitt?"

"We've talked."

"So it's you," said Gunther.

"Nobody else."

"I can see. What do you think of this tonight?"

"It's complicated."

"It's vulgar; what's so complicated about that?"

"Maybe wealth is vulgar no matter what it does."

"I'm not vulgar. Are you vulgar, Chris?"

"I'm not rich enough to be vulgar."

"The Hasids and the milkmaids are going to dance," said Hitt. "It's an act; I've seen them before. The men dance with the women, and then the men dance with the men and they balance large bottles of vodka on their heads and do Russian dances. It's religion as show biz. Someday the Catholic Mass will be done in Vegas, and the bar mitzvah will be performed at La Scala like a Handel opera for castrati. They'll have countertenors singing the part of the boys. The full orthodox service in Hebrew, with choir. Very expensive to put on. It's going to be beautiful. That's all that's going to remain of these things, Griffin. Too many Christians at a Passover seder and I feel like I'm putting on a floor show luau. The ritual becomes entertainment—that is, if religion doesn't destroy the world before we can get the world to destroy religion. But that's Hollywood's job. It's too bad you quit. You were a good soldier in the battle against religion, Griffin."

"Is that what I was doing?"

"It's what the world of religion thinks of Hollywood, so it must be true."

"It wasn't conscious."

"You'd have run the Studio if it had been conscious. You'd be chairman of the board if you knew what you were really doing, if you knew what was at stake in the battle between Hollywood and God. And I mean God as a brand name, not as anything real. But it's hard for Americans to hear someone say that; even the most secular Americans are still afraid of the idea of God. And this is what's at stake, Griffin Mill. The religions want the world to end now because they're afraid of losing control, they're all Jim Jones, all of them. Masada, the Coliseum, suicide bombers, immolated Buddhists, it's all the same: death instead of this life now. Hollywood doesn't want the world to die except in fantasy, and then it wants to collect the royalties on everyone coming back to relive that fantasy on home video. Hollywood is positive, the most positive force in nature. But it's a precarious situation. We could lose. Someone could blow up the studios, you know that, if they wanted to destroy the Temple Mount, just get a drive-on pass, and pull the pin or set the timer. *Boom.* Blow up the Oscars. *Boom.*

"Look, Griffin, I was just saying this to Chris; I was telling him this story. The world is given notice that in three days the polar ice caps are going to melt, the world is going to be irretrievably flooded, and humanity will be drowned. The pope goes on television and says to the world, 'We have three days to repent. Confess now and you will join Christ in Heaven.' The Dalai Lama says, 'We have three days to recognize that life and death are just an illusion.' Meanwhile, the rabbis pull together a team of the smartest Jews they can find and tell them, 'Boys, we've got three days to figure out how to live underwater.' I don't know what to do anymore, Griffin, and that's the truth. Chris, do you know?"

"Not me. Griffin?"

Where did this motherfucker get the authority to tease me? Griffin wanted to know, but had to answer quickly and lightly.

"It's pretty humbling when everyone is looking to me for the answers."

Gunther put an arm on Griffin's shoulder, to steady him to his responsibility. "Not just you, boy. Not just you."

Griffin had nothing left to say to either man. Not even offering a good-bye, he turned and joined the crowd among the jugglers, stilt walkers, and magicians. The band inside the sound stage was playing "Hava Nagilah," and the guests were rushing in to join hands and dance. Griffin followed the crowd. He saw Lisa inside, holding hands with Candace Netter near the center of the dance floor. Everyone was singing. All the Christian kids of the LA private schools knew "Hava Nagilah" better than they did "Onward, Christian Soldiers," better than they knew the Lord's Prayer. If only Judaism could be this wild all the time, thought Griffin, it might catch on, but it was only with this song and this dance that the Jews ever really lost their European reserve and went native without shame.

Cousins and uncles pulled Squire into the center of the dance and others dragged a chair from a table, and then he sat on the chair and the uncles, cousins, and out of the crowd even his strange terrifying father took a leg of the chair and held the back and lifted him over their heads.

The videographers and photographers had him covered from every angle, but the purity of the moment overwhelmed the power of the cameras to make everyone an extra in the boy's documentary, and instead the crowd absorbed the cameras and made them just another element of the celebration. Everything was whirl, spin, and song. Singing words in Hebrew whose meaning he didn't know and didn't want to know, Griffin reminded himself that Gunther Hitt was a German and, if that didn't matter, a European, which did matter, who admitted that Europeans couldn't understand American religious exuberance. Neither could Griffin, really, except for this one song-

and-dance, when grown-ups lifted kids overhead, in the middle of a three-hundred-thousand-dollar celebration of the boy's entrance into some kind of covenant with God and the Jewish community.

Griffin watched Phil Ginsberg as he took his turn on the chair and his brothers and cousins or whoever lifted him overhead and danced with him. Ginsberg did not flinch from ecstasy. Even Candace cheered him, and then it was her turn for the chair, and the women in the room pushed the men away as they grabbed the chair legs, as the women held hands defensively against any man getting through their circle and danced around Candace and sang for her, sang to her, she lifting her hands and clapping, blowing kisses, offering her hands. The women kissed them, kissed each other, held each other, lifted their hero higher, singing in Hebrew, singing what Griffin couldn't understand, except that he knew that all of this was for him.

. . .

June parked the car and braced herself to smile at the mom, and if she was offered a glass of wine she'd take it and hang around, because she had nothing else to do. Griffin and Lisa would get home on their own time, and Ethan would tell her about the party and the service after he woke up, in the late morning. She'd make whatever he wanted for breakfast, maybe some blueberry muffins.

A few dads were ahead of her, going for their kids. The party was on the tennis court. The DJ was taking his system apart, and the only music, just a bit louder than polite for the hour, came from a stereo in the house. Votive candles in paper bags lined the court. There was a half-dead chocolate cake on a table, like the rubble of a bombed city, and bowls of chips and M&Ms and jugs of diet soda. The girls clustered on the far side of the court, in the shadows. The girls outnumbered the boys, most of them at the edge of things while the girls stood together in a dense pack, some of them freak-dancing, grinding into one another for a few beats, enough to tease and then back away, some of them watching but all of them close, with a field of high sexual energy, because it was only for each other and too much for the boys to get around. Even the dads didn't know what to do, didn't know how to call their daughters out of the crowd.

She scanned quickly: Willa and Jessa weren't there. She passed the girls and the helpless scared fathers. The men looked ridiculous, irrelevant, trying to talk to their daughters. When the girls did leave the pack, hugging each other lightly, collarbone to collarbone, with a cheery "Love yoooooooo," they flipped from sluts in heat to daddy's little girls too quickly for the fathers to sustain their fear of the implications of what they had witnessed, the modern realization of the Bacchic celebration, of the nymphs about three minutes before the satyrs show up with the booze.

June wanted sympathy. She wanted to tell someone, a stranger, My ex-husband is out with his wife, while I have to babysit their daughter because she's not safe with her mother.

. . .

The mom was with a few other moms and a few cool dads and probably a friend or two of the mom, drinking wine in the breakfast room, hidden and hiding from the birthday party, with a few joints on the table. The mom assumed that June knew her name and introduced her quickly. Hard to know who was divorced and who was just picking the kid up alone. Hard to tell even which of the men were attached to which of the women. She took the wine and tapped a joint and one of the men said "Allow me" and lit it for her. There were no children around but she still felt awkward. The mom said, "Go into the maid's room, turn on the shower fan, then step into the shower, close the shower door, and exhale into the fan if you're worried; otherwise just stand at the window."

June stood at the window and had three good hits. It was strong pot, but these were wealthy people so it figured. It was physical pot and she wanted to fuck.

They were all talking about children and schools, they were talking about real estate and movies, they were talking about what an asshole George Bush was, and they were talking about global warming. They were talking about Arnold Schwarzenegger and would he run again, they were talking about hybrid cars and Esa-Pekka Salonen, they were talking about the drive to Mammoth Mountain and massages in Koreatown, they were talking about Larchmont Village and the yoga studio, they were talking about rescue dogs and JetBlue, they were talking about SAT prep courses and admissions to college, they were talking about the Oscars and terrorism. June wanted to tell them that she had just now realized the compulsion of exhibitionism, and if someone would put on the right band, she would allow one of the men to slap her cunt for their amusement. But instead she asked, "Are my daughters around?" She remembered that much, through the pot, that if one girl was hers and the other was her sister, and she was in charge of both, the safety of both, then she was their mother and they were her daughters, and the meaning of this was absolute, solid, like the table, like the wedding rings that most of them at the table were wearing, but not all of them. The mom pointed upstairs. She had a wedding ring but none of the men at the table made sense as her husband.

It was one of those houses with a weekend night nanny, who supervised whatever was going on in the children's wing. This one was watching over a couple of thick-haired seven-year-old boys killing whores on a video game. No one looked up at June, who continued down the children's hall, past the heavily carpeted bedrooms and the captain's beds high enough for three sets of drawers for whatever shit the kids weren't using now, and in one room, in the middle of a comforter, sat an eight-year-old girl in a spandex Vegas stripper's top with rhinestones on one shoulder, watching *Bring It On* for the fifth time. The kids' halls in these houses always had the same contradictory atmosphere, story-book princess silence and at the same time, beside the silence, the noise of televisions, the clicking of keyboards as the kids IM'ed each other, massacres on computer games, small sounds leaking from iPod earphones, freshly downloaded cell-phone ring melodies, a girl in another room yakking on a conference call to three girls like her in other houses, all being groomed for Penn. June found Willa and Jessa by themselves in another bedroom, sitting on the floor, talking to each other. They looked up at her, and they knew more about her than she knew about them. She took them home. She asked them, "Did you have a nice time?"

Twelve

After the bar mitzvah, Griffin and Lisa took Ethan to their house and the girls slept at June's. Ethan went online in his bedroom at Griffin and Lisa's house and chatted with Eli for another two hours. He told him that he didn't like Squire, or Squire's friends, and if they were anything like the other kids at Coldwater, high school was going to be horrible. Ethan told Eli they made him feel spoiled. He'd never before felt like he was just another rich kid, but he didn't know another way to define himself.

On Sunday, Griffin and Lisa went to June's house for breakfast. Ethan was already gone. The girls had already eaten their breakfast and were watching *Family Guy.* The adults were finally by themselves. June asked about the bar mitzvah. Griffin encouraged Lisa to answer. Lisa talked about the service, how it had moved her and how this feeling stayed with her even later, at the party, which should have wrecked the profound and beautiful confusion she'd felt in the synagogue. June asked Lisa what the women were wearing, and Griffin cleaned up the kitchen, his old kitchen. He knew where everything went. It tickled him, in the midst of all this, that he had fucked both of these women and now they were laughing with each other. He had an impulse to sum things up, to insert his dick into the conversation. Then he remembered the keystroke tracker on Ethan's computer.

Ethan and Eli had set up an account and constructed an identity, GOTHSEXNOW, a couple: HE, 32; SHE, 29. The boys had lifted a photograph from the profile of another couple, both naked. SHE had the dauntingly clever look of an art school graduate who ran an animation department, the heavy plastic frames, the black hair with short bangs, and the nipple ring, belly button ring, and future primitive Maori Goes to College black tattoos on both arms, above her skinny biceps. SHE had wide breasts, Griffin thought from nursing. SHE had no pubic hair. HE had an ample gut, shaved head, and a goatee, a style of man some smart women liked these days, the large stomach not a referent to couch-potato laziness but to Mexican gangbanger and cautious biker intelligence wrapped in Burning Man exuberance—these endorsements assured by the spirited trendiness of his hairless genitals, his cock hanging there like he was showing off the hybrid of a dead Chihuahua and a vintage Zippo.

And the profile statement seemed real; Griffin doubted the boys could have constructed their self-advertisement.

GOTHSEXNOW: We live the dark side, shadows, night, and if we could be anywhere, we'd let Anne Rice send us there. We're 4 real and expect the same. No answers without a picture, NO SINGLE MEN. We have a gallery of pictures of us as you'd like to see us, and we'll trade them for yours, and if we all like what we see, we can travel. If you want to know more about us, just click here.

Griffin clicked on a few links that brought him to: PRIVATE EYE, their photo gallery, two categories: OURS, THEIRS. Under OURS, Griffin played SLIDESHOW, fifteen pictures of GothSexNow in a PLAY SLIDESHOW titled NAKED ROUTE 66. All right, thought Griffin, I've got you now, you're Route 66ers, that's as much a tribe as drag queen Lucies, you think you're Goth, but . . . no . . . they didn't call themselves Goth, that's what the boys named them, and they probably borrowed that name from someone else on another Web site, because there was nothing Anne Rice in any of the pictures, and Griffin decided that he'd been off by a few degrees about the guy's style; it wasn't so interesting or diseased. Vampires don't pose naked in front of high-desert abandoned Mobil stations in the middle of the day, or stop the car near the railroad tracks, put the camera on a tripod, wait for the purple sky of a '62 Corvette sunset, just as the big Santa Fe engines of a mile-long freight train are behind them, and the woman drops to her knees and sucks her fat husband's cock. It was a pretty good picture, thought Griffin, and it was turning him on. Griffin took the suck-and-fuck tour of America's Historical Highway.

While the slide show continued, a little yellow icon flashed on the screen and a dialogue box opened.

BUDDIES ON LINE NOW: PERVO_LOIS&CLARK

PERVO_LOIS&CLARK: How have you been?

Griffin understood that PERVO_LOIS&CLARK were friends in some way of GOTHSEXNOW and wanted to chat. He answered.

GOTHSEXNOW: Really really horny . . . :) U?

PERVO_LOIS&CLARK: Complicated days. But we're managing. How's life in Detroit?

GOTHSEXNOW: Hot, but could be hotter, connect with anyone lately?

PERVO_LOIS&CLARK: No, not here. Family stuff. Heavy. Wait a sec . . . Clark wants to say hello.

PERVO_LOIS&CLARK: Clark here, who's this?

GOTHSEXNOW: New best friend.

PERVO_LOIS&CLARK: Are you the he or the she?

GOTHSEXNOW: The he.

PERVO_LOIS&CLARK: (Lois) You connect with anyone lately? Any good swingergoths?

GOTHSEXNOW: Tons. All over. Big goth orgy 2 nites ago. Everyone is fucking now!!!

Griffin giggled when he wrote it out that way; he felt creative and wonderful and powerful.

PERVO_LOIS&CLARK: Amazing, isn't it? Amazing. I am utterly amazed that group sex has slunk out of its cheesy ring a ding kind of Peter Lawford meets the Maytag Man's daughter's swingerdom and burst upon the "scene." There's something obvious about it, but still shocking enough that I'm sure Jerzy Kosinski is clawing at the dirt above him. I went into it looking for the chance to fuck Monica Vitti on the golf course with Alain Delon and Maurice Ronet taking turns with Lois, or at the least a little bit of Bunuelish bourgeois indiscretion, but instead it's mostly the people in line for, at best, Jay Leno. And we have no objection to fucking the vapid and the repulsive and the no-doubt criminal—at least not most of the time.

GOTHSEXNOW: Huh?

PERVO_LOIS&CLARK: Lois here. . . . Clark, they live in Motor City, not Tinsel Town. Goth, love,

Delon and Ronet were in the French version of
The Talented Mr. Ripley, in the 60s. And that's
what he says he wanted but I know he would have
traded it all in for Gloria Grahame with a dildo.

PERVO_LOIS&CLARK: I never said I didn't, darling, but the big dream is everyone in the Mis-
fits, even Thelma Ritter. And these days they
think Eyes Wide Shut is sexy.

GOTHSEXNOW: I don't know what you're talking about. I don't go to movies much.

While they typed to each other, PERVO_LOIS&CLARK sent a link
for a QuickTime movie. A black-and-white film—from the 50s, not
the 40s, guessed Griffin—with a blond actress, adorable in her time,
a sassy not-so-dumb blonde saying, "Travel, expenses, excitement,
what's wrong with that?"

PERVO_LOIS&CLARK: . . . Lois?

PERVO_LOIS&CLARK: Oy. It made me think that
if Kubrick hadn't been on an airplane in thirty
years, he also probably hadn't had a good fuck.
Sad.

GOTHSEXNOW: I like seeing people put their
faces online, sucking cock.

PERVO_LOIS&CLARK: i can't think of anyone
we've ever met in "the lifestyle" (oy, gott) who
wasn't more or less stupid, or at least circum-
scribed in his or her cultural/intellectual
sphere, again inversely as he/she was a more active pursuer of sexual satisfaction—so many calls
for qualification, so little time, and would I

prefer to meet georges bataille, or sade or
arthur koestler or jerzy kosinski to the con-
tractors (sic sic sick) and nurses and dental
hygienists (yuck) we've encountered? (although
Hermann Broch or Alfonso Reyes or many of their
paramours wouldn't be so bad.)

GOTHSEXNOW: The blond chick Gloria Grahame?

PERVO_LOIS&CLARK: (ClarK) yes, yes. No one
has a memory anymore!

PERVO_LOIS&CLARK: (Lois)—honeyyyy, let them
be, relax, relax.

PERVO_LOIS&CLARK: (CLARK) where the fuck am
I, anyway? RIGHT. Sorry to be a jerk about your
not knowing Gloria Grahame, it's not like you're
in the business and should know. I'm sure there
are plenty of music references you have that I
should have too. Isn't that part of the point of
all of this, only connect? if only our parents
knew. maybe we just don't know their screen names.

GOTHSEXNOW: Gotta go. Later!

And Griffin logged out. He googled PERVO_LOIS&CLARK but
came up empty. It was a real handle but not accessible through normal channels. They were jerks, he thought, pompous jerks. But he
was pretending to be one thing, maybe they were pretending to be
something too.

. . .

He heard Lisa and June in the kitchen, laughing like first-graders
at a slumber party, giggling, then controlling themselves, then giggling into tears of laughter, topping each other with laughing. He

had no idea what to think about anything right now, a feeling that was becoming familiar. He made no effort to put on any kind of face when he interrupted them.

"Can you tell me?"

They both looked at him and then opened the gates for a swarm of bigger laughs. June answered. "She told me something that she thought was news."

"She always knew, Griffin."

"I think I knew the first time we talked after I got the word about David. As soon as they said you'd gone to see him, I knew it was you. The way you kept coming around. The way you acted. You were so tender to me, much more than you needed to be. I didn't have any hard proof that you killed him, but neither did the police, although they swore to me that you were the one and I should be careful. After you left me for Lisa they called me, just to see how I was doing and to ask if I'd ever told you anything. I said no. I said the most you'd said is that it was awful how David died and you hoped that his killer found justice, somewhere, someday. Even Lisa kind of sensed it; that's what we were laughing about."

Lisa poured Griffin a cup of coffee. "We weren't laughing at you, you have to understand this. We don't know if we love you. You're a shit, a murderous, adulterous shit. But we married you, knowing this. Well, she knew you were a murderer, and I knew you were an adulterer. So what do we have to complain about? Really. We did this too."

Griffin said, "Things are getting better."

. . .

On Monday morning, Alicia told him he could have his own computer, Internet connection, and a phone. Until his own computer arrived she gave him her desktop and replaced that with her laptop.

She had not erased the history from her browser, which went back twenty-one days and was filled with porn. She liked a few Web sites: DoctorTushy.com, Adult Friend Finder, Clips Hunter, Craigslist Casual Encounters. The usual.

This is what has been given me and I am too tired and scared to fight. I will look.

He had an idea, finally, and called Phil Ginsberg, who heard the idea and invited him to the Telluride Group, to make a presentation.

. . .

There was an electric hair dryer on a bracket in the bathroom on Phil Ginsberg's jet, and Griffin switched it on, just to hear the difference between a jet engine and a hair dryer. He had a malicious thought, an uncommonly malicious fantasy, that he would call Greg Swaine and blow the hair dryer toward the phone. He wouldn't tell him, *I'm on the jet, loser,* he would just think it, but a goad to provoking envy comes as standard equipment on these things, and Griffin made a conscious decision to just relax into this arrogance so long as he didn't act on it, because his speech to the group was in two days, and he wanted to rid himself of the impurities of contempt.

He returned to the cabin and watched as the Arizona desert met the mountains of Colorado, and he inhaled the idea of the mountains. Even Ginsberg, on the phone during the flight, had to stop talking when he saw the tall peaks. Griffin wondered if this was a sign of humanity or an instinctual response that signified nothing. He wondered this about both of them.

Telluride sits in a long box canyon, the deep end filled with toxic tailings from the old mines, the highest and most remote aerie of America's hideouts for the rich. The approach to the short runway at the end of the valley demands that the plane turn sharply over the valley and descend quickly in a short space.

· · ·

That night Griffin called Lisa from his suite and told her that he loved her.

"I love you too, Griffin."

"You gave me the encouragement, you pushed me, you loved me enough to push me, and you loved me enough to show me Candace Netter's book, thank you, thank you, which helped me more than I can tell you, because if I hadn't read that book I wouldn't have been able to handle Phil Ginsberg. When he introduces me to the Telluride Group, I almost want to thank his wife for *Sharing His Closet.*"

"That's probably a bad idea."

"It's a terrible idea, I know that, I was just saying. Oh, my God, Lisa. I'm here, I'm finally here. I made it. We made it. We're going to have one of those lives now that people read and dream about. I've had a great life so far but nothing like what we're about to have. I feel blessed. You blessed me. I love you. Anything you want, I will give it to you."

"I just want you to be happy."

"I am happy. I didn't even know what it meant to be happy. I didn't know that happiness is a buffet line with billionaires behind me, just kidding around and making jokes."

"Are there a lot of wives there?"

"Yes. And you'll be here next year."

"What are they wearing?"

"T-shirts that say TELLURIDE."

"Really?"

"Yeah, and jewels so big they have little slave girls from Indonesia holding up their arms."

"Willa wants to say good night."

"Hi, Daddy."

"Willa, love. Willa, Willa, Willa. I'll bring you back here in the winter and we'll go skiing."

"Can I bring a friend?"

"You can bring anyone you want."

"What if they don't want to come with me?"

"Honey . . . Wills. Don't worry about that now."

"But I am worrying about it. What if I invite someone and she doesn't want to come with me?"

"Maybe she won't be able to come because she's got other plans with her own family. You invite someone else, someone who's free."

"Yeah, but—but if I invite my second choice, then maybe I won't have as much fun."

Griffin heard June, in the background, telling Willa to give the phone back to Lisa. Willa said to June, "But I'm not going to have a good time if I ski alone, and I can't invite anybody because I don't have any friends."

June took the phone. "Don't worry, Griff, everything is under control. Kill them tomorrow, we all need it."

"Thanks," said Griffin.

"We love you!" Lisa called out.

. . .

Phil Ginsberg took the microphone. "As the world gets smaller, as resources are dwindling, as the population grows, as the air is warming up, as we face inevitable changes that will mean mass starvation or war or famine or disease, how—to be crude about it—are we going to make lots of money quickly? I asked that question of Griffin, and he's going to tell you what we're doing."

As Griffin walked to the podium, he felt the vast unfolding within himself of greatness, but not the start of a new story, no, finally he saw the eternal truths in the stories he had thought were dead. He saw that he had not been through his own crisis of purification until now, because until he gave the money to Coldwater, he had never taken the great risk called for to truly be a hero. The demon monster, like all demon monsters, had only been himself, his double, distorted by vanity. And now he could see the pattern behind him. June and Lisa were his two comic spirit guides. Ginsberg was his shape-shifting messenger.

The computer was ready for the PowerPoint presentation. He cued for the music, Don Henley singing Leonard Cohen's "Everybody Knows."

"Hi. I'm Griffin Mill. It's an honor to be here. Why do people look at porn? It doesn't matter, but they do and it doesn't go away. There's something in the air. They need it. Porn is bigger than the movies. Porn is where the stories have gone. Porn is in its infancy, and it's time for porn to grow up.

"You all know what pornography looks like. It looks like this: devil women and satanic imagery; it's vulgar and creepy and makes you feel dirty. It's a huge business, we know that. And it's not a well-organized business, we also know that. Some of us here make some money off of porn by holding it at arm's length and not looking closely, cable companies and hotels that have video on demand. The biggest money in porn goes to really sleazy operators in places like the San Fernando Valley, or in Russia for the violent stuff. It's degrading. But—it's part of our lives. We're not going to get rid of it. And what Phil and I are going to do is put together a global production and distribution company to market pornography in a way that's never been attempted. We're talking about higher production values, better scripts, the work of artists that could cross over. David Lynch, for example, is a brilliant pornographer never given full rein. The younger horror directors would be brilliant at porn: the Wachowski brothers of *The Matrix,* for example. Porn is a larger business than movies or video games. It needs global distribution to overwhelm a market that's currently saturated with stuff that, frankly, is put out by various mafias. We will not be that. The ratings system doesn't change. The viewers don't necessarily change except for this: We will advertise, not just to attract business but to win for ourselves the legitimacy that will make government regulation something we can control to our benefit."

Gunther Hitt raised his hand. "I'd like to say something, may I?"

"Of course," said Griffin.

"Are there any journalists in the room? No? Good. You pervert. You sick disgusting pervert. Is this some sort of game out of a college seminar on Genet and Bataille? You took a class in the history of porn at the University of California in Santa Barbara? Is this a sign of cleverness? Phil, will you explain to us, please, what the fuck you had in mind by endorsing such a stupid idea? Don't try, actually. I don't want to know. It's a bad idea, but not for the reasons you think, you stupid fuck."

Griffin had felt the audience's support for the idea and didn't want to back down from a fight. This was his chance; he knew it. "Listen, Gunther, don't you think I thought this through? Don't you

think I was prepared for all the objections? Do you think your objections are original?"

"No, they're not original. That's why I'm voicing them. They're
basic."

"And what's your point, the moral objection of the world?"

"The degradation of the world by bringing the underground
to the surface!" Hitt shouted. "Some things are better left unexpressed. There will be a backlash. And it will come to hurt us. Not
everyone watches dirty movies; it's just that simple. Not everyone
is as sick as you and I are. That's right. I like them too. I like weird
sex, and I have the money and the charisma for any kind of sex I
want. A lot of us in this room are perverts. But I know that my
freedom is not universal. I have to be on guard all the time to be
mindful that my pleasures and my desires are not universal. If I try
to maintain the same posture and air of virtue before people whose
suspicion of my vices I want to suppress, I have no gauge at hand
from which to determine how much the aura of my vices has gradu-
ally segregated me from the normal ways of life. You're asking
for too much. Keep the revenue where it is, from hotels and cable,
and let the Mafia handle production and make the most money.
Don't try to take them over. You want to buy a business from the
Mafia?"

"What's the difference between porn and gambling? We bought
Vegas from the Mafia. Why not buy porn?"

"That's the first good point you've made, but I still say no. We
bought casinos but we surrounded them with hotels, swimming pools,
and magic shows."

"And the family-resort angle failed, so we came up with the advertising line, *What happens here, stays here.* Or maybe it should be *What
happens here, stays here—until you run for public office.* Ha-ha-ha." While

Griffin answered him, he watched Phil Ginsberg leave the room without looking back.

"Don't be a wiseass, Griffin, we're talking about money."

"All right, but what is that campaign about except sex with people you don't know, either for money or for adventure? It's not about losing money at the tables. And it's not about seeing strippers, either. It's about fucking."

"Good answer. But porn is not about fucking. That's what's wrong with it. That's why your idea is bad. You don't understand it. You're at the surface; you put together a few statistics and a banal observation. Yes, it's a big business, and it makes more than Hollywood. So what? Are we supposed to sell cocaine now?"

"Plenty of big banks handle drug money, you know that."

"But the banks don't sell the shit themselves. That's the difference. Your idea is clumsy. I'm disappointed."

Griffin had nothing left to say in defense, because he knew that Hitt was right.

"Thank you, Gunther. Are there any other comments?"

There were none. Griffin left the podium, a dead man.

There had been no comic spirit guides. There had been no purification. No mentor. No double in the mirror. He wasn't even the villain. He was a troll, one of those monsters along the hero's path, who makes a lot of noise at the entrance to his bone-littered cave. Not even that big. He was the nameless bodyguard in the Bond film shot down from the catwalk, one of those deaths that serve as punctuation to a larger action. He was too small for even the villain to know by name, and if there were heroes in the world, the whole meaning of his miserable death was that he was too unimaginative to even know that heroes exist.

He went back to his hotel room and packed. A knock at the

door: Chris Tryon. Griffin let him in. Tryon had a large manila envelope for him.

"Your plane ticket. You're flying out of Grand Junction."

"I shouldn't be so petty about this, but it's kind of crude of him: he brought me here and now he's taking the plane away."

"He took the plane home half an hour ago."

"Who are you, Chris? What are you? What do you do? I don't get it, I don't get you, I just don't know."

"I work for the right people at the right time. I'm a kind of cipher, I know that. It comes from having a small role in the lives of large people, but my role is important. A spy is no one, and I'm not a spy, but I keep my eyes open, and I have a memory, and I have a discerning sense of judgment, and I'm always right, even if I can't say why. I'm right about you. You'll do fine. You just need more information. You haven't had the right life experiences yet. Until today you haven't been disoriented as much as you need to be. Even the fact that you've killed someone—that only helped you for a while."

"I figured they knew. They told you?"

"You've got this backward. I didn't tell them. This is between you and me"—

In the microsecond before Tryon continued his thought, Griffin wondered how Tryon would have known about the murder of David Kahane, but he didn't mean Kahane, he meant Swaine.

—"and Warren Swaine, may he rest in peace, a good peace; he deserves it. Here's the medicine he was reaching for." And out of the envelope Tryon removed a photograph and text, downloaded from the Internet, a picture of Greg Swaine and Elixa, their faces distorted, but not enough to fool anyone who knew them. The picture was taken in a hip hotel room, one of those rooms with gray walls and a good photograph of William Burroughs horsing around with Jack Kerouac.

Beside the photograph, Greg and Elixa were leaning against the wall; he was in a dark suit, she was in tight red latex. They looked like sex. It was their ad on Adult Friend Finders.

```
PERVO_LOIS&CLARK


By day we're part of the crowd, doing our best.
By night we're movie stars. We're new to the Life-
style and we're looking for folks pretty much like
ourselves, sophisticated, friendly and nasty.
We're both bi and very oral. We're looking for
people not just to have sex with but to be friends
with. We're educated and would love to meet others
like us, a bit surprised to be here, but no less
delighted. We're on the West Coast, and while we
don't live in San Francisco we travel there often.
We love discovering new restaurants. Then we like
to go back to a sexy hotel room—like the W—and
fuck our brains out. No (tobacco) smokers, please!
```

"I watched your meeting with Mr. Swaine on a computer in the house—the office had a few hidden cameras—and I saw everything and I heard everything. You thought he had medicine in that drawer, didn't you? That's why you held it closed with your knee. He did have medicine, in the top drawer, but he wanted to show you something that was more important to him than his own life. Powerful stuff, Griffin, you know? He was saying to you, *You don't know a thing about my son.* And all he wanted to do was show you this picture, to explain why he wasn't going to pay for Eli's tuition. Until I saw the picture I thought he was being harsh."

"Why didn't you come in and save him?"

"Because if I had, you wouldn't have been able to send your son to Coldwater as easily as you did, because there wouldn't have been any money for Eli. Right?"

"How did you figure that out?"

"Because you were asking him to pay for his grandson's tuition. I heard everything, Griffin. And then you made your move on Phil. It was a great move too. You took advantage of the situation like you'd planned it. And Swaine was just trying to tell you how much his son disgusted him. Look at the picture. It's not even that bad."

"Can I keep this?" asked Griffin.

"You killed for it, dude. It's yours."

. . .

He took a cab home from LAX. He had to wait in line with tourists and businessmen without limousines to meet them—the loveless, he supposed, people with no one to pick them up. He didn't even know what the cab was going to cost, and that made him sick. He was out. He wasn't even on the way down. It was all over. *This was the name of the ghost: David Kahane. The name of the ghost had always been David Kahane. You can't get away with murder.* His children would end up in public school while Greg Swaine's kids got the trust-fund free ride. Lisa will leave me and take what she can. *My son will hate me. Willa will go insane. Jessa—what will Jessa do? I don't know her. I left her too young.*

He asked the cabdriver to go around the block twice. He didn't care what kind of weird impression he made, but then he thought, *I have to be careful. I may be working with this guy in a few months.* Griffin had the feeling of waking up after a one-night stand, the feeling of having burned a carpet with a cigarette after not smoking for ten years, an important carpet, the carpet of your father's boss, and you fucked his wife on the carpet and it was her cigarette and you'd taken one drag and choked and dropped the cigarette, and you're so drunk you pass out and then in the morning you wake up naked on the carpet, your father's boss's wife snoring beside you, and her husband wakes you up with a kick to your ribs. That's not a good feeling, and it was all that Griffin knew.

• • •

He didn't push the doorbell because he didn't want the children to rush up to him in their automatic enthusiasm for his return. He was sure that if he looked at himself in a mirror he would see his dissolution, something he wanted to hide from his children at least for a few minutes longer, and protect himself from the sudden retreat of their happiness on seeing him, as their fear of the changes in their father confused them.

• • •

He went into the house he shared with Lisa and the first voice he heard was June's, calling up the stairs to tell Jessa to finish her homework. Willa heard him and came out of the dining room to give him a hug. Lisa followed, but saw, looking at his eyes, that the trip had failed.

"You're home early. I thought you were coming back in three days."

"I don't want to talk right now." He patted Willa, knowing he owed her more, left his bag in the hall, and went upstairs. He could hear Ethan listening to music and went in. He didn't knock on Ethan's door.

Ethan slouched on his bed, surrounded by posters and stickers.

"I thought you were coming back after the weekend."

"I finished what I had to do."

"How did it go?"

"I failed you, Ethan. I'm sorry. I don't know what to tell you except, I don't know, learn Chinese. That's it. Learn Chinese and study something real, like engineering, and you should also learn something practical and basic, like plumbing, just in case."

"What are you talking about, Dad?"

"The end of the world as we know it."

"I hate that song. REM is your generation, not mine. My generation has hope."

"Why?"

"Because your generation grew up with the fantasy that things were getting better. That's fucked up."

"Is that why the movies don't work anymore? The three-act structure is based on the idea that things will change?"

"I don't know. Some movies are good."

"But I don't mean some movies, I mean *the movies*, as this cultural thing. Solve the crime, win the game. That's not really change, is it? I mean in story terms. The CSI shows. Nothing changes. Guilt is found out. That's not a story, is it? Not in the old sense. Marriage, that's a story."

"Dad, what can I do to help you?"

Griffin hugged his son, because Ethan had never looked at him and shown Griffin that he was seen whole. "You can see how bad things are with me, can't you?"

"All of you. You and Mom and Lisa and Willa, everyone except Jessa. Mom? Wow, let me show you something."

Ethan sat up and went to the computer. He typed in a Web site, ICARRYMYLIFE.blogspot.com. It was just a standard green blog page and the author of the blog called herself JB.

The most recent entry, a few days old, said:

Here's something I've been thinking about doing for a long time, and now I've done it. I may have only two readers in the whole wide world, but they helped me. Thank you, guys, I love you! I was going to have a link here to the posting, but you'd still need a password, so here it is, straight from the personals on Nerve.

The previous entry was her first.

HOW DO YOU CARRY YOUR LIFE?

I carry mine badly these days. If I could write a novel about it I would. But right now I can't because I can't stop seeing that my ex was cruel to me and he's in a mess because he did horrible things that he might not be able to heal. Really horrible. The worst. And I have to help him, at the same time, to help the children. This disgusts me. And then I think, no, I am an adult. He did what he did, I have done what I did. I have to find a way to help.

I like the blogosphere because no one knows who you are, so you can be yourself in a sea of other selves. This feels to me like a regression to something beautiful and primordial. I like the way the blog entries are stacked, not even backwards, but down. It's sedimentary. Sentimental sediment, all the way down to the bedrock, a long cylinder of memories. Someday in the future, there are going to be computer programs that sift through the blogs the way geologists and biologists today read the history of the natural world through the pollen embedded in the layers of glaciers and river bottoms, and the programs will track the changing world through the simultaneous deposits of digitized human emotion. They'll see the broad strata like the layers at the Grand Canyon, or like tree rings. They'll find out the deep patterns of emotion, like which years saw the worst lovers, which saw the advance of tenderness and mercy, which years contained the richest silt of love, which years were nothing but disasters of frustration and fear, the years of increased friendships and connections, the years that men turned away from real women, the years that men came back, and so on and so on and so on.

And this is only the beginning of what they'll do. They will measure the layers against history and weather, they will understand the connections between political leadership and human emotion, global warming and group sex, massacre and plague and jealousy and acid rain and cyclones and the rise of divorce. The scientists and specialists will argue among themselves about cause and effect, but they will have a way to connect the physical record with the emotional record, the record of human stories with the record of animal extinction. Perhaps they'll find that human emotion changed the weather, that it wasn't just carbon dioxide that caused global warming, but something else,

```
something powerful inside the heart, the human
heart.
    I know what happened this year. This year
everything fell apart.
```

"This is your fault, Dad." And then Ethan surprised himself by slamming the door on his father and running downstairs. He went to the kitchen and pulled down the pots and pans hanging from the rack.

. . .

While Griffin was in Ethan's room, Lisa helped Willa with an old homework assignment she hadn't finished at school, a crayon copy of the Duc de Berry's illustrated manuscript *Book of Hours,* a typical Children's Lincoln assignment, contrived to flatter cash out of the wealthier grandparents who held their children in contempt for having rejected the sophistication taught at home, where they grew up with expensive limited-edition copies of Renaissance art, instead of coffee-table books like *The Art of The Lord of the Rings* and *Hip Hotels.* June was worried about Lisa's short fuse with Willa after Griffin had come into the house in such a low mood, and whatever Ethan was doing in the kitchen now could only be as an alarm to summon his mother, but she had promised Maya Hernandez to protect Willa, and Ethan would have to wait or come out to find her.

Willa drew blackbirds in her blue sky, too many, until this batswarm representation of her turmoil became a cloud that ate the sun, and Lisa, afraid of anyone's opinion of the obvious significance of this symbol, could find no other way to ask Willa to work on another section of the page than to say, "Honey, over here, in the sky? Those birds are getting kind of busy, do you know what I mean?

You don't want anyone to look at this beautiful page and then look up here at the birds and think, hmmm, that's kind of sloppy."

Willa threw her crayon across the room. Lisa could see the tantrum rise triumphantly through her daughter like Jerry Lewis announcing a telethon fund-raising record.

"I'm not being *soppy*. I'm doing the best I can."

June heard the dropped consonant bounce from the floor to the ceiling and then ricochet around the room, a Daffy Duck *sproing.*

Compelled by who knows what kind of ancestral will to doom, Lisa said, "Sloppy."

"That's what I said."

"You said *soppy.*" Lisa ripped the book and wailed at June, "I can't do this! I can't do this anymore!" And she ran out of the room.

June sat quickly beside Willa. "Your mom is tired. Let's let her get a glass of water, and while she drinks it you and I can start this drawing over again. You can draw it any way you want. And if you want me to help you, all you have to do is ask."

Willa picked up the black crayon. "I'm going to draw the birds."

"Do you want to draw the sky first?"

"No. I'm going to draw the birds. See? This is a bird. And this is another bird. And these are birds: all of these are birds."

. . .

"What are you doing on the floor?" Lisa asked Ethan, when she found him in the kitchen, surrounded by stockpots, saucepans, two roasting pans, five ceramic mixing bowls in five colors, and every bag or box of anything dry from the pantry—flour, sugar, salt, kosher salt, uncooked pinto beans, uncooked long-grain brown rice, uncooked organic basmati rice, muesli, Jell-O, dried wasabi, dried chickpeas, Special K, Cocoa Puffs, bags of whole coffee beans,

Starbucks House Blend, Starbucks Decaf French Roast—and he was emptying each of the bags into the pots, pouring one variety of grain and legume on top of the next until level with the top, and then above, making a little Vesuvius that fell under the weight of the stream. He had put the empty bags into the garbage.

"What is everybody screaming about in the living room?"

"That I'm a bad mother. Basically. Why are you here?"

"Because my father is a bad father."

"But that's probably how it looks to you because, if you look at it, why you're really here is because I'm a bad mother. Willa and I wouldn't need your mother here tonight if I were a good mother. I hit her."

"There's worse things."

"I don't want to think about them."

"Sometimes parents do things they think no one knows about."

"Like what?"

"I don't know."

"You have to be thinking of something, otherwise you wouldn't have said that."

"Never mind."

"You're going to have to throw all that out. It costs a lot of money."

"What does all this cost, a hundred dollars? More or less?"

"Something like that, although you'd be surprised at how quickly it all adds up when you check it out at the supermarket. It could be a hundred and seventy-five dollars, right there. That's a lot of money."

"Not really. And even if it is, so what? My father is rich."

"Not really."

"Does he have more than a million dollars in the bank?"

"I don't know."

"Yes, you do."

"I don't know how much he has, not really."

"You know; I know you know. You have to know."

"Do you know?"

"Yes, because my mother told me."

"So why ask me?"

"To see if you'd be honest with me."

"There's a difference between honesty and telling a child something he doesn't really need to know."

"Never mind."

"Did your father get mad at you for something?"

"Could I be alone, please? Could I just be alone?"

"I came in here for a drink of water."

"So get your water and leave me alone."

"That's not a nice way to talk to me."

"Are you going to hit me too?"

Lisa kicked a frying pan filled with white rice, then a six-quart stockpot filled with coffee beans, flour, and muesli. Bound by the heavy flour, a delta of the grains and beans sprayed across the floor in streaked layers like tailings from the mine in Telluride.

"Clean it up, Ethan." Forgetting to pour a glass of water, Lisa left the kitchen, slammed the door of the empty maid's room, and knelt on the floor beside the sofa, thinking about pills, many pills, how many it would take to die.

. . .

Jessa heard the screaming, the slamming, and the pots and pans. Her mother and father would never know of Jessa's hatred of them. She hated Lisa too, hated them all without knowing yet the words to define the nuance of her contempt, more like a vibration she could align with. She will find others like her in a few years, in high school, and more of them in college and after—the ones who don't complain, the quiet ones, the ones who don't cheat, the ones who make their own beds—and what they will do when they arrive together with language, mind, memory, instinct, education, ambition, and hatred—hatred for their divorced parents, hatred for their badly married parents who suffered in silence or noise for the sake of their children, hatred for their angry fathers and crazy mothers, hatred for the alcoholics and hatred for the parents in recovery, hatred for the ugly rich and hatred for their lackeys—they might just stand their parents against a wall and fire when ready, fire at will, fire until they empty the guns and then reload and fire again. They might. They probably will. They probably should. Jessa knows this, not in words.

. . .

Ethan, lying face down on the floor, gritty like a desert highway after a sandstorm, waved a hand without looking up. After Lisa walked out, Ethan emptied all the spice jars on the floor. His face was powdered yellow with turmeric, on his lips a black crust of poppy seeds.

. . .

Griffin heard the noise downstairs, and June, calling him.

Jessa heard her father, on the stairs, call for Lisa. June called out for Jessa. She opened her door. "Yes, Mother."

"Would you be with Willa for a bit?"

"Yes. Come on up, Willa."

"Thank you, hon. Willa, why don't you go up to your sister and just be with her for a bit?"

. . .

Griffin and June walked to the maid's room through the mess, rice and cereal creaking like icy snow. Neither had anything to say to Ethan. The photograph of June rising from the swimming pool and kissing Jessa, through the camera was held by a magnet to the refrigerator door.

Lisa asked for a glass of water. Griffin waited for June to say, "I'll get it," or "Griffin, would you?" but instead June said, "You know where the glasses are."

Lisa went for the water and Ethan waved at her as he had waved to his parents, and Lisa said, "Hey."

. . .

June sat on the floor, looking up at Griffin and Lisa on the couch.

"We have a very bad situation right now."

"I'm sorry, June."

"This is not the time to apologize for murdering my boyfriend in cold blood, Griffin. That's the easy way out of your problems, it's always been the easy way out. That's why you married me."

"That's why he married me too," said Lisa. "Because it was easier for him to get divorced and me pregnant than for him to look you in the eye and make love to you, but now he can't even make love to me."

"And that's not important now either," said June. "The only thing that matters is that we have three children in the house and they all need both of their parents. The sofa opens up to a bed. I'm going to tell you what I've been thinking. And I'm going to say some things that sound weird, but it's the only way. First of all, I believe that you can never get divorced. Once you've been married, you're married forever. When you get legally divorced, the altar cries because it knows the pain you're facing. The souls are bound together; the flesh and spirit grow together. That's what children are for, to prove in flesh the bonding of the souls. But I also believe that when you get divorced and you remarry, then that's a real marriage too. God hears the vow—don't interrupt me—God hears the vow and accepts the vow and blesses the vow. So we're stuck with a big problem. Griffin, you're married to me and you're married to Lisa, and Lisa and I are sort of married to each other because of that, because we both carried your children, half of us is in your children and half of you, and in some way that I can't explain, Lisa and I mix together because of that. It's the reason for divorce being so painful. You're tearing the spirit, which won't be torn without screaming, and it keeps trying to grow back. We have to live together. We have to live under one roof. Griffin, Lisa, listen to me. Willa will never feel safe with you, Lisa, not completely; she needs protection, and I'm the only one who gives it to her, me and Jessa. And Ethan needs his father—that's all—and not just a few days a week. He needs to see his father become a man. You're not a man yet, Griffin, not even with blood on your hands. Do you understand me? I'm not asking you to just live under the roof, do you understand where I'm going with this? I'm lonely. I haven't been fucked hard in so long I can't remember."

"Neither can I," said Lisa.

June applauded. "Then you know a little bit of what I feel, but not all of it, because you may not get fucked, but you do get cuddled, a man holds you in his arms at night, or you roll over in bed and put one hand on his head and your other hand on his hip and a foot between his feet and a knee against his knee, and you hold him for your own comfort. A man doesn't know what that feels like to a woman, the pure animal security of that feeling, the friendship with a man when you know more about him than he knows about you, and you know he's a better man than he knows."

"There's more to it than that," said Lisa. "When he's asleep you can hold the man you want him to be, and if you breathe with him and into him with enough love, he'll absorb your love and be stronger for it. We know this isn't true, and men don't understand the love we give them, but we try anyway."

"But we sometimes fail them too," said June. "And I've been thinking about this. In what department of marriage do we fail them the most? We fail our men by not holding them accountable. This is tricky because I don't mean responsibility; that's a category that doesn't need explanation, and it's the category by which the men fail us when they don't do the work they owe us. Men have duties they owe their women. And we have duties we owe them. But our failure to hold them accountable means that we know our men keep a secret ledger of their lives, and by not helping them with the balance, the marriage falls into moral and romantic bankruptcy. That's the beginning of hatred and divorce. Accountability means time. What they do with their time, when they use time secretly, and we close our eyes. We just try to force our way through. Most marriages are like the Little Engine That Could, huffing and puffing up the hill to a golden anniversary. But half the trains get uncoupled, because they just can't pull the weight anymore, and instead of blaming the worn-out engines, we blame the drivers. I'm happy for the marriages between people who earned their love for each other, but the three of us don't have that, not yet. The three of us failed at marriage. Lisa failed at marriage when she fucked a married man, and then when she hit her child. Griffin failed at marriage because he didn't marry for love, he married out of guilt and fear."

"I loved you."

"How do you know? Because you got a hard-on around me? Because my skin is smooth? Because I let you fuck me in the ass more than once? Because I pushed you around a little and you liked it? Because I slapped you sometimes? Because you took me to Cannes? Because I went with you to the Oscars? Because you bought me a BMW? You must have loved me, because otherwise why would you buy me a BMW? That's the way most of the guys around here know they love their wives, by how much shit they buy them and how big a suite they get at the Four Seasons on Maui. Or did you love me because you gave me children and then left me for Lisa?

"And I failed at marriage because I couldn't find another husband, and I tried. I debased myself and I tried. I made a fool of myself, a schmuck of myself, if you want to know. You can't believe what I went through. But the only good was, and I'm going to tell you this so you understand everything, I found the one true American God, and his angel, Moroni, as introduced to me by two girls, Shifra from New Zealand and Puah from Idaho. They were named for the first two women mentioned in Exodus, the midwives who saved the life of baby Moses. If I hadn't gone to Park City with this disaster of a man, I wouldn't be saying this now. There wasn't any one thing wrong with him, but nothing was right. There must be twenty million men like this guy. Lisa, you have someone to talk to and watch the news with. You have someone to pick up something you need on his way home from work. You have a grown-up in the house. I don't. And I had two children with you, Griffin. I tried to find another man but I couldn't, and I never will. Not a good man, not a bad man, no man. I have two kids and I don't bring much more to the table than that. I look good enough, but I'm forty-two and I'm not rich. I need you just as much as Lisa needs you. And Lisa needs you just as much as I need you. In every way."

She stopped talking and took the glass of water from Lisa and drank what remained. Lisa refilled the glass from the bathroom sink instead of going back into Ethan's disaster in the kitchen.

"We're going to live together, the three of us. You're going to sell both houses, and get one big house with an apartment above a detached garage, and that's where I'm going to live. And when the children are all grown and in college, we'll have linked bedrooms in the main house. We'll remodel so we can have that."

Griffin needed clarification. "Do you mean we're going to fuck each other?"

June lifted a hand and tilted the palm to Lisa, who said, "We'll have to, at least once, to get it out of the way. And if we like it, we'll do it again."

"But the point of this," said June, "isn't group sex, the point is the children. You'll have your public life together. I can live without a public social life if I have to, for the children."

"But you're talking about a private life with us, and the children will see us in bed together."

"No," said June. "Some things can't be changed, and you'll wake up with Lisa. But there will be some nights when you come to me or I come to you. And there will be nights when you and I have the kids, nights when you and Lisa have them, and we can take turns just going out to the movies or doing whatever we want to do."

"Fucking included?"

"Yes. That's the point. This is it. This is the solution. This is the answer to the dilemma of the modern marriage. This is the accountability. You want to fuck, and we want our children to have fathers. We can pretend that men follow the rules and don't fuck around and then, when they do, punish them as though that's a singular offense. So there we have it. We can lie to ourselves or we can admit that only a few men are really faithful to one woman. Most want it, and what they want they get, or try to get."

Griffin said, "It's late. The kids have school tomorrow. Let's put them to bed. We'll clean the kitchen later. What a mess."

Thirteen

Two years later, the second week of July, and Gunther Hitt finishes his introduction: "Our friend, our colleague, our leader, our genius, Griffin Mill." Griffin is a few joyful weeks from his fifty-fourth birthday, his life extended by the applause for him as he walks to the lectern in front of the big projection screen. He has $750 million—all in one stock, that's true, but the Initial Public Offering price was $15 a year ago and today, at the market's opening, the price was $48. At the end of the meeting, when he finishes his presentation, the fund managers and investment bankers in the room, the stock analysts for brokerage houses, and the financial reporters for the newspapers and news channels will all have seen the future, and they will recommend that investors buy before the stock goes to $70. The company has no debt and a growing community of subscribers. Phil Ginsberg now has a little more than $2.3 billion; Gunther Hitt has even more. In gratitude, Ginsberg has bought Griffin a private jet for $25 million and, as he said, "for the heck of it," is paying the fuel bill for two years. In an hour, after Griffin finishes his talk, he'll meet his two wives and three children, plus a big fluffy dog, at the Telluride airport and fly to his island.

"It's great to be here with all of you. We're happy today. We should be. And we're going to be happier, once I show you Only Connect Release Two. But as I lead you through the new design, I want you to remember that it's human loneliness that makes us so successful. There's a big word we make fun of too often, *alienation*, but it's the modern condition. Let's face it. Most of us are trapped in jobs we don't like—if we have jobs—in careers over which we have no control, in a service economy that requires perpetual numbing belligerent happiness. Most of us feel like shit. Most of us hate ourselves and can't imagine anyone loving us. This even happens in most of our marriages. But the human heart, the soul, the flesh, they all cry out for contact. This is natural, and yet most of us live in solitary confinement, surrounded by a billion others in the same condition. This isn't true for everyone; we know that. Some of us are blessed. But for the rest, all we want is to connect, only connect.

"Two years ago, people, some of you in this room, said, It can't work. OnlyConnect can't work because every Internet service provider already has a dating program, and there's also Craigslist, and Lavalife, and Nerve.com, and Match.com, and Jdate, and so on. We said, We have a new idea. Those of you who bet on us were right. We knew we were right.

"Now I'm going to take you through the new OnlyConnect. I'm going to show you what we've changed, now that technology has finally been able to deliver full-screen streaming video. So look at the monitor."

With a keypad and mouse on the podium, Griffin clicks on the OnlyConnect icon.

"OnlyConnect is already the most successful relationships-and-romance portal in the history of the Internet, and we've achieved that status with what, until today, has been a standard interface, pages of head shots beside biographical text. All of that is about to change. This is big news and I'm announcing it here.

"Part one: OnlyConnect has acquired the W Hotels group. W Hotels is a large chain where each hotel provides a level of high design that feels personal, a hotel that, without embarrassment and without being coy, promises sex and discretion and, more than that, surroundings that are so perfect that everyone looks beautiful. The secret is cinematic lighting. I come from Hollywood, so I know how lighting is sometimes everything; if the lighting is right you can look like a movie star and be someone that others will fall in love with. That's what we want here, not just for people to meet and screw—there's plenty of that on the Internet—we want a site that encourages love and commitment. A site that encourages honesty. And we have it. Look at the monitors. You're looking at a hotel lobby. You see people coming and going. Each one of those moving figures onscreen that looks so real is a computer graphic representation of an OnlyConnect member. So now I can announce Part Two: OnlyConnect has signed an exclusive joint partnership with Pixar Animation Studios and our good friends at Starbucks Coffee.

"Watch the monitors. What you see is the first of two thousand reconfigured Starbucks outlets. Eventually we'll have kiosks like this in every mall in the world. The world! Fifteen thousand kiosks is what we're expecting to install. They're simple to run, as you can see. Watch the model, that's Gavin Whalley, our head of customer service. Gavin is walking into the OnlyConnect booth at a Starbucks —this is actually the original Starbucks in Seattle—and he's standing in front of a green screen. Here you see the trained OnlyConnector placing twenty-five reflective disks on Gavin's face and body. This is the same technique that the genius director Peter Jackson used to endow King Kong with such brilliant emotions. Now you see Gavin follow a few simple directions, raising and lowering his arms, turning around, smiling, frowning, making a happy face and an angry face, and laughing. Then we record his voice, first his speaking voice, reading the beautiful sonnet "How do I love thee? Let me count the ways . . ." and then singing "Jingle Bells." The combination of both reading and speaking voices gives the avatar tremendous warmth. All the data are entered into the computer, and presto! the new member of the community now has his personal avatar, the member's online physical representation. As you can see, the computer graphic detail is pretty damn lifelike. Ready for love, or ready for adventure.

"So, watch the monitor. Home page. The hotel. Your avatar is ready. Look at it. All those other avatars you see in the street and coming and going into the hotel are the avatars of members of our community online right now, in real time. Look at the quality of that image. In the beginning of the computer era, it was the military, it was atomic war, that pushed the computer into advanced technology. And then it was the entertainment industry, the military entertainment complex, if you will, that pushed the computer into greater speed and capacity. And now—well, now it's love. It's love that drives the quality of those graphics; the believability of their movements and expressions is at the very highest advanced state of the art. There is nothing available to surpass what we have developed for OnlyConnect. The avatars on screen look like people, move like people, and talk like people.

"Now, a quick demonstration of the basic plot. You see these people crossing the lobby. You click on whoever interests you and follow that person out of the lobby to what we call the Lounge. And whoever you're interested in takes you to the lounge of their sexual affinity or their romantic dream.

"There's Friends Lounge, for people who aren't looking for something as dramatic as love, they just want someone to see movies and hang out with. Men and women together; it's very loose. Then, of course, there's Dating Lounge. We tried different names but they seemed a bit forced—Love Lounge, Romance Lounge, there was too much pressure in those names for the hotel guests to succeed. Dating is a pretty neutral word; it is what it is. Then there's the Lesbian Lounge and the Gay Lounge, for lesbians and gay men; there's Alternate Lounge, for BDSM, transgendered people, and we've made it a bit Goth, just to be playful. And then there's Couples Lounge. We're not calling it Swingers Lounge or Lifestyles Lounge because we find those words a little too—can I say, seventies? You know? And this is the future, not the disco past. And then we have the national minority lounges: India Lounge, Latin Lounge, and so on. These can be developed as subscribers look for ethnicity; the categories expand as subscribers define themselves according to whatever labels they want to use. This can be a hotel of a thousand lounges.

"Now, the person you follow from the lobby continues into the lounge and you are met by the Host or Hostess, and this changes randomly, so we're not guilty of sexism. Men and women can be met by either gender. Now we're in the Dating Lounge. If you're looking for BDSM, we've got a big old leather man who won't tell you his name, to give you the grilling—I like the way he says, 'I ask all the questions, bitch'—and for the couples we have a host and hostess couple, Troy and Heidi. Troy and Heidi are forty years old, both carry a little extra weight, and they're dressed by Land's End, no gold chains, no leering, a committed couple who love each other and want to preserve their marriage but not kill themselves by squelching all desire. They do not ask you what you're looking for. Instead, they propose their own introductions, because that's the scariest question of all, isn't it? *'What are you looking for?'* And that's where OnlyConnect broke the old mold. At all the other relationships sites it was on the questionnaire—What you are looking for, What do you dislike, What are your turn ons, What are your turn offs?—compose a little self-serving statement about yourself and hope for the best, and don't fuck too many strangers and lose your self-respect or get that bad aura of the unhappily promiscuous. OnlyConnect developed the patent for Transparency. We said, 'Throw away the questionnaire; don't ask the member any questions at all.' None. We make one demand: Disable anything on your computer that blocks our access to your cookies and to your Web-browsing history and favorites. We said, We'll ask one question, the one question that can give us the answer to all questions. And that question is, 'What is your social security number?' And millions of people out there said, Here, here is my social security number. They gave us permission to do a complete search of their lives, everything, their credit cards, their phone bills, the books they buy from Amazon, movies they rent from Netflix, the shows they TiVo, flowers they buy, when and for whom, medical records, speeding tickets, library fines, long-distance calls, pornographic chat lines, charitable deductions, the percentage you leave as tips, all of it, you name it, whatever your social security card can unlock, we unlock. And then, beyond geography and a few basic parameters, we don't ask who you're looking for or what you're looking for, because the divorce rate in Western civilization is proof that most of us don't know! With Transparency, we can make some amazing suggestions about the people you should meet, the people you're really looking for, and they're not the ones you're likely to meet on any of the other sites, because the questions on those sites are guaranteed to do nothing but create a narcissistic ideal, impossible to meet, instead of introducing you to a flesh-and-blood person (or persons), who link to you through interests, hobbies, health issues, education, and favorite books and records. And then, adding some spice to it, we make suggestions about people you might like to meet who don't quite fit the profile but could.

"That's the heart of it, because the more you allow the host to know about you, the better the host can find who or what you're looking for. So on any given visit, the Host or Hostess asks you where you want to go, in real life, what city, how far you're willing to travel, and then does the rest.

"Now let's stroll back to the Dating Lounge and go through a typical introduction. We'll be a thirty-seven-year-old woman, a single mom with two kids, because she's hard to find someone serious for, and she wants to get married.

"By the way, a twenty-five-year-old graduate of Arizona State who majored in business administration, spent most of her time on the cheerleading squad, and just moved to New York as a researcher for MTV and is just looking for a hunky guy—she isn't hard to find matches for. Our research tells us she wants a New York City fire-fighter. Also by the way, anyone in uniform—firefighters, police officers, members of the Armed Forces—get a fifteen-percent dis-count for joining the community; I knew you'd like that.

"Okay, so, our thirty-seven-year-old woman. Call her Pamela. Pamela enters the Dating Lounge and the Hostess, Becky, asks if she wants to stay local or travel. Pamela says she wants local today. Becky says, "Let me go see who's here," and in all of about ten seconds Becky comes back and leads Pamela through the lounge. Now you go through the lounge and here's where we had another of our really genius inspirations: The lounge is a party, there's men and women mingling, chatting, there's laughter, music, the sound of drinks be-ing refilled—unless of course you go to the Sober Living party, where there's laughter but it's gentler, and instead of mixed drinks we serve coffee and tea; you hear the sound of porcelain mugs being set down, not ice rattling in a glass.

"When Pamela enters, some of them look at her; she's being checked out. Now every man there is someone with an identity. If Pamela is also into women, everyone at the party is potentially a date, but if she's into couples, she has to go back to the lobby and find her way to Heidi and Troy. Okay, so she touches the shoulder of this

guy or that, and then she finds out who he is. If he's talking to another woman he tells that woman "Excuse me" and turns. The Jeremy figure on the screen is talking to another woman. When I move
the cursor to his shoulder and click on it, he says, "Excuse me," to
the woman and turns to face Pamela. And that's Jeremy's voice. Listen to him."

*"I'm Jeremy, I'm thirty-five, and I'm looking for more than love for myself, I'm
looking for love for my children too. I have to say that up front, because I've been on the
dating scene for a few years now and I'm tired of the games. My children are learning-
challenged. I'm looking for someone who has a lot of patience and also doesn't mind that
I slept with a lot of women and I have herpes. Are you real? I'm an aviation law
attorney, I don't make a fortune, but I know how to have a good time. I like to hike,
fish, and camp, but I also like to check out the latest art at the local galleries, and I really
love gourmet food, so if you like to cook, I like to eat. I'm living a sober life, one day at
a time, but I don't insist on having a sober partner. I have to say all this because I don't
want to waste your time. I'm a real person. Oh, and I'm also very physical, and that's
an important part of life for me, being able to express myself when words are not enough.
I take a blood-pressure drug, and I've had a hair transplant. I've wasted time in the
past because I lied about myself. Now I'm being honest. Enough about me. Who are
you? How do you carry your life? What's your social security number?"*

And now Pamela answers.

*"Hi, Jeremy, I'm Pamela. I'm thirty-seven. I also have sole custody of two
children: Ryan, nine, and Kersti, fourteen. Kersti just came back from a tough love
academy in Baja California and she's fine. I know how hard it is to raise children
alone, and I know how hard it is to raise a child who is challenged. And I have
herpes too. We should definitely talk about this. Maybe we can meet for coffee and
look at some art together. I like that you like art, because I spent three thousand two
hundred eighty-seven dollars and fifteen cents on art last year. I'm not much of an*

outdoors person, but I'd love to try, if you'll show me how. I had knee surgery and I wear shoes that are different sizes. I'm old-fashioned, I came back to Prozac after switching to Effexor, which is like going back to Coke Classic, if you know what I mean. I've had a few bad relationships, because no one was honest. I'm being honest. That's how I carry my life."

"Isn't that better than five first dates and the same old story that tastes like stale toast every time you hear yourself telling it? People are looking for connection in the world. We want to meet them at the center of their confused emotions, and the only way to find any happiness in life is by being honest. That's what we want. We're tired of our secrets—and they come out anyway. Privacy is dead. Get over it. So let's see past the sins and crimes to the heart. If you'll walk into the next room, we have fifty terminals set up, for private experiences with OnlyConnect. Enjoy yourselves. If you want to find the happiness you're missing, just answer one single question. What's your social security number?"

Griffin walks off the podium to a standing ovation. They come to him, surround him, shake his hand, tell him what a great thing he has here, tell him how excited they are, tell him that this is something they've never seen before, and he thanks them.

Phil Ginsberg holds up his hand like a school crossing guard, threatening the cautious driver who has already seen the children, and, without saying more, leads his partner to the door.

"Griffin, thank you. Thank you for coming into my life. Really. I was looking for money and what did I find? I found something good, I found a person who was good. And I didn't know that kind of shit matters, it never did before, but there's something about you, Griffin, I don't know what it is, maybe it's just wisdom, but you know something about the world. You've grown up. You're a different man from when I met you."

"Phil, you're embarrassing me, but I think I know what you mean. And the truth is, I didn't like who I was. Now I'm learning to like who I am. But don't tell anyone I said that."

"Griffin, I won't do anything you don't want me to do."

The two men hug, the money hug, solid grip on each other's shoulders, but backs arched away so they can look each other in the eye, equality, fraternity, and lots and lots of cash. Griffin says good-bye and leaves for the airport.

Fourteen

Griffin has a sixteen-million-dollar house on Martha's Vineyard, nineteen acres overlooking Squibnocket Pond. He shares his cove with a guy who made a fortune on Nortel and Global Crossing, selling early, so Griffin in spite of his own larger pile, can't help but hate him, like he's some kind of Argentinean dirty war criminal who got away with general amnesty, not that Squibnocket Pond is where the Enron pensioners who lost it all could go for a protest parade; they'd be stopped at the ferry.

But the Vineyard is not the haven Griffin used to dream of. He has that too, an island he owns with Phil Ginsberg in the Fijian chain, five square miles with a jet strip: one stop to refuel from fuel tanks hidden in Hawaii and then it's on to safety when they need it, *if* they need it. Hidden beneath the houses that he and Ginsberg built for themselves, on a bluff above mean high tide (should the polar ice cap melt within the next thirty-five years) are bunkers filled with food and weapons. So he doesn't need the Vineyard's illusions of island omnipotence, he needs the perfection that only wealth in New England in the summer can give, the true northern religion, not air and mood but cash and air and mood, cash and résumé, cash and the Ivy League, cash and who you come from, who you know. Griffin isn't Ivy League, and on Martha's Vineyard no amount of cash levels that part of the social balance, even if you own a big house, even if you give a ton of dough to the Nature Conservancy, but his children will go where they want, even Willa, because they're smart and because Griffin knows the right people.

Griffin likes the ponds near Menemsha, where he sails a small boat with his children, Jessa especially. He's building a three-hundred-foot schooner in Holland, and he keeps four boats in the ponds, a thirty-five-foot picnic boat with huge twin engines, for fuck-them-all speed and exuberance and overnight visits to anyplace within two hundred miles; a twenty-eight-foot modern version of a classic New England day sailer, which he takes into Narragansett Bay when the wind pipes up; and a sixteen-and-a-half-foot sloop for Wednesday afternoon races. June and Lisa share a Boston Whaler, a simple shallow-draft outboard, although theirs is equipped for ocean navigation, but they never do more with the boat then cruise slowly around the ponds to visit friends. Everyone knows that the three are living together as man and wife and wife. The children are just darling, so who's to say they're wrong?

At night the three of them close the door on the world and play their bedtime games. Griffin has no sexual fantasies anymore, only memories and plans. Sometimes June plays the role of a NASA scientist measuring Lisa for a space suit. Sometimes Lisa is a gynecologist demonstrating the conductivity of a gel used for electro-cardiograms with sensors placed in the cervix. Sometimes Griffin is a fifteen-year-old boy picked up in Central Park and taken home by two nuns who want an orgy. Sometimes June asks Lisa, "Will it bother you if Griffin fucks me?" Lisa likes to watch. Sometimes they just roll around and giggle. There are days of jealousy and resentment; there are days of quiet gratitude.

They taught him to kiss, and he learned to be gentle; he learned, from watching and from their encouragement and chastisement, how to make love like a woman and still be the man a woman wants and needs. Only this summer do they really, finally, see their future together. At night he holds them both, loving them differently and equally.

An invitation comes from the Rhines, across the pond. He's a real estate guy who bought old malls and fixed them up. It's an interesting invitation, the Rhine boy was marine ROTC at Penn, and Hillary Clinton is inducting him into the marines. It's a weird kind of event on this island, but the Rhines are New Yorkers and Hillary's the New York senator and they give her a lot of money for her campaigns, and it's a marine custom that the senator from your home state can induct you wherever you are, so the Rhines have invited a couple of hundred people who would come to their house anyway, because why not? It's a beautiful home and they have a great view and they're rich and they serve great food, but underneath a canopy to keep the sun off, this boy of privilege is going to be inducted by Hillary Clinton, surrounded by a U.S. Marine honor guard, and of course, Bill Clinton is tagging along. The Clintons make it to Martha's Vineyard a few times each summer, and they take turns being houseguests among their friends, and tonight they're not with the Rhines, but what difference does it make? None.

Griffin wants to ride the Boston Whaler across the pond, but for the Clintons' security they have to go in the car. So Griffin and Lisa and June drive over to the Rhines, show their invitation to the Secret Service guys and are passed along to the valet, and then they walk down the flagstone path and around the house to the broad lawn.

Griffin could not decide if this is vulgar or beautiful, dress blues in the garden of an eight-million-dollar house, but he is impressed by a son of wealth, in a time of war, who chooses dangerous service. The other parents around him on the lawn surely stumble through their confused impressions. They feel glee for achieving an invitation to such a cool event yet contain their electric satisfaction; for most of them this is better than fucking. They also contend with envy and respect for the parents of a courageous son, braver than their own, willing to die for their protection, which opens the door to dread for their own children, cultured and weak. Who among them has ever suggested to their Zeke and their Josh, their Sarah and their Kristen, their Thom and their Amelia, that any *patria* is worth *mori*? This may be a disgusting country, thought Griffin, with cancer in the water and starving babies near the railroad, but who among us isn't here because the country let us, or even our grandparents, work hard and win a seat at the table for our own merits? Even Clinton walked here from Dogpatch. We own the American Dream, we have reached the point where our lives cost us basically nothing, and only one family among us accepts that their letter of gratitude for opportunity and choice might come home in a coffin.

Griffin watches the honor guard laughing with Clinton. This man had been hated by the military for dodging the Vietnam draft, but the young marines are so relaxed and happy with him that they look ready to fight for his return to the Oval Office. This is a man who loves people, thinks Griffin, and people love to be loved. Clinton loves these marines and they love him in return.

Griffin advances closer, to hear what Clinton is saying, and as he leaves the ragged perimeter of the crowd, stands alone. Clinton looks at him and calls out, "Don't be nervous, the guns aren't loaded."

"Yes they are, Mr. President," says one of the marines.

"Stay away then," Clinton adds, and Griffin stops. "No, no, no. Come on. These men are as shy as North Dakota virgins. They'll climb a rock face with Arabs firing stingers at their asses, but they won't get in line for the buffet. Who are you?"

"Griffin Mill."

"From Hollywood."

"Yes. How do you know?"

"Everybody knows Griffin Mill, Mr. OnlyConnect_ In_Uniform dot com. Meet the men." Griffin takes the hands of each of the marines; Clinton keeps talking. "It's a great day, isn't it? I was telling them that I really hated the Vietnam war and just didn't think it was worth going over there to die for, but I've never felt good about anybody dying in my place. We were talking about duty and honor. I told them I know a lot more about dishonor. And then we swapped a couple of jokes. Did you serve?"

"No."

"That's not to our credit. These are men."

"I know that."

"I can see you do. That's why you were watching us instead of networking this valuable crowd."

One of the marines says, "You sound a little ambivalent about that crowd, Mr. President."

"I suppose I do because I am. Every conversation is politics, and it's a complicated process. Democracies are messy and take a lot of time. But no one's invented anything better that I've studied."

There is a silence, which Clinton genially pops, to avoid forcing them to hang on words he finds too familiar.

"Men, it's been really great talking, but now I'm afraid I really do have to work the tent. I hope I see you again, and if I don't, remember me kindly."

They say they will. Clinton salutes with a wink, and puts his hand on Griffin's shoulder. "I see that OnlyConnect is a big hit with the market. Do you miss working with Stella?"

"It's still show business."

"You wanted to make some money, I understand that. You know, I didn't get rich while I was in office; that came after, and don't tell me that if I'd lost the race for my first term, the big Wall Street law firms were waiting to pay a few million a year for the ex-governor of Arkansas to bring them business. I might have ended up teaching government at Georgetown and been grateful for the salary. Of course, I have a pretty free ride now, but basically I'm just Mickey Mantle shaking hands at Caesar's Palace. I know that."

"Sir, this may be forward of me, but I'd like to talk to you about this. To be honest, I need to talk to you about just what you said, or what you're hinting at."

"We can talk now."

"People need your attention, and I think that once we get started, we might talk a long time."

"That's fair. All right. I'm on the island for two more days, but it's best if we meet tonight. I'll get you invited to dinner at the Fleischmanns', and you'll be the last to leave. Your wives can drive home, and I'll get a car to take you back when we're finished."

"I'll give you the number," Griffin says, dizzy with the easy way Clinton invited Lisa and June.

"Griffin, we'll find you." And with that, Clinton dives back into the ocean of money.

. . .

That night Griffin sits across a round table with Clinton and ten others. He looks across the table at June and Lisa. He wonders how long they can live this way. June is in such a strange position, the older wife and also the junior wife. He regrets the pain he has brought her, or might still bring to her.

Griffin is pretty sure he's the richest at the table, or will be in a year if the stock moves as expected. The host is an investment banker whose wife made an ugly comment about Griffin's two wives before some charity art thing or other, and word came back to

Griffin, and he refused to go, because June had been insulted enough in her life. So now Griffin is here at the invitation of William Jefferson Clinton, and the banker has asked twice after both June's and Lisa's children.

Two good-looking live-in tutors for the SATs follow the banker's twins around, high school juniors, just back from helping build a youth center for a Guatemalan fair-trade shade-grown coffee collective, after a summer stint on Capitol Hill learning to shake hands. Before he was wealthy, it annoyed Griffin that the admissions officers at Harvard were so susceptible to such obvious pumping of steroids into the applications, but now that he's been shown the real map of the world and given the seven-figure pass code for the gates to the hidden canyons and empty beaches, he understands.

Griffin watches the other men at the table. Dinner with the man they believe was the greatest president of their lifetimes elevates their narcissism into the red zone, and in the morning they'll pay for the fever of their enthusiasm and the embarrassment of their crush on him. Clinton releases too much sexual confusion, and to seek a solution to what he stirs up, everyone wants to know more about him, which only drags them deeper into his thrall. Whatever anyone knows, Clinton knows more. A man at the table mentions something about Nabokov's butterflies, and Clinton quotes a page from *Speak, Memory*, and then butterflies leads him to a screaming eagle decal on one of Reggie Jackson's restored Trans-Ams. He talks to the men about golf and the women about their parents' diseases. Fleischmann collects handmade ice-fishing lures from backwoods America, and Clinton explores the obsession in a way that gives these simple carvings the grandeur of Phoenician glassware. Bill Clinton adds to everyone's knowledge of themselves. For that, these men are willing to let him fuck their wives. Clinton is a genius, and Griffin knows what to ask him, which is, simply, everything.

When the other couples at the party go home to their children, Clinton asks Griffin to stay behind. June and Lisa say good night. The Fleischmanns leave the two men alone, and Clinton invites Griffin outside, where he can smoke a cigar.

"Do you smoke?" asked Clinton.

"No, sir."

"I don't inhale." Clinton studies Griffin for a reaction.

"This is why I want to talk to you, because you can say that. I know that's funny, but I'm past the point of laughter."

"You'll have a drink, though? They have some nice brandy here. Come on." Clinton leads Griffin back to the bar and pours them each two fingers of something old. They return to the deck, and a half moon, and a few clouds. A gust of wind shakes light and dark shadows from the trees.

"You cold?" asks Clinton.

"No, sir."

"We'll go in when I finish this," and he lights the cigar. "You want to know how I can live with guilt, don't you?"

"How did you know?"

"It's all that anyone intelligent wants to know about me, that and my marriage, what it really is."

"And what is your marriage?"

"I've been married to the same woman, my only wife, for thirty years. We wanted to be the parents of a happy brood but agreed, sadly, that we could not attend to the needs of more than one child. Our daughter is intelligent and poised, and through the worst storms that I dragged my family into, she kept her dignity. She has never been arrested for drinking or drugs, never made an ass of herself in public, never traded on her position in the world for access to movie stars and nightclubs. She's had fun, of course, she's no prude, but she's a modest person. Where does a child get such character except from the home?"

"But you fucked around."

"Yes, I did. I also changed welfare, cleaned up the air, saved more land for national parks and monuments than my last three predecessors combined, and would have achieved peace in Israel if I hadn't been subjected to impeachment."

"Do you really believe that?"

"Oslo was the beginning. You have to be patient for the Messiah. But this isn't why we're talking. You wanted something from me, what everyone wants, permission or absolution. For what?"

"My crimes and sins."

"Should I ask you what they are?"

"I'd rather you didn't."

Clinton smokes in silence. Griffin studies his head, monstrous in size compared to other men; one could imagine a larger brain residing there, with layers of consciousness in folds of tissue unknown to science.

"Have you killed anyone?" asks Clinton.

Griffin whispers the answer, the truth.

"King David sent Uriah to die in battle so he could marry Bathsheba. His only punishment, that I can see, is that God gave the honor of building the Temple to his son, Solomon, but if you ask me who's the better man, it's David. He died in bed, an old man, with Abishag, a teenage starlet of her day, dancing for him and keeping him warm. It isn't clear about sex, if they had it or not, but the girl's beauty and her youth gave him clarity of vision and inspired him to make a difficult decision about who would succeed him. He needed that girl for the deepest comfort. And you know who sent for her? Bathsheba. There's a wife. That's a marriage. The only thing I was fairly charged with was for the appearance of helping that woman get a job after she'd blown me. And there's some truth to it, but don't tell me there aren't a thousand women who pass through Washington, work for an elected official or high appointment, and jump into bed. And she begins a worthy advance through the system. Like it or not, there are things learned in bed, and only in bed, that can move a man or a woman to something great within themselves. Promiscuity can focus the senses, the faculties of mind and insight. Very few of the people who make a dent on history can get enough of such wisdom from only one bed. And that's what the American people understand, and in a moment of panic and weakness I didn't trust them. America has one heart. The American people said all of that to me with every poll that showed them enraged with my enemies. I let them down by not respecting their intelligence. Give them as much of the truth as the world can stand without needing more, get that out of the way, and you deflate your enemies because they'll be screaming at the American people for not being shocked. And who really wants to be screamed at? I may be depraved, but I, William Jefferson Clinton, am the pure product of America, and the truth is, so is everyone else. So are you."

"Why did Hillary put up with it?"

"She knows who I am."

"Do you love her?"

"Yes, I love her, I support her, and I'm proud of her. She is not a natural politician, which means she can't easily make the usual pact of self-absorption with the people who elect them, like Arnold Schwarzenegger, the agreement to accept each other's bullshit without calling the other to account. It's ridiculous that he's governor, ridiculous, and again, he wouldn't be governor if I hadn't already proven that the American people don't give a shit about your private life. The man forced himself on more pussy than Fritz the Cat, and look at his skinny-ass wife, starving herself or something, I don't know. That's a tangent. It's good brandy."

"That violates what you just said about respecting the intelligence of the American people, who rejected the impeachment, as I think you were telling me, because they didn't elect you as pope but as president. Now you're saying they supported you through the impeachment because they didn't want Congress to remind them of their own moral crimes."

"If you can't see that it's both, even with the contradiction, you'll never get what you want in life. What offended some people is that I was bringing a homosexual style into heterosexual life. Do you understand the real threat posed by the homosexuals? It's not AIDS or pedophilia."

"Are you asking me?"

"Yeah, I'm asking you to tell me why Americans are so afraid of homosexuals, especially the Americans who hate me and want my wife beaten to death on the steps of the Capitol."

"They want to get fucked up the ass and they're afraid of it?"

"No. Americans are afraid of homosexuals because homosexuals know the difference between love and sex and don't apologize. And the homosexual *lifestyle* is what most Americans are afraid of because the idea of pleasure for its own sake is dangerous. Most Americans are afraid they'll be left out of the orgy, and they don't want anyone else having fun. Meanwhile, and this is not a small disparity, the homosexuals want to get married and have children, and this also upsets those people who hate me and want Hillary soaked in kerosene, hoisted to the top of the Washington Monument, and put to the torch. Why? Because they know that homosexual fidelity includes some room for fun, and the people who hate me are tortured by visions of other ways of living. They're the same people who came to the New World and could not understand a functioning humanity that had never heard the good word of the gospels, so those whom they couldn't convert, they killed. Griffin, I'm as much a real part of this world as those marines you saw me talking to this afternoon, and that's why they talked to me, because I'm a country boy just like them. The first time I ever saw a gun fired, it was my stepfather shooting at my mother. The George Bush I followed and the George Bush who followed me had fathers who loved them enough to show them the path. Why does a boy whose father loves him grow up to be selfish? Did your father love you?"

"Yes, but he didn't teach me anything."

"Then he didn't love you. That's why you and I are friends."

"I thought you didn't have any friends."

"Griffin Mill, you're my friend. Maybe my only friend. Yes, my only friend, and this is the last time we'll ever talk."

"What's so special about the way a North Dakota virgin is shy?"

"I have no idea."

"But the marines laughed."

"Do you smoke?" asks Clinton, refusing to say more.

"I told you. No."

"You should, once in a while. It won't kill you, and even if it does, sometimes you need a little poison if you want to see behind the curtain. Don't you want to see behind the curtain?"

Clinton waves the cigar like a magician's wand, and in the shifting cloud Griffin sees the Founding Fathers at the signing of the Declaration of Independence, from the tricornered caps to the carving of the setting or rising sun on the back of Washington's chair. As that cloud of smoke dissolves, the last good president of the United States waves the cigar in the other direction, and the smoke this time collects itself as a moving picture of George Washington, in New York for his second inauguration, warning the people of the United States against their own tyranny. Clinton once again waves the cigar, turning to another cardinal direction, and the cloud of smoke is the Jefferson Memorial, but as the cloud passes over Griffin he sees instead the Lincoln Memorial and Marian Anderson singing "America the Beautiful" after the Daughters of the American Revolution had banned this child of slaves from their hall. William Jefferson Clinton waves it again, and the next curtain of smoke replays that old film of him when he was fifteen, stepping out of a crowd of young scholars to shake the hand of John Fitzgerald Kennedy, but the picture shifts and there is Clinton in a motel room somewhere, getting a blow job. The next wave of the cigar and Kosovo is bombed from the air, which then mixes itself into the relentless massacres of history, and Griffin thinks this miracle is too sentimental, too kitsch, even for a miracle, and then Clinton takes another puff on the cigar and blows the smoke into a ring, and the ring drifts into the form of Griffin Mill strangling David Kahane and, after that, Linda Tripp taping Monica Lewinsky.

The Journey of the Hero

My name is Griffin Mill. This is my wife, Lisa Kaplan Mill, and our daughter, Willa. This is my first wife, June Mercator Mill, and our children, Ethan and Jessa. I live with them all. I want to make this clear. I live as husband and wife and wife. I had an affair with Lisa while I was married to June. Over the last few years, after Lisa hit our daughter in public, my dear June—come here, June—my dear June brought us all together and healed us with the power of her love. And now June and I are having another baby. Actually, that's why we're here today. For our children, all of our children.

Thousands of men have stood before the people of this country and asked for your votes and lied to you about who they were, and, lying about themselves, they lied about their promises. I'm telling you the truth about myself, and I won't make any promises. I won't talk about anything except the way things really are. I'll tell you the truth about the way you and I live today.

Some of you are shocked by what I just told you, but my private life has nothing to do with the climbing rate of asthma in the inner cities. What does my private life have to do with substitute teachers who don't know how to read? What does my adultery or my polyamory have to do with the government's war on unions, a minimum wage that can't support a family of four, when the family that owns Wal-Mart has a hundred billion dollars while paying its workers a small cut above minimum wage? You've been electing your slave masters because they distract you with scandal. I want to tell you the names of the rich who don't pay taxes. I want to talk seriously about global warming and the melting of the polar ice cap, and they got you in a big foamy lather about what kind of wine Michael Jackson gave little boys to get them drunk or if Brad and whoever are going to have a baby.

You elected Al Gore. You elected John Kerry. You elected weak men who couldn't fight for the people who supported them, so George Bush stole the elections, not from Al Gore and John Kerry but from you. You voted for men who spent too much of their energy proving themselves to their mothers and fathers, men who imagined their ordinary shames were great sins, who dragged their small shadows slowly on the parade ground and then wanted us to applaud them for courage as if they were six-year-olds jumping into a swimming pool. Our greatest presidents have been vicious, sexual, complicated. Abraham Lincoln slept with men, did you know that? You wanted leaders who had good reason to lie. Since the Democrats fielded such puny dull men, you accepted the Republicans, who at least were bold enough to be thieves. You paid a terrible price for this, in the blood of your children, in war. And you lost heart.

For a long time I had lost heart. I didn't care about society because I believed the earth was dead, and trying to save the earth was a waste of time, and the best strategy was an exit strategy. But I have three children and another on the way. And I can't teach them to give up.

Governor Schwarzenegger has been a failure. He borrows money and says he's not raising taxes, but all he's doing is having your children pay for his *true lies*. He's saying *hasta la vista* to public services. Your lives are harder, and he's *terminating* your security. The Republicans in this country, and plenty of Democrats, are *predators*, like the people in the nineties who told you to buy stocks they knew were bad and told you to buy them while they were selling. A lot of people are still hurting because of that. I've been fortunate to make money in what I hope is an ethical way, bringing people together when they know the truth about each other. I know who you are because I know what you want.

You don't want lies. And like a married couple who really want to honor their covenant with each other, you want someone to go first and take the scary step of telling the other everything he's done or she's done: all the sins, all the mistakes, and all the fears. We're all scared, for good reason. But I believe that even if we can't save the world, we have to try, and we have to admit that we're scared and that maybe we'll fail. In a marriage, each wants the other to take the first step. I'm taking that step now. But I don't want to leave. I want to stay.

I want to be your governor. And I am declaring my candidacy today. I want to be the next governor of California.

· · ·

Jessa says to Lisa, "You're going to be the First Lady in Washington; you know that, don't you? You and my mom. You're going to both be First Ladies, and Daddy's going to be the President of the United States."

Lisa wants to tell her that Daddy is still lying about his sins, because he told the American people nothing about the murder of David Kahane. And then she thinks, No, he's not lying, all he did was leave it out. And it's none of their business.